THE PHANTOM
OF THE OPERA

THE PHANTOM OF THE OPERA

Gaston Leroux

WORDSWORTH CLASSICS

This edition published 1995
by Wordsworth Editions Limited
Cumberland House, Crib Street, Ware,
Hertfordshire SG12 9ET

ISBN 1-57335-383-3

*Printed and bound in Great Britain
by Mackays of Chatham plc, Chatham, Kent
Typeset in the Uk by R & B Creative Services Ltd*

INTRODUCTION

GASTON LEROUX IS LISTED in the *Larousse Illustré* as a journalist and writer of detective stories, and in particular as the creator of the reporter/detective, Rouletabille, hero of his celebrated 'locked-room' novel, *The Mystery of the Yellow Room*, and of many others. No mention is made of *The Phantom of the Opera*, and yet it would be hard to find an ordinary person in the Western world who does not know the thrilling title. Curiously, the publication of the ingeniously plotted novel that Leroux produced in just three months of 1911 passed almost unnoticed, and it was ten years before Universal Pictures made the classic horror film that brought *The Phantom of the Opera* international fame. Subsequent versions of the film and, more recently, Andrew Lloyd-Webber's sensational stage musical, have now made the *Phantom* a household name, yet there remain few who know Leroux's brilliant original text.

Leroux had made his reputation as an investigative journalist by exposing a corrupt Prefect of Police and clearing the name of an accused man in a sensational case whilst he was working as a court-reporter for *L'Echo de Paris*. He had always been a theatre-lover, but his attempts to write for the stage were not successful. During a visit to the Opera House, he heard the legend of the bizarre figure, thought by many to be a ghost, who had lived secretly in the cavernous labyrinth of the Opera cellars, and apparently engineered so many awful events. Convinced of some truth behind the weird stories, Leroux's natural instincts induced him to investigate, and he was ultimately moved to write his famous story.

The Opera building in Paris, with its extraordinary maze-like structure, its necessary stage devices and its subterranean lake, makes an ideal setting for a horror story, particularly one that is concerned to such an extent as *The Phantom of the Opera*, with illusion. Leroux's apparently sincere belief in the human existence of Erik, the Opera Ghost, and in the veracity of his own story is conveyed consistently throughout the novel. He writes his own introduction to the book, explaining the research he has done, citing his sources, and claiming to have made his own connection between the doings of the horrific legendary creature and a real, unsolved drama at the Opera which had involved the discovery of a corpse, and the disappearance of a young opera singer and her lover. He gives excellent references to his chief witnesses so that the novel is effectively cast as the account of a genuine enquiry. This effect is repeatedly reinforced by Leroux's frequent and illuminating footnotes, the calm, Holmes-like logic of his discerning explanations, and his emphatic epilogue.

The Phantom of the Opera makes compulsive reading. It abounds with wonderful descriptions, extraordinary events, tragedy, horror, pathos, tremendous humour, and a gallery of charming minor characters. Leroux's portrait of the hideous musician, crazed by his own extreme ugliness, shows compassionate insight into a criminally insane mind. Music infuses the story, enriching the many dimensions of the novel which is steeped in the glamour of life at the Opera. The author's knowledge of the building itself and the extraordinary history of its construction are used to create a basis of realism in the story. Incredible, seemingly supernatural elements are artfully fused with real facts, with references to real people, places and events, so that the novel is a dazzling blend of illusion and reality, between which it is hard to distinguish. This naturally intensifies every chilling moment, making Gaston Leroux's *The Phantom of the Opera* one of the greatest horror stories of all time.

Gaston Leroux was born in Paris in 1868 during the course of a train journey to Normandy. Leroux grew up in Normandy where he developed a passion for literature and began to write poetry and stories. He studied law in Paris and qualified for the Bar which he swiftly abandoned in favour of journalism. In 1890 he took a job as a court reporter for L'Echo de Paris, and by 1892 he had made his name as France's first investigative journalist by solving a sensational case before it came to trial. By the age of thirty, Leroux was the most celebrated travelling reporter of his day. His dangerous excursions around the hot-spots of the world provided rich source material for the novels that he began to write seriously in 1907. His first book, Le Mystère de la Chambre Jaune, which introduced the journalist/amateur-detective Rouletabille, who, like Sherlock Holmes, uses cool reasoning to solve mysteries whilst the police remain in confusion, was an immediate success. Leroux went on to write sixty-three more novels of various genres. He died of uraemia in 1927.

Further reading:

Foreword by Peter Haining in the W.H. Allen edition, London 1985

AUTHOR'S INTRODUCTION

*In which the author of this singular work informs the reader how he
acquired the certainty that the Opera ghost really existed*

THE OPERA GHOST REALLY EXISTED. He was not, as was long
believed, a creature of the imagination of the artists, the superstition of the managers, or the absurd and impressionable brains of the
young ladies of the ballet, their mothers, the box-keepers, the cloak-
room attendants, or the concierge. No, he existed in flesh and
blood, though he assumed all the outward characteristics of a real
phantom, that is to say, of a shade.

When I began to ransack the archives of the National Academy
of Music, I was at once struck by the surprising coincidences
between the phenomena ascribed to 'the ghost' and the most extraordinary and fantastic tragedy that ever excited the minds of the
Paris upper classes; and I was soon led to think that this tragedy
might reasonably be explained by the phenomena in question. The
events do not date more than thirty years back; and it would not be
difficult to find at the present day, in the foyer of the ballet itself,
old men of high repute – men upon whose word one could
absolutely rely – who would remember as though they happened
yesterday the mysterious and dramatic conditions that attended the
kidnapping of Christine Daaé, the disappearance of the Vicomte de
Chagny and the death of his elder brother, Count Philippe, whose
body was found on the bank of the lake that exists in the lower cellars of the Opera on the Rue-Scribe side. But none of these witnesses had until that day thought that there was any reason for
connecting the more or less legendary figure of the Opera ghost
with that terrible story.

The truth was slow to enter my mind, puzzled by an enquiry that,
at every moment, was complicated by events which, at first sight,
might be looked upon as superhuman; and more than once I was
within an ace of abandoning a task in which I was exhausting myself
in the hopeless pursuit of a vain image. At last, I received the proof
that my presentiments had not deceived me; and I was rewarded for
all my efforts on the day when I acquired the certainty that the
Opera ghost was more than a mere shade.

On that day, I had spent long hours over *The Memoirs of a Manager*, the light and frivolous work of the over-sceptical Moncharmin, who, during his term at the Opera, understood nothing of the mysterious behaviour of the ghost and who was making all the fun of it that he could at the very moment when he became the first victim of the curious financial operation that went on inside 'the magic envelope.'

I had just left the library in despair, when I met the delightful acting-manager of our National Academy, who stood chatting on a landing with a lively and well-groomed little old man, to whom he introduced me gaily. The acting-manager knew all about my investigations and how eagerly and unsuccessfully I had been trying to discover the whereabouts of the examining-magistrate in the famous Chagny case, M Faure. Nobody knew what had become of him, alive or dead; and here he was back from Canada, where he had spent fifteen years; and the first thing he had done, on his return to Paris, was to come to the secretarial offices at the Opera and ask for a free seat. The little old man was M Faure himself.

We spent a good part of the evening together; and he told me the whole Chagny case as he had understood it at the time. He was bound to conclude in favour of the madness of the viscount and the accidental death of the elder brother, for lack of evidence to the contrary; but he was nevertheless persuaded that a terrible tragedy had taken place between the two brothers in connection with Christine Daaé. He could not tell me what became of Christine or the viscount. When I mentioned the ghost, he only laughed. He too had been told of the curious manifestations that seemed to point to the existence of an abnormal being, residing in one of the mysterious corners of the Opera, and he knew the story of 'the envelope;' but he had seen nothing in the story worthy of his attention as magistrate in charge of the Chagny case; and it was as much as he had done to listen to the evidence of a witness who appeared of his own accord and declared that he had often met the ghost. This witness was none other than the man whom all Paris called 'the Persian' and who was well known to every subscriber to the Opera. The magistrate simply took him for a visionary.

I was immensely interested by this story of the Persian. I wanted, if there were still time, to find this valuable and eccentric witness. My luck began to improve; and I discovered him in his little flat in the Rue de Rivoli, where he had lived ever since and where he died five months after my visit. I was at first inclined to be suspicious; but, when the Persian, with child-like candour, had told me all that he knew about the ghost and handed me his proofs of the ghost's existence – including the strange correspondence of Christine Daaé – to do as I pleased with, I was no longer able to doubt. No, the ghost was not a myth !

I have, I know, been told that this correspondence may have been forged from first to last by a man whose imagination had certainly been fed on the most seductive tales; but fortunately I discovered some of Christine's writing outside the famous bundle of letters; and on a comparison of the two, all my doubts were removed. I also went into the past history of the Persian and found that he was an upright man, incapable of inventing a story that might have defeated the ends of justice.

This, moreover, was the opinion of the more serious people who, at one time or other, were mixed up in the Chagny case, who were friends of the Chagny family and to whom I showed all my documents and set forth all my inferences. In this connection, I should like to print a few lines which I received from General D—:

'SIR,

'I cannot urge you too strongly to publish the results of your enquiry. I remember perfectly that, a few weeks before the disappearance of that great singer, Christine Daaé, and the tragedy which threw the whole of the Faubourg Saint-Germain into mourning, there was a great deal of talk, in the foyer of the ballet, on the subject of "the ghost;" and I believe that it only ceased to be discussed in consequence of the later affair that excited us all so greatly. But, if it be possible – as, after hearing you, I believe – to explain the tragedy through the ghost, then I beg you, sir, to talk to us about the ghost again. Mysterious though the ghost may at first appear, this ghost will always be more easily explained than the gruesome story in which malevolent people have tried to picture two brothers killing each other who had worshipped each other all their lives.

'Believe me, etc.'

Lastly, with my bundle of papers in my hand, I once more went over the ghost's vast domain, the huge building which he had made his kingdom. All that my eyes saw, all that my mind perceived corroborated the Persian's documents precisely; and a wonderful discovery crowned my labours in a very definite fashion. It will be remembered that, later, when digging in the substructure of the Opera, preparatory to burying the phonographic records of the artists' voices, the workmen laid bare a corpse. Well, I was at once able to prove that this corpse was that of the Opera ghost. I made the acting-manager test this proof with his own eyes; and it has now become a matter of supreme indifference to me if the papers pretend that the body was that of a victim of the Commune.

The wretches who were massacred, under the Commune, in the cellars of the Opera, were not buried on this side; I will tell where their skeletons can be found, in a spot very far removed from that immense crypt, which, during the siege, was stocked with all sorts of provisions. I came upon this track while in the act of looking for the remains of the Opera ghost, which I should never have discovered but for the great stroke of luck described above.

But we will speak again of the corpse and of what should be done with it. For the present, I must conclude this very necessary introduction by thanking M Mifroid (who was the commissary of police called in for the first investigations after the disappearance of Christine Daaé); M Rémy, the late secretary; M Mercier, the late acting-manager; M Gabriel, the late chorus-master; and, more particularly, Mme la Baronne de Castelot-Barbezac, who was once the 'Little Meg' of the story (and who is not ashamed of it), the most charming star of our admirable *corps de ballet*, the eldest daughter of the worthy Mme Giry, now deceased, who had charge of the ghost's private box. All these have been of the greatest assistance to me; and, thanks to them, I shall be able to reproduce those hours of pure love and sheer terror, in their smallest details, before the reader's eyes.

And I should be ungrateful indeed if I omitted, while standing on the threshold of this dreadful and veracious story, to thank the present management of the Opera, which has so kindly assisted me in all my enquires, and M Massager in particular, together with M Gabion, the acting-manager, and the most amiable of men, the architect entrusted with the preservation of the building, who did not hesitate to lend me the works of Charles Garnier, although he was almost sure that I would never return them to him. Lastly, I must pay a public tribute to the generosity of my friend and former collaborator, M J.-L. Croze, who allowed me to dip into his splendid theatrical library and to borrow rare editions of books by which he set great store.

Gaston Leroux

CONTENTS

THE PHANTOM
OF THE OPERA

CHAPTER I

Is It The Ghost?

IT WAS THE EVENING on which MM Debienne and Poligny, the managers of the Opera, were giving a farewell gala performance to make their retirement. Suddenly the dressing-room of La Sorelli, one of the principal dancers, was invaded by half a dozen young ladies of the ballet, who had come up from the stage after 'dancing' *Polyeucte*. They rushed in amid great confusion, some giving vent to forced and unnatural laughter, others to cries of terror. Sorelli, who wished to be alone for a moment to 'polish up' the speech which she was to make to the resigning managers, looked round angrily at the mad and tumultuous crowd. It was little Jammes – the girl with the tip-tilted nose, the forget-me-not eyes, the rose-red cheeks and the lily-white neck and shoulders who gave the explanation in a trembling voice:

'It's the ghost!'

And she locked the door.

Sorelli's dressing-room was fitted up with commonplace, official elegance. A pier-glass, a sofa, a dressing-table and a cupboard or two provided the necessary furniture. On the walls hung a few engravings, relics of the dancer's mother, who had known the glories of the old Opera in the Rue Le Peletier: portraits of Vestris, Gardel, Dupont, Bigottini. But the room seemed a palace to the chits of the *corps de ballet*, who were lodged in common dressing-rooms where they spent their time singing, quarrelling, smacking the dressers and hair-dressers and buying one another glasses of *cassis*, beer, or even rum, until the call-boy's bell rang.

Sorelli was very superstitious. She shuddered, when she heard little Jammes speak of the ghost, called her a silly little fool and then, as she was the first to believe in ghosts in general and the Opera ghost in particular, at once asked for details:

'Have you seen him?'

'As plainly as I see you now!' moaned little Jammes, whose legs were giving way beneath her, and she dropped into a chair.

Thereupon little Giry – the girl with eyes black as sloes, hair black as ink, a swarthy complexion and a poor little skin stretched over poor little bones – little Giry added:

'If that's the ghost, he's very ugly!'

'Oh yes!' cried the chorus of ballet-girls.

And they all began to talk together. The ghost had appeared to them in the shape of a gentleman in dress-clothes, who had suddenly stood before them in the passage, without their knowing where he came from. He seemed to have loomed through the wall.

'Pooh!' said one of them, who had more or less kept her head. 'You see the ghost everywhere!'

And it was true. For several months there had been nothing discussed at the Opera but this ghost in dress-clothes who stalked about the building, from top to bottom, like a shadow, who spoke to nobody, to whom nobody dared speak and who vanished as soon as he was seen, no one knowing how or where. As became a real ghost, he made no noise in walking. People began by laughing and making fun of this spectre clad like a man of fashion or an undertaker; but the ghost legend soon swelled to enormous proportions among the *corps de ballet*. All the girls pretended to have met this supernatural being more or less often. And those who laughed the loudest were not the most at ease. When he did not show himself, he betrayed his presence or his passing by accidents, comic or serious, for which the general superstition held him responsible. Had any one met with a fall, or suffered a practical joke at the hands of one of the other girls, or lost a powder-puff, it was at once put down to the ghost, the Opera ghost.

Yet who had actually seen him? You meet so many men in dress-clothes at the Opera who are not ghosts. But this dress-suit had a peculiarity of its own: it clothed a skeleton. At least, so the ballet-girls said. And, of course, it had a death's-head.

Was all this serious? The truth is that the idea of the skeleton came from the description of the ghost given by Joseph Buquet, the chief scene-shifter, who had really seen the ghost. He had run up against the ghost on the little staircase, by the footlights, which leads straight down to the 'cellars'. He had seen him for a second – for the ghost had fled – and to any one who cared to listen to him he said:

'He is extraordinarily thin and his dress-coat hangs on a skeleton frame. His eyes are so deep that you can hardly see the fixed pupils. All you see is two big black holes, as in a dead man's skull. His skin, which is stretched across his bones like a drumhead, is not white, but a dirty yellow. His nose is so little worth talking about that you can't see it side-face; and *the absence* of that nose is a horrible thing *to look at*. All the hair he has is three or four long dark locks on his forehead and behind the ears.'

This chief scene-shifter was a serious, sober, steady man, very slow at imagining things. His words were received with interest and amazement; and soon there were other people to say that they too had met a man in dress-clothes with a death's-head on his shoulders. Sensible men, hearing the story, began by saying that Joseph Buquet had been the victim of a joke played by one of his assistants. And then, one after the other, there came a series of incidents so curious and so inexplicable that the very shrewdest people began to feel uneasy.

For instance, a fireman is a brave fellow! He fears nothing, least of all fire! Well, the fireman in question,[1] who had gone to make a round of inspection in the cellars and who seems to have ventured a little further than usual, suddenly reappeared on the stage, pale, scared, trembling, with his eyes starting out of his head, and practically fainted in the arms of the proud mother of little Jammes. And why? Because he had seen, coming towards him, *at the level of his head, but without a body attached to it, a head of fire!* And, as I said, a fireman is not afraid of fire.

The fireman's name was Pampin.

The *corps de ballet* was flung into consternation. At first sight, this fiery head in no way corresponded with Joseph Burquet's description of the ghost. But the young ladies soon persuaded themselves that the ghost had several heads, which he changed about as he pleased. And, of course, they at once imagined that they were in the greatest danger. Once a fireman did not hesitate to faint, leaders and front-row and back-row girls alike had plenty of excuses for the fright that made them quicken their pace when passing some dark corner or ill-lighted corridor. Sorelli herself, on the day after the adventure of the fireman, placed a horse-shoe on the table in front of the stage-door-keeper's box, for every one who entered the Opera other than as a spectator to touch before setting foot on the first tread of the staircase. This horse-shoe was not invented by me – any more than any other part of this story, alas! – and may still be seen on the table in the passage outside the stage-door-keeper's box, when you enter the Opera through the yard known as the Cour de l'Administration.

To return to the evening in question:

[1] I have the anecdote, which is quite authentic, from M Pedro Gailhard himself, the late manager of the Opera.

'It's the ghost!' Little Jammes had cried.

An agonizing silence now reigned in the dressing-room. Nothing was heard but the hard breathing of the girls. At last, Jammes, flinging herself into the furthest corner of the wall, with every mark of real terror on her face, whispered:

'Listen!'

Everybody seemed to hear a rustling outside the door. There was no sound of footsteps. It was like light silk gliding along the panel. Then it stopped.

Sorelli tried to show more pluck than the others. She went up to the door and, in a quavering voice, asked:

'Who's there?'

But nobody answered. Then, feeling all eyes upon her, watching her least movement, she made an effort to show courage and said, very loudly:

'Is there anyone behind the door?'

'Oh yes, there is! Of course there is!' cried that little dried plum of a Meg Giry, heroically holding Sorelli back by her gauze skirt. 'Whatever you do, don't open the door! Oh lord, don't open the door!'

But Sorelli, armed with a dagger which she always carried, turned the key and drew back the door, while the ballet-girls retreated to the inner dressing-room and Meg Giry moaned:

'Mother! Mother!'

Sorelli looked into the passage bravely. It was empty: a gas-flame, in its glass prison, cast a red and sinister light into the surrounding darkness, without succeeding in dispelling it. And the dancer slammed the door again, with a deep sigh:

'No', she said, 'there is no one there.'

'Still, we saw him!' Jammes declared, returning with timid little steps to her place beside Sorelli. 'He must be somewhere, prowling about. I sha'n't go back to dress. We had better all go down to the foyer together, at once, for "the speech," and then come up again together.'

And the child reverently touched the little coral finger which she wore as a charm against bad luck, while Sorelli stealthily, with the tip of her pink right thumb-nail, made a St Andrew's cross on the wooden ring which adorned the fourth finger of her left hand. She said to the little ballet-girls:

'Come, children, pull yourselves together! I daresay no one has ever seen the ghost. . . .'

'Yes, yes, we saw him . . . we saw him just now!' cried the girls.

'He had his death's-head and his dress-coat, just as when he appeared to Joseph Buquet!'

'And Gabriel saw him too!' said Jammes. 'Only yesterday! Yesterday afternoon . . . in broad daylight.'

'Gabriel, the chorus-master?'

'Why, yes, didn't you know?'

'And he was wearing his dress-clothes, in broad daylight?'

'Who? Gabriel?'

'Why, no, the ghost!'

'Certainly! Gabriel told me so himself. That's what he knew him by. Gabriel was in the stage-manager's office. Suddenly, the door opened and the Persian entered. You know, the Persian has the evil eye. . . .'

'Oh yes!' answered the little ballet-girls in chorus, warding off ill-luck by pointing their fore-finger and little finger at the absent Persian, while their second and third fingers were bent on the palm and held down by the thumb.

'And you know how superstitious Gabriel is,' continued Jammes. 'However, he is always polite, and, when he meets the Persian, he just puts his hand in his pocket and touches his keys. . . . Well, the moment the Persian appeared in the doorway, Gabriel gave one jump from his chair to the lock of the cupboard, so as to touch iron! In so doing, he tore a whole skirt of his overcoat on a nail. Hurrying to get out of the room, he banged his forehead against a hat-peg and gave himself a huge bump; then, suddenly stepping back, he skinned his arm on the screen, near the piano. He tried to lean on the piano, but the lid fell on his hands and crushed his fingers. He rushed out of the office like a madman, slipped on the staircase and came down the whole of the first flight on his back. I was just passing with Mother. We picked him up. He was covered with bruises and his face was all over blood. We were frightened out of our lives, but, all at once, he began to thank Providence that he had got off so cheaply. Then he told us what had frightened him. He had seen the ghost behind the Persian, *the ghost with the death's-head*, just like Joseph Burquet's description!'

Jammes had told her story ever so quickly, as though the ghost were at her heels, and was quite out of breath at the finish. A silence followed, while Sorelli polished her nails in great excitement. It was broken by little Giry, who said:

'Joseph Buquet would do better to hold his tongue.'

'Why should he hold his tongue?' asked somebody.

'That's Ma's opinion,' replied Meg, lowering her voice and looking about her, as though fearing lest other ears than those present might overhear.

'And why is it your mother's opinion?'

'Hush! Ma says the ghost doesn't like being talked about.'

'And why does your mother say so?'

'Because . . . because . . . nothing. . . .'

This reticence exasperated the curiosity of the young ladies, who crowded round little Giry, begging her to explain herself. They were there, side by side, leaning forward simultaneously in one movement of entreaty and fear, communicating their terror to one another, taking a keen pleasure in feeling their blood freeze in their veins.

'I swore not to tell!' gasped Meg.

But they left her no peace and promised to keep the secret, until Meg, burning to say all she knew, began, with her eyes fixed on the door:

'Well, it's because of the private box. . . .'

'What private box?'

'The ghost's box!'

'Has the ghost a box? Oh, do tell us, do tell us! . . .'

'Not so loud!' said Meg. 'It's Box 5, you know, the box on the grand tier, next to the stage-box, on the left.'

'Oh, nonsense!'

'I tell you it is. . . . Ma has charge of it. . . . But you swear you won't say a word?'

'Of course, of course. . . .'

'Well, that's the ghost's box. . . . No one has had it for over a month, except the ghost, and orders have been given at the box-office that it must never be sold. . . .'

'And does the ghost really come there?'

'Yes. . . .'

'Then somebody does come?'

'Why, no! . . . The ghost comes, but there is nobody there.' The little ballet-girls exchange glances. If the ghost came to the box, he must be seen, because he wore a dress-coat and a death's-head. This was what they tried to make Meg understand, but she replied:

'That's just it! The ghost is not seen. And he has no dress-coat and no head! . . . All that talk about his death's-head and his head of fire is nonsense! There's nothing in it . . . . You only hear him, when he is in the box. Ma has never seen him, but she has heard him. Ma knows, because she gives him his programme.'

Sorelli interfered:

'Giry, child, you're getting at us!'

Thereupon little Giry began to cry:

'I ought to have held my tongue. . . . If Ma ever got to know! . . . But it's true enough, Joseph Buquet had no business to talk of things that don't concern him . . . it will bring him bad luck . . . Ma was saying so last night. . . .'

There was a sound of heavy and hurried footsteps in the passage; and a breathless voice cried:

'Cecile! Cecile! Are you there?'

'It's Ma's voice,' said Jammes. 'What's the matter?'

She opened the door. A respectable lady, built on the lines of a Pomeranian grenadier, burst into the dressing-room, and dropped groaning into a vacant arm-chair. Her eyes rolled madly in her brick-dust-coloured face.

'How awful!' she said. 'How awful!'

'What? What? . . .'

'Joseph Buquet . . .'

'What about him?'

'Joseph Buquet is dead!'

The room became filled with exclamations, with astonished outcries, with scared requests for explanations. . . .

'Yes, he was found hanging in the third-floor cellar!'

'It's the ghost!' blurted little Giry, as though in spite of herself; but she at once corrected herself, with her hands pressed to her mouth. 'No, no! . . . I didn't say it! . . . I didn't say it! . . .'

All around her, her panic-stricken companions repeated, under their breaths:

'Yes . . . it must be the ghost! . . .'

Sorelli was very pale:

'I shall never be able to recite my speech,' she said.

Ma Jammes gave her opinion, while she drained a glass of liqueur that happened to be standing on the table: 'The ghost must have had something to do with it. . . .'

The truth is that no one ever knew how Joseph Buquet met with his death. The verdict at the inquest was 'natural suicide.' In his *Memoirs of a Manager*, M Moncharmin, one of the joint lessees who succeeded MM Debienne and Poligny, describes the incident as follows:

'A grievous accident spoilt the little party which MM Debienne and Poligny gave to celebrate their retirement. I was in the managers' office, when Mercier, the acting-manager, suddenly came darting in. He seemed half mad and told me that the body of a scene-shifter had been found hanging in the third cellar under the stage, between a set piece and a scene from the *Roi de Lahore*. I shouted:

' "Come and cut him down!"

'By the time I had rushed down the staircase and the Jacob's ladder, the man was no longer hanging from his rope!'

So this is an event which M Moncharmin treats as natural. A man hangs at the end of a rope; they go to cut him down; the rope has disappeared. Oh, M Moncharmin found a very simple explanation! Listen to him:

'It was just after the ballet; and leaders and dancing-girls lost no time in taking their precautions against the evil eye.'

There you are! Picture the *corps de ballet* scuttling down the Jacob's ladder and dividing the suicide's rope among themselves in less time than it takes to write! When, on the other hand, I think of the exact spot where the body was discovered – the third cellar underneath the stage – I imagine that *somebody* must have been interested in seeing that the rope disappeared after it had effected its purpose; and time will show if I am wrong.

The horrid news soon spread all over the Opera, where Joseph Buquet was very popular. The dressing-rooms emptied and the little ballet-girls, crowding round Sorelli like timid sheep around their shepherdess, made for the foyer through the ill-lit passages and staircases, trotting as fast as their little pink legs could carry them.

CHAPTER II

The New Margarita

ON THE FIRST LANDING, Sorelli ran against the Comte de Chagny, who was coming upstairs. The count, who was generally so calm, seemed greatly excited:

'I was just coming to you,' he said, taking off his hat. 'Oh,

Sorelli, what an evening! And Christine Daaé: what a triumph!'

'Impossible!' said Meg Giry. 'Six months ago, she sang like a carrion-crow! But do let us get by, my dear count,' continued the chit, with a flippant curtsey. 'We are going to enquire after a poor man who has been found hanging by the neck.'

Just then, the acting-manager came fussing past and stopped when he heard this remark:

'What!' he exclaimed, roughly. 'Have you girls heard so soon? . . . Well, please forget about it for to-night, . . . and, above all, don't let MM Debienne and Poligny know: it would upset them, on their last day.'

They all went on to the foyer of the ballet, which was already full of people. The Comte de Chagny was right: no gala performance had ever equalled this. All the great composers of the day had conducted their own works in turn. Faure and Krauss had sung; and, on that evening, Christine Daaé had revealed her true self, for the first time, to the astonished and enthusiastic audience. Gounod had conducted the *Funeral March of a Marionnette;* Reyer, his beautiful overture to *Sigurd;* Saint-Saëns, the *Danse macabre* and a *Rêverie orientale;* Massenet, an unpublished Hungarian march; Guiraud, his *Carnaval;* Delibes, the *Valse lente* from *Sylvia* and the *pizzicati* from *Coppélia.* Mlle Krauss had sung the bolero in the *Vespri Siciliani;* and Mlle Denise Bloch the drinking-song in *Lucrezia Borgia.*

But the real triumph was reserved for Christine Daaé, who had begun by singing a few passages from *Romeo and Juliet.* It was the first time that the young artist sang in this work of Gounod, which had not yet been transferred to the Opera and which had been revived at the Opéra Comique long after its first production at the old Théâtre Lyrique by Mme Carvalho. Those who heard her say that her voice, in these passages, was seraphic; but this was nothing to the superhuman notes that she gave forth in the prison scene and the final trio in *Faust,* which she sang in the place of La Carlotta, who was ill. No one had ever heard or seen anything like it.

Daaé revealed a new Margarita that night, a Margarita of a splendour, a radiance hitherto unsuspected. The whole house went mad, rising to its feet, shouting, cheering, clapping, while Christine sobbed and fainted in the arms of her fellow-singers and had to be carried to her dressing-room. A few subscribers, however, protested. Why had so great a treasure been kept from them all that time? Till then, Christine Daaé had played a good Siebel to Carlotta's rather too splendidly massive Margarita. And it had needed Carlotta's incomprehensible and inexcusable absence from this gala night for little Daaé, at a moment's warning, to show all that she could do in a part of the programme reserved for the Spanish diva! Now what the subscribers wanted to know was, why had MM Debienne and Poligny applied to Daaé, when Carlotta was taken ill? Did they know of her hidden genius? And, if they knew of it, why had they kept it hidden? And why had she kept it hidden? Oddly enough, she was not known to have a professor of singing at that moment. She had often said that she meant to practise by herself in future. The whole thing was a mystery.

The Comte de Chagny, standing up in his box, listened to all this frenzy and took part in it by loudly applauding. Philippe Georges Marie Comte de Chagny was just forty-one years of age. He was a great aristocrat and a good-looking man, above the middle height and with attractive features, in spite of his hard forehead and his rather cold eyes. He was exquisitely polite to the women and a little haughty to the men, who did not always forgive him his social successes. He had an excellent heart and an irreproachable conscience. On the death of old Count Philibert, he became the head of one of the oldest and most distinguished families in France, whose arms dated back to the fourteenth century. The Chagnys owned a great deal of property; and, when the old count, who was a widower, died, it was no easy task for Philippe to accept the management of so large an estate. His two sisters and his brother Raoul would not hear of a division and waived their claim to their respective shares, leaving themselves entirely in Philippe's hands, as though the right of primogeniture had never ceased to exist. When the two sisters married, on the same day, they received their portion from their brother, not as a thing belonging to them, but as a dowry for which they thanked him.

The Comtesse de Chagny, née de Moerogis de La Martynière, had died in giving birth to Raoul, who was born twenty years after his elder brother. At the time of the old count's death, Raoul was twelve years old. Philippe busied himself actively with the youngster's education. He was admirably assisted in this work, first by his sisters and afterwards by an old aunt, the widow of a naval officer, who lived at Brest and gave young Raoul a taste for the sea. The lad entered the *Borda* training-ship, finished his course with honours and quietly made his trip round the world. Thanks to powerful influence, he had just been appointed a member of the official expedition on board the *Requin*, which was to be sent to the Arctic Circle in search of the survivors of the *D'Artois* expedition, of whom nothing had been heard for three years. Meanwhile, he was enjoying a long furlough, which would not expire for another six months; and already the dowagers of the Faubourg Saint-Germain were pitying the handsome and apparently delicate stripling for the hard work in store for him.

The shyness of the sailor-lad – I was almost saying his innocence – was remarkable. He seemed to have but just left the women's apron-strings. As a matter of fact, petted as he was by his two sisters and his old aunt, he had retained from this purely feminine education manners that were almost candid, stamped with a charm which nothing had yet been able to sully. He was a little over twenty-one years of age and looked eighteen. He had a small, fair moustache, beautiful blue eyes and a complexion like a girl's.

Philippe spoilt Raoul. To begin with, he was very proud of him and pleased to expect a glorious career for his junior in the navy, in which one of their ancestors, the famous Chagny de La Roche, had held the rank of admiral. He took advantage of the young man's leave of absence to show him Paris, with all its luxurious and artistic delights. The count considered that, at Raoul's age, it is not good to be too good. Philippe himself had a character that was very well-balanced in work and pleasure alike; his demeanour was always faultless; and he was incapable of setting his brother a bad example. He took him with him wherever he went. He even introduced him to the foyer of the ballet. I know that the count was said to be 'on terms' with Sorelli. But it could hardly be reckoned as a crime for this nobleman, a bachelor, with plenty of leisure, especially since his sisters were settled, to come and spend an hour or two after dinner in the company of a dancer who, though not so very, very witty, had the finest eyes that ever were seen! And, besides, there are places where a true Parisian, when he has the rank of the Comte de Chagny, is bound to show himself; and, at that time, the foyer of the ballet at the Opera was one of those places.

Lastly, Philippe would perhaps not have taken his brother behind the scenes of the Opera if Raoul had not been the first to ask him, repeatedly renewing his request with a gentle obstinacy which the count remembered at a later date.

On that evening, Philippe, after applauding the Daaé, turned to Raoul and saw that he was quite pale.

'Don't you see,' said Raoul, 'that the woman's fainting?'

'You look like fainting yourself,' said the count. 'What's the matter?'

But Raoul had recovered himself and was standing up:

'Let's go,' he said, in a trembling voice.

'Where do you want to go to, Raoul?' asked the count, astonished at the excitement shown by his younger brother.

'Let's go and see her. She never sang like that before.'

The count gave his brother a curious, smiling glance and seemed quite pleased. They were soon at the door leading from the house to the stage. Numbers of subscribers were slowly passing through. Raoul tore his gloves without knowing what he was doing; and Philippe had much too kind a heart to laugh at him for his impatience. But he now understood why Raoul was absent-minded when spoken to and why he always tried to turn every conversation to the subject of the Opera.

They reached the 'tray' and pushed through the crowd of gentlemen, scene-shifters, supers and chorus-girls, Raoul leading the way, his face set with passion, feeling that his heart no longer belonged to him, while Count Philippe followed him with difficulty and continued to smile. At the back of the stage, Raoul had to stop before the inrush of the little troop of ballet girls who blocked the passage which he was trying to enter. More than one chaffing phrase darted from little made-up lips, to which he did not reply; and at last he was able to pass and dived into the semi-darkness of a corridor ringing with the name of 'Daaé! Daaé!' The count was surprised to find that Raoul knew the way. He had never taken him to Christine's himself and he came to the conclusion that Raoul must have gone there alone while the count stayed talking in the foyer with Sorelli, who often asked him to wait until it was her time to 'go on' and sometimes handed him the little gaiters in which she ran down from her dressing-room to preserve the spotlessness of her satin dancing-shoes and her flesh-coloured tights. Sorelli had an excuse: she had lost her mother!

Postponing his usual visit to Sorelli for a few minutes, the count followed his brother down the passage that led to Daaé's dressing-room and saw it had never been so crammed as on that evening, when the whole house seemed excited by her success and also by her fainting-fit. For the girl had not yet come to; and the doctor of the theatre had just arrived at the moment when Raoul entered at his heels. Christine, therefore, received the first aid of the one, while opening her eyes in the arms of the other. The count and many more remained crowding in the doorway.

'Don't you think, doctor, that these gentlemen had better clear the room?' asked Raoul coolly. 'There's no breathing here.'

'You're quite right,' said the doctor.

And he sent every one away, except Raoul and the maid, who looked at Raoul with eyes of the most undisguised astonishment. She had never seen him before and yet dared not question him; and the doctor imagined that the young man was acting as he did because he had every right to. The viscount, therefore, remained in the room and watched Christine slowly return to life, while even the joint managers, Debienne and Poligny, who had come to offer their sympathy and congratulations, found themselves thrust back into the passage among the crowd of dandies. The Comte de Chagny, who was one of those standing outside, laughed:

'Oh, the rogue, the rogue!' And he added, under his breath, 'Those youngsters with their school-girl airs! So he's a Chagny after all!'

He turned to go to Sorelli's dressing-room, but met her on the way, as we have seen, with her little troop of trembling girls.

Meanwhile, Christine Daaé uttered a deep sigh, which was answered by a groan. She turned her head, saw Raoul and started. She looked at the doctor, on whom she bestowed a smile, then at her maid, then at Raoul again:

'Monsieur,' she said, in a voice not much above a whisper, 'who are you?'

'Mademoiselle,' replied the young man, kneeling on one knee and pressing a fervent kiss on the diva's hand, '*I am the little boy who went into the sea to rescue your scarf.*'

Christine again looked at the doctor and the maid; and all three began to laugh.

Raoul turned very red and stood up:

'Mademoiselle,' he said, 'since you are pleased not to recognize me, I should like to say something to you in private, something very important.'

'When I am better, do you mind?' And her voice shook. 'You have been very good.'

'Yes, you must go,' said the doctor, with his pleasantest smile. 'Leave me to attend to mademoiselle.'

'I am not ill now,' said Christine, suddenly, with strange and unexpected energy.

She rose and, passing her hand over her eyelids:

'Thank you, doctor. . . . I should like to be alone. . . . Please go away, all of you. . . . Leave me. . . . I feel very restless this evening. . . .'

The doctor tried to make a short protest, but, perceiving the girl's evident agitation, thought that the best remedy was not to thwart her. And he went away, saying to Raoul, outside:

'She is not herself to-night. . . . She is usually so gentle. . . .'

Then he said good night; and Raoul was left alone. The whole of this part of the theatre was now deserted. The farewell ceremony was no doubt taking place in the foyer of the ballet. Raoul thought that Daaé might go to it; and he waited in the silent solitude, even hid himself in the kindly shadow of a doorway. He still felt a terrible pain at his heart; and it was of this that he wished to speak to Daaé without delay.

Suddenly, the dressing-room door opened and the maid came out by herself, carrying bundles. He stopped her and asked how her mistress was. The woman laughed and said that she was quite well, but that he must not disturb her, for she wished to be left alone. And she passed on. A single idea crossed Raoul's burning brain: of course, Daaé wished to be left alone *for him!* Had he not told her that he wanted to speak to her privately?

Hardly breathing, he went up to the dressing-room and, with his ear to the door to catch her reply, prepared to knock. But his hand dropped. He had heard a *man's voice* in the dressing-room, saying, in a curiously masterful tone:

'Christine, you must love me!'

And Christine's voice, infinitely sad and trembling, as though accompanied by tears, replied:

'How can you talk like that? *When I sing only for you?* . . .'

Raoul leant against the panel to ease his pain. His heart, which had seemed gone for ever, returned to his breast and was throbbing loudly. The whole passage echoed with its beating; and Raoul's ears were deafened. Surely, if his heart continued to make such a noise, they would hear it inside, they would open the door and the young man would be turned away in disgrace. What a position for a Chagny! To be caught listening behind a door! He seized his heart in his two hands to make it stop.

The man's voice spoke again:

'Are you very tired?'

'Oh, to-night, I gave you my soul and I am dead!'

'Your soul is a beautiful thing, child,' replied the man's grave voice, 'and I thank you. No emperor ever received so fair a gift. *The angels wept to-night.*'

Raoul heard nothing after that. Nevertheless, he did not go away, but, as though fearing lest he should be discovered, returned to his dark corner, determined to wait for the man to leave the room. At one and the same time, he had learnt what love meant and hatred. He knew that he loved. He wanted to know whom he hated. To his great astonishment, the door opened and Christine Daaé appeared, wrapt in furs, with her face hidden in a lace veil, alone. She closed the door behind her, but Raoul observed that she did not lock it. She passed him. He did not even follow her with his eyes, for his eyes were fixed on the door, which did not open again.

When the passage was once more deserted, he crossed it, opened the door of the dressing-room, went in and shut the door. He found himself in absolute darkness. The gas had been turned out.

'There is some one here!' said Raoul, with his back against the closed door, in a quivering voice. 'What are you hiding for?'

All was darkness and silence. Raoul heard only the sound of his own breathing. He quite failed to see that the indiscretion of his conduct exceeded all bounds.

'You sha'n't leave this room until I let you!' he exclaimed. 'If you don't answer, you are a coward! But I'll expose you!'

And he struck a match. Its flame lit the room. There was no one in the room! Raoul, first turning the key in the door, lit the gas-jets. He went into the dressing-closet, opened the cupboards, hunted about, felt the walls with his moist hands. Nothing!

'Look here!' he said, aloud. 'Am I going mad?'

He stood for ten minutes listening to the gas flaring in the silence of the empty room. Lover though he was, he did not even think of stealing a ribbon that would have given him the perfume of the woman he loved. He went out, not knowing what he was doing nor where he was going. At a given moment in his wayward progress an icy draught struck him in the face. He found himself at the foot of a staircase down which, behind him, a procession of workmen were carrying a sort of stretcher, covered with a white sheet.

'Which is the way out please?' he asked of one of the men.

'Straight in front of you. The door is open. But let us pass.'

Pointing to the stretcher, he asked, mechanically:

'What's that?'

The workman answered:

' "That" is Joseph Buquet, who was found in the third cellar, hanging between a set piece and a scene from the *Roi de Lahore*.'

He took off his hat, fell back to make way for the procession and went out.

CHAPTER III

Why The Managers Resigned

DURING THIS TIME, the farewell ceremony was taking place. I have
already said that a magnificent performance had been given on the
occasion of the retirement of M Debienne and M Poligny, who
had determined to 'die game,' as we say nowadays. They had been
assisted in the realization of their ideal, though melancholy programme by all that counted in the social and artistic world of
Paris. All these people met, after the performance, in the foyer of
the ballet, where Sorelli waited for the arrival of the retiring managers with a glass of champagne in her hand and a little prepared
speech at the tip of her tongue. Behind her, the members of the
corps de ballet, young and old, discussed the events of the day in
whispers, or exchanged discreet signals with their friends, a noisy
crowd of whom surrounded the supper-tables arranged along the
slanting floor.

A few of the dancers had already changed into ordinary dress;
but most of them still wore their skirts of gossamer gauze; and all
had thought it the right thing to put on a special face for the occasion: all, that is, except little Jammes, whose fifteen summers –
happy age! – seemed already to have forgotten the ghost and the
death of Joseph Buquet. She never ceased to laugh and chatter, to
hop about and play practical jokes, until MM Debienne and
Poligny appeared on the steps of the foyer, when she was severely
called to order by the impatient Sorelli.

Everybody remarked that the retiring managers looked cheer-
ful, as is our Paris way. None will ever be a true Parisian who has
not learnt to wear a mask of gaiety over his sorrows and one of
sadness, boredom, or indifference over his inward joy. You know
that one of your friends is in trouble; do not try to console him: he
will tell you that he is already comforted; but, should he have met
with good fortune, be careful how you congratulate him: he thinks
it so natural that he is surprised that you should speak of it. In
Paris, our lives are one masked ball; and the foyer of the ballet is
the last place in which two such sophisticated persons as MM

Debienne and Poligny would have made the mistake of betraying their sorrow, however genuine. And they were already beaming rather too lavishly upon Sorelli, who had begun to recite her speech, when an exclamation from that little madcap of a Jammes broke the smile of the managers so brutally that the expression of distress and dismay that lay beneath it became apparent to all eyes:

'The Opera ghost!'

Jammes yelled these words in a tone of unspeakable terror and her finger pointed, among the crowd of dandies, to a face so pallid, so lugubrious and so ugly, with two such deep black cavities under the straddling eyebrows, that the death's-head in question immediately scored a huge success.

'The Opera ghost! The Opera ghost!'

Everybody laughed and pushed his neighbour and wanted to offer the Opera ghost a drink; but he was gone. He had slipped through the crowd; and the others vainly hunted for him, while two old gentlemen tried to calm little Jammes and while little Giry stood screeching like a peacock.

Sorelli was furious: she had not been able to finish her speech; the managers had kissed her, thanked her and run away as fast as the ghost himself. No one was surprised at this, for it was known that they were to go through the same ceremony on the floor above, in the foyer of the singers, and that finally they were themselves to receive their personal friends, for the last time, in the great lobby outside the managers' office, where a sit-down supper would be served.

Here they found the new managers, MM Armand Moncharmin and Firmin Richard, whom they hardly knew; nevertheless, they were lavish in protestations of friendship and received a thousand flattering compliments in reply, so that those of the guests who feared that they had a rather tedious evening in store for them at once assumed brighter faces. The supper was almost gay; and a particularly clever speech of the representative of the government, mingling the glories of the past with the successes of the future, caused the greatest cordiality to prevail.

The retiring managers had already made over to their successors the two little master-keys which opened all the doors – thousands of doors – of the Opera-house. And those tiny keys, the object of general curiosity, were being passed from hand to hand, when the attention of some of the guests was diverted by their discovery, at the end of the table, of that strange, wan, fantastic face, with the hollow eyes, which had already appeared in the foyer of that ballet and been greeted by little Jammes's exclamation:

'The Opera ghost!'

There sat the ghost, as natural as could be, except that he neither ate nor drank. Those who began by looking at him with a smile ended by turning away their heads, for the sight of him at once provoked the most funereal thoughts. No one repeated the joke of the foyer, no one exclaimed:

'There's the Opera ghost!'

He himself did not speak a word and his very neighbours could not have stated at what precise moment he had sat down between them; but every one felt that, if the dead did ever come and sit at the table of the living, they could not cut a more ghastly figure. The friends of Firmin Richard and Armand Moncharmin thought that this lean and skinny guest was an acquaintance of Debienne's or Poligny's, while Debienne and Poligny's friends believed that the cadaverous individual belonged to Firmin Richard and Armand Moncharmin's party. The result was that no request was made for an explanation, no unpleasant remark, no joke in bad taste, which might have offended this visitor from the tomb. A few of those present who knew the story of the ghost and the description of him given by the chief scene-shifter – they did not know of Joseph Buquet's death – thought, in their own minds, that the man at the end of the table might easily have passed for him; and yet, according to the story, the ghost had no nose, whereas the person in question had. But M Moncharmin declares, in his *Memoirs*, that the guest's nose was transparent: 'long, thin and transparent' are his exact words. I, for my part, will add that this might very well apply to a false nose. M Moncharmin may have taken for transparency what was only shininess. Everybody knows that orthopædic science provides beautiful false noses for people who have lost their noses naturally or as the result of an operation.

Did the ghost really take a seat at the managers' supper-table, that night, uninvited? And can we be sure that the figure was that of the Opera ghost himself? Who would venture to assert as much? I mention the incident, not because I wish for a second to make the reader believe – or even try to make him believe – that the ghost was capable of such a sublime piece of impudence, but because, after all, the thing is possible.

M Armand Moncharmin, in chapter xi. of his *Memoirs*, says:

'When I think of this first evening, I cannot dissociate the secret confided to us by MM Debienne and Poligny, in their office, from the presence at our supper of that *ghostly* person whom none of us knew.'

What happened was this: MM Debienne and Poligny, sitting at the centre of the table, had not seen the man with the death's-head. Suddenly, he began to speak:

'The ballet-girls are right,' he said. 'The death of that poor Buquet is perhaps not as natural as people think.'

Debienne and Poligny gave a start:

'Is Buquet dead?' they cried.

'Yes,' replied the man, or the shadow of a man, quietly. 'He was found, this evening, hanging in the third cellar, between a set piece and a scene from the *Roi de Lahore*.'

The two managers, or rather ex-managers, at once rose and stared strangely at the speaker. They were more excited than they need have been, that is to say, more excited than any one need be by the announcement of the suicide of a chief scene-shifter. They looked at each other. They had both turned whiter than the table-cloth. At last, Debienne made a sign to MM Richard and Moncharmin; Poligny muttered a few words of excuse to the guests; and all four went into the managers' office. I leave M Moncharmin to continue the story:

'MM Debienne and Poligny seemed to grow more and more excited,' he says, in his *Memoirs*, 'and they appeared to have something very difficult to tell us. First, they asked us if we knew the man, sitting at the end of the table, who had told them of the death of Joseph Buquet; and, when we answered in the negative, they looked still more concerned. They took the master-keys from our hands, stared at them for a moment and advised us to have new locks made, with the greatest secrecy, for the rooms, closets and presses that we might wish to have hermetically closed. They said this so funnily that we began to laugh and to ask if there were thieves at the Opera. They replied that there was something worse, which was the *ghost*. We began to laugh again, feeling sure that they were indulging in some joke that was intended to crown our little entertainment. Then, at their request, we became 'serious,' resolving to humour them and enter into the spirit of the game. They told us that they would never have spoken to us of the ghost, if they had not received formal orders from the ghost himself to ask us to be pleasant to him and to grant any request that he might make. However, in their relief at leaving a domain where that tyrannical shade held sway, they had hesitated until the last moment to tell us this curious story, which our sceptical minds were certainly not prepared to entertain, when the announcement of the death of Joseph Buquet came to serve them as a brutal reminder that, whenever they had disregarded the ghost's wishes, some fantastic or disastrous event had brought them back to a sense of their dependence.

'During these unexpected utterances, made in a tone of the most secret and important confidence, I looked at Richard. Richard, in his student days, had acquired a great reputation for practical joking and he seemed to relish the dish which was being served up to him in his turn. He did not miss a morsel of it, though the seasoning was a little gruesome because of the death of Buquet. He nodded his head sadly, while the others spoke, and his features assumed the air of a man who bitterly regretted having taken over the Opera, now that he knew that there was a ghost mixed up in the business. I could think of nothing better than to give a servile imitation of this attitude of despair. However, in spite of all our efforts, we could not, at the finish, help bursting out laughing in the faces of MM Debienne and Poligny, who, seeing us pass straight from the gloomiest state of mind to one of the most outrageous merriment, acted as though they thought that we had gone mad.

'The joke became a little tedious; and Richard asked, half seriously and half in jest:

' "But, after all, what does this ghost of yours want?"

'M Poligny went to his desk and returned with a copy of the lease. The Opera lease begins with the well-known words setting forth that "the management of the Opera shall give to the performances of the National Academy of Music the splendour that becomes the first lyric stage in France," and ends with Clause 98, which says that the privilege can be withdrawn if the manager infringe the conditions stipulated in the lease. This is followed by the conditions, which are four in number.

'The copy produced by M Poligny was written in black ink and was exactly similar to that in our possession, except that, at the end, it contained a paragraph in red ink and in a queer, laboured handwriting, as though produced by dipping the heads of matches in the ink, the writing of a child that has never got beyond the downstrokes and has not yet learnt to join its letters. This paragraph ran, word for word, as follows:

' "5. Or if the manager, in any month, delay for more than a fortnight the payment of the allowance which he shall make to the Opera ghost, an allowance of 20,000 francs a month, say, 240,000 francs a year."

'M Poligny pointed with a shaking finger to this last clause, which we certainly did not expect.

' "Is this all? Doesn't he want anything more?" asked Richard, with the greatest coolness.

' "Yes, he does," replied Poligny.

'And he turned over the pages of the lease until he came to the clause specifying the days on which certain private boxes were to be reserved for the free use of the President of the Republic, the ministers and so on. At the end of the clause, a line had been added, also in red ink:

' "Box 5 on the grand tier shall be placed at the disposal of the Opera ghost for every performance."

'When we saw this, there was nothing for us to do but to rise from our chairs, shake our two predecessors warmly by the hand and congratulate them on thinking of this charming joke, which proved that the old French sense of humour was never likely to become extinct. Richard added that he now understood why MM Debienne and Poligny were retiring from the management of the National Academy of Music. Business was impossible with so unreasonable a ghost.

' "Certainly, 240,000 francs are not to be picked up for the asking," said M Poligny, without moving a muscle of his face. "And have you considered what the loss over Box 5 meant to us? We did not sell it once; and not only that, but we had to return the subscription: why, it's awful! We really can't work to keep ghosts! We prefer to go away."

' "Yes," echoed M Debienne, "we prefer to go away. Let us go."

'And he stood up. Richard said:

' "But, after all, it seems to me that you were much too good to the ghost. If I had such a troublesome ghost as that, I should not hesitate to have him arrested. . . ."

' "But how? Where?" they cried, in chorus. "We have never seen him!"

' "But when he comes to his box?"

' *We have never seen him in his box!*"

' "Then sell it."

' "Sell the Opera ghost's box! Well, gentlemen, you try it!"

'Thereupon we all four left the office. Richard and I had never laughed so much in all our lives.'

CHAPTER IV

Box 5

ARMAND MONCHARMIN WROTE such voluminous *Memoirs* during the fairly long period of his co-management that we may well ask if he ever found time to attend to the affairs of the Opera other than by gossiping of what went on there. M Moncharmin did not know a single note of music, but he called the minister of education and fine-arts by his Christian name, had dabbled a little in society journalism and enjoyed a considerable private income. Lastly, he was a charming fellow and showed that he was not lacking in intelligence, for, as soon as he made up his mind to be a sleeping partner in the Opera, he selected the best possible active manager by going straight to Firmin Richard.

Firmin Richard was a very distinguished composer, who had published a number of successful pieces of all kinds and who liked every form of music and every sort of musician. Clearly, therefore, it was the duty of every sort of musician to like M Firmin Richard. The only thing to be said against him was that he was rather masterful in his ways and endowed with a very hasty temper.

The first few days which the partners spent at the Opera were given over to the delight of finding themselves the heads of so magnificent an enterprise; and they had forgotten all about the curious, fantastic story of the ghost, when an incident occurred which proved to them that the joke – if joke it were – was not over. M Firmin Richard reached his office that morning at eleven o'clock. His secretary, M Rémy, showed him half a dozen letters which he had not opened because they were marked 'private.' One of the letters at once attracted Richard's attention, not only because the envelope was addressed in red ink, but because he seemed to have seen the writing before. He soon remembered that it was the red handwriting in which the lease had been so curiously completed. He recognized the clumsy, childish hand. He opened the letter and read:

'DEAR MR MANAGER.

'I am sorry to have to trouble you at a time when you must be so very busy renewing important engagements, signing fresh contracts and generally displaying your excellent taste. I know what you have done for Carlotta, Sorelli and little Jammes, not to mention others whose admirable qualities of talent or genius you have suspected.

'Of course, when I use these words, I do not mean to apply them to La Carlotta, who sings like a cockroach and who ought never to have been allowed to leave the Ambassadeurs and the Café Jacquin; nor to La Sorelli, who owes her success mainly to the coach-builders; nor to little Jammes, who dances like a calf in a field. And I am not speaking of Christine Daaé either, though her genius is certain, whereas you jealously prevent her from creating any important part. When all is said, you are free to conduct your little business as you think best, are you not?

'All the same, I should like to take advantage of the fact that you have not yet turned Christine Daaé adrift by hearing her this evening in the part of Siebel, as that of Margarita has been withheld from her since her triumph of the other night; and I must ask you not to dispose of my box to-day *nor on the following days*. For I cannot end this letter without telling you how disagreeably surprised I have been lately, on arriving at the Opera, to hear that my box had been sold, at the box-office, *by your orders*.

'I did not protest, first, because I dislike scandal and secondly, because I thought that your predecessors, MM Debienne and Poligny, who were always charming to me, had neglected, before leaving, to mention my little fads to you. I have now received a reply from these gentlemen to my letter asking for an explanation; and this reply proves that you know all about *my clause in the lease* and, consequently, that you are treating me with outrageous contempt. *If you wish us to live in peace, you must not begin by taking away my private box.*

'Believe me to be, dear Mr Manager, without prejudice to these little observations,

'your most humble and obedient servant,

'OPERA GHOST.'

The letter was accompanied by a cutting from the agony column of the *Revue théâtrale*, which ran:

'O. G. – There is no excuse for R. and M. We told them about it and called their attention to your clause in the lease. Kind regards.'

M Firmin Richard had hardly finished reading this letter, when M Armand Moncharmin entered carrying one exactly similar. They looked at each other and burst out laughing:

'They are keeping up the joke,' said M Richard, 'but I don't call it funny.'

'What does it all mean?' asked M Moncharmin. 'Do they imagine that, because they have been managers of the Opera, we are going to let them have a box for an indefinite period?'

'I am not in the mood to allow myself to be humbugged much longer,' said Firmin Richard.

'It's harmless enough,' observed Armand Moncharmin. 'What is it they really want? A box for to-night?'

M Firmin Richard told his secretary to give Box 5 on the grand tier to MM Debienne and Poligny, provided it was not sold. It was not. It was sent round to them. Debienne lived at the corner of the Rue Scribe and the Boulevard des Capucines; Poligny in the Rue Auber. O. Ghost's two letters had been posted at the Boulevard-des-Capucines post-office, as Moncharmin remarked after examining the envelopes.

'You see!' said Richard.

They shrugged their shoulders and regretted that two men of that age should amuse themselves with such childish tricks.

'They might have been civil, for all that!' said Moncharmin. 'Did you notice how they treat us with regard to Carlotta, Sorelli and little Jammes?'

'Why, my dear fellow, those two are mad with jealousy! . . . To think that they went to the expense of an advertisement in the *Revue théâtrale!* . . . Have they nothing better to do?'

'By the way,' said Moncharmin, 'they seem to be greatly interested in little Christine Daaé!'

'You know as well as I do that she has the reputation of being quite good,' said Richard.

'Reputations are easily obtained,' replied Moncharmin. 'Haven't I a reputation for knowing all about music? And I don't know one key from another.'

'Don't be afraid; you never had the reputation,' Richard declared.

Thereupon he ordered the artists to be shown in who, for the last two hours, had been walking up and down outside the door behind which fame and fortune – or dismissal – awaited them.

The whole day was spent in discussing, negotiating, signing or cancelling contracts; and the two over-worked managers went to bed early, without so much as casting a glance at Box 5 to see whether M Debienne and M Poligny were enjoying the performance.

Next morning, the managers received a card of thanks from the ghost:

'DEAR MR MANAGER,

'Thanks. Charming evening, Daaé exquisite. Choruses want waking up. Carlotta a splendid commonplace instrument. Will write you soon for the 240,000 francs, or 233,424 fr 70 c, to be correct. MM Debienne and Poligny have sent me the 6575 fr 30 c representing the first ten days of my allowance for the current year; their privileges finished on the evening of the 10th inst.

'Kind regards.

'O. G.'

On the other hand there was a letter from MM Debienne and Poligny:

'GENTLEMEN,

'We are much obliged for your kind thought of us, but you will easily understand that the prospect of again hearing *Faust*, pleasant though it be to ex-managers of the Opera, cannot make us forget that we have no right to occupy Box 5 on the grand tier, which is the exclusive property of *him* of whom we spoke to you when we went through the lease with you last. See Clause 63, final paragraph.

'Accept, gentlemen, etc.'

'Oh, those fellows are beginning to annoy me!' shouted Firmin Richard, snatching up the letter.

And, that evening, Box 5 was sold.

The next morning, MM Richard and Moncharmin, on reaching their office, found an inspector's report relating to an incident that had happened, the night before, in Box 5. I give the essential part of the report:

'I was obliged to call in a municipal guard twice, this evening, to clear Box 5 on the grand tier, once at the beginning and once in the middle of the second act. The occupants, who arrived as the curtain rose on the second act, created a regular scandal by their laughter and their ridiculous observations. There were cries of "Hush!" all around them; and the whole house was beginning to protest, when the box-keeper came to fetch me. I entered the box and said what I thought necessary. The people did not seem to me to be in their right minds; and they made stupid remarks in reply to my observations. I said that, if the noise was repeated, I should be compelled to clear the box. The moment I left, I heard the laughing again, with fresh protests from the house. I returned with a municipal guard, who turned them out. They protested, still laughing, saying they would not go unless they had their money back. At last they became quiet and I allowed them to enter the box again. The laughter at once recommenced and, this time, I had them turned out definitely.'

'Send for the inspector,' said Richard to his secretary, who had already read the report and marked it in blue pencil.

M Rémy, the secretary, had foreseen the order and called the inspector in at once.

'Tell us what happened,' said Richard, bluntly.

The inspector began to splutter and referred to the report.

'Well, but what were those people laughing at?' asked Moncharmin.

'They must have been dining, sir, and seemed more inclined to lark about than to listen to good music. The moment they entered the box, they came out again and called the box-keeper, who asked them what they wanted. They said, "Look in the box: there's no one there, is there?" "No," said the woman. "Well," said they, "when we went in, we heard a voice saying *that the box was taken!*"'

M Moncharmin could not help smiling as he looked at M Richard; but M Richard did not smile. He himself had done too much in that way in his time not to recognize, in the inspector's story, all the marks of one of those practical jokes which begin by amusing and end by enraging their victims. The inspector, to curry favour with M Moncharmin, who was smiling, thought it best to give a smile too. A most unfortunate smile! M Richard glared at his subordinate, who, from that moment, made it his business to display a face of utter consternation.

'Still, when those people arrived,' roared Richard, 'there was no one in the box, was there?'

'Not a soul, sir, not a soul! Nor in the box on the right, nor in the box on the left: not a soul, sir, I swear! The box-keeper told me so often enough, which proves that it was all a joke.'

'Oh, you agree, do you?' said Richard, 'You agree! It's a joke! And you think it funny, no doubt?'

'I think it in very bad taste, sir.'

'And what did the box-keeper say?'

'Oh, she just said that it was the Opera ghost. That's all she said!'

And the inspector grinned. But he soon found that he had made a mistake in grinning, for the words were no sooner out of his mouth than M Richard, from gloomy, became furious:

'Send for the box-keeper!' he shouted. 'Send for her! This minute! This minute! And bring her in to me here! And turn all those people out!'

The inspector tried to protest, but Richard closed his mouth with an angry order to hold his tongue. Then, when the wretched man's lips seemed shut for ever, the manager commanded him to open them once more:

'Who is this "Opera ghost"?' he snarled.

But the inspector was by this time incapable of speaking a word. He managed to convey, by a despairing gesture, that he knew nothing about it, or rather that he did not wish to know.

'Have you ever seen him, have you seen the Opera ghost?'

The inspector, by means of a vigorous shake of the head, denied ever having seen the ghost in question.

'Very well!' said M Richard, coldly.

The inspector's eyes started out of his head, as though to ask why the manager had uttered that ominous 'Very well!'

'Because I'm going to settle the account of anyone who has not seen him!' explained the manager. 'As he seems to be everywhere, I can't have people telling me that they see him nowhere. I like people to work for me when I employ them!'

Having said this, M Richard paid no further attention to the inspector and discussed various matters of business with his acting-manager, who had entered the room meanwhile. The inspector thought he could go and was gently – oh, so gently! –

sidling towards the door, when M Richard nailed the man to the floor with a thundering:

'Stay where you are!'

M Rémy had sent for the box-keeper to the Rue de Provence, close to the Opera, where she was engaged as a portress. She soon made her appearance.

'What's your name?'

'Mame Giry. You know me well enough, sir; I'm the mother of little Giry, little Meg, what!'

This was said in so severe and solemn a tone that, for a moment, M Richard was impressed. He looked at Mame Giry, in her faded shawl, her worn shoes, her old taffeta dress and dingy bonnet. It was quite evident from the manager's attitude that he either did not know or could not remember having met Mame Giry, nor even little Giry, nor even 'little Meg!' But Mame Giry's pride was so great that the celebrated box-keeper imagined that everybody knew her.

'Never heard of her!' the manager declared. 'But that's no reason, Mame Giry, why I shouldn't ask you what happened last night to make you and the inspector call in a municipal guard. . . .'

'I was just wanting to see you, sir, and talk to you about it, so that you mightn't have the same unpleasantness as M Debienne and M Poligny. . . . They wouldn't listen to me either, at first. . . .'

'I'm not asking you about all that. I'm asking you what happened last night.'

Mame Giry turned purple with indignation. Never had she been spoken to like that! She rose as though to go, gathering up the folds of her skirt and waving the feathers of her dingy bonnet with dignity; but, changing her mind, she sat down again and said, in a haughty voice:

'I'll tell you what happened. The ghost has been annoyed again!'

Thereupon, as M Richard was on the point of bursting out, M Moncharmin interfered and conducted the interrogatory, whence it appeared that Mame Giry thought it quite natural that a voice should be heard to say that a box was taken, when there was nobody in the box. She was unable to explain this phenomenon, which was not new to her, except by the intervention of the ghost. Nobody could see the ghost in his box, but everybody could hear him. She had often heard him; and they could believe her, for she always spoke the truth. They could ask M Debienne and M

Poligny and anybody who knew her; and also M Isidore Saack, who had had a leg broken by the ghost!

'Indeed! ' said Moncharmin, interrupting her. 'Did the ghost break poor Isidore Saack's leg?'

Mame Giry opened her eyes with astonishment at such ignorance. However, she consented to enlighten those two poor innocents. The thing had happened in M Debienne and M Poligny's time, also in Box 5 and also during a performance of *Faust*. Mame Giry coughed, cleared her throat – it sounded as though she were preparing to sing the whole of Gounod's score – and began:

'It was like this, sir. That night, M Maniera and his lady, the jewellers in the Rue Mogador, were sitting in the front of the box, with their great friend, M Isidore Saack, sitting behind Mme Maniera. Mephistopheles was singing' – Mame Giry here burst into song herself – 'Catarina, while you play at slee-eeping,' and then M Maniera heard a voice in his right ear (his wife was on his left) saying, "Ha, ha! *Julie's* not playing at sleeping!" His wife happened to be called Julie. So M Miniera turns to the right to see who was talking to him like that. Nobody there! He rubs his ears and asks himself if he's dreaming. Then Mephistopheles went on with his serenade. . . . But perhaps I'm boring you, gentlemen?'

'No, no, go on. . . .'

'You are too good, gentlemen,' with a smirk. 'Well, then, Mephistopheles went on with his serenade' – Mame Giry burst into song again – ' "Saint, unclose thy portal holy and accord the bliss, to a mortal bending lowly, of a pardon-kiss." and then M Maniera again hears the voice in his right ear, saying, this time, "Ha, ha! Julie wouldn't mind according a kiss to *Isidore!*" Then he turns round again, but this time to the left; and what do you think he sees? Isidore, who had taken his lady's hand and was covering it with kisses through the little opening in the glove . . . like this, gentlemen' – rapturously kissing the bit of palm left bare in the middle of her thread glove. 'Then they had a lively time between them! Bang! Bang! M Maniera, who was big and strong like you, M Richard, gave two blows to M Isidore Saack, who was small and weak like M Moncharmin, saving his presence. There was a great uproar. People in the house shouted, "That will do! Stop them! He'll kill him!" Then, at last, M Isidore Saack managed to run away. . . .'

'Then the ghost had not broken his leg?' asked M Moncharmin, a little vexed to think that his figure had made so little impression on Mame Giry.

'He did break it for him, sir,' replied Mame Giry, haughtily. 'He broke it for him on the grand staircase, which he ran down too fast, sir, and it will be long before the poor gentleman will be able to go up it again!'

'Did the ghost tell you what he said in M Maniera's right ear?' asked M Moncharmin, with a gravity which he thought exceedingly humorous.

'No, sir, it was M Maniera himself. So. . . .'

'But you have spoken to the ghost, my good lady?'

'As I'm speaking to you now, *my good sir!*'

'And, when the ghost speaks to you, what does he say?'

'Well, he tells me to bring him a footstool!'

This time, Richard burst out laughing, as did Moncharmin and Rémy, the secretary. Only the inspector, warned by experience, was careful not to laugh, while Mame Giry went so far as to adopt an attitude that was positively threatening:

'Instead of laughing,' she cried, indignantly, 'you'd do better to do as M Poligny did, who found out for himself. . . .'

'Found out what?' asked Moncharmin, who had never been so much amused in his life.

'About the ghost, of course! . . . Look here. . . .'

She suddenly calmed herself, feeling that this was a solemn moment in her life:

'*Look here,*' she repeated. 'They were playing the *Juive*. M Poligny thought he would watch the performance from the ghost's box. . . . Well, when Leopold cries, "Let us fly" – you know – and Éléazer stops them and says, "Whither go ye?". . . well, M Poligny – I was watching him from the back of the next box, which was empty – M Poligny got up and walked out quite stiffly, like a statue, and before I had time to ask him, "Whither go ye?" like Éléazer, he was down the staircase, but without breaking his leg. . . .'

'Still, that doesn't tell us how the Opera ghost came to ask you for a footstool,' insisted M Moncharmin.

'Well, from that evening, no one tried to take the ghost's private box from him. The manager gave orders that he was to have it at each performance. And, whenever he came, he asked me for a footstool. . . .'

'Tut, tut! A ghost asking for a footstool! Then this ghost of yours is a woman?'

'No, the ghost is a man.'

'How do you know?'

'He has a man's voice, oh, such a lovely man's voice! This is what happens: when he comes to the Opera, it's usually in the middle of the first act. He gives three little taps on the door of Box 5. The first time I heard those three taps, when I knew there was no one in the box, you can think how puzzled I was! I opened the door, listened, looked: nobody! And then I heard a voice say, "Mame Jules" – my poor husband's name was Jules – "a footstool, please." Saving your presence, gentlemen, it made me feel all overish like. But the voice went on, "Don't be afraid, Mame Jules: I'm the Opera ghost!" And the voice was so soft and kind that I hardly felt frightened at all. *The voice was sitting in the corner chair, on the right, in the front row.'*

'Was there any one in the box to the right of Box 5?' asked Moncharmin.

'No, Box 7 and Box 3, the one on the left, were both empty. The curtain had only just gone up.'

'And what did you do?'

'Well, I brought the footstool. Of course, it wasn't for himself he wanted it, but for his lady! But I never heard her nor saw her. . . .'

Eh? What? So now the ghost was married! The eyes of the two managers travelled from Mame Giry to the inspector, who, standing behind the box-keeper, was waving his arms to attract their attention. He tapped his forehead with a distressful forefinger, to convey his opinion that the Widow Jules Giry was most certainly mad, a piece of pantomime which confirmed M Richard in his determination to get rid of an inspector who kept a lunatic in his service. Meanwhile, the worthy lady went on about her ghost, now depicting his generosity:

'At the end of the performance, he always gives me two francs, sometimes five, sometimes even ten, when he has been many days without coming. Only, since people have begun to annoy him again, he gives me nothing at all. . . .'

'Excuse me, my good woman,' said Moncharmin, while Mame Giry tossed the feathers in her dingy hat at this persistent familiarity, 'excuse me. . . . How does the ghost manage to give you your two francs?'

'Why, he leaves it on the little shelf in the box, of course. I find it with the programme which I always give him. Some evenings, I find flowers in the box, a rose that must have dropped from his lady's bodice . . . for he brings a lady with him sometimes: one day, they left a fan behind them.'

'Oh, the ghost left a fan, did he? And what did you do with it?'

'Well, I brought it back to the box next night.'

Here the inspector's voice was raised:

'You've broken the rules; I shall have to fine you, Mame Giry.'

'Hold your tongue, you fool!' muttered M Firmin Richard.

'You brought back the fan. And then?'

'Well, then, they took it away with them, sir; it was not there at the end of the performance; and in its place they left me a box of English sweets, which I'm very fond of. That's one of the ghost's pretty thoughts. . . .'

'That will do, Mame Giry. You can go.'

When Mame Giry had bowed herself out, with the dignity that never deserted her, the managers told the inspector that they had decided to dispense with that old madwoman's services; and, when he had gone in his turn, they instructed the acting-manager to make up the inspector's accounts. Left alone, the managers told each other of the idea which they both had in mind, which was that they should look into that little matter of Box 5 for themselves.

CHAPTER V

The Enchanted Violin

CHRISTINE DAAÉ, owing to a series of intrigues to which I will return later, did not immediately continue her triumph at the Opera. After the famous gala night, she sang once at the Duchesse de Zurich's; but this was the last occasion on which she was heard in society. She refused, without plausible excuse, to appear at a charity concert to which she had promised her assistance. She acted throughout as though she were no longer the mistress of her own destiny and as though she dreaded a fresh triumph.

She knew that the Comte de Chagny, to please his brother, had done his best on her behalf with M Richard; and she wrote to thank him and also to ask him to cease speaking in her favour. Her reason for this curious attitude was never known. Some pretended that it was due to overweening pride; others spoke of her divine modesty. But people on the stage are not so modest as all that; and I think that I shall not be far from the truth if I ascribe her action simply to fear. Yes, I believe that Christine Daaé was frightened by what had happened to her. I have a letter of Christine's (it forms part of the Persian's collection), relating to this period, which suggests a feeling of absolute terror:

'I don't know myself when I sing,' writes the poor child.

She showed herself nowhere; and the Vicomte de Chagny tried in vain to meet her. He wrote to her, asking leave to call upon her, but had given up all hope of receiving a reply, when, one morning, she sent him the following note:

'MONSIEUR,

'I have not forgotten the little boy who went into the sea to rescue my scarf. I feel that I must write to you to-day, when I am going to Perros, in fulfilment of a sacred duty. To-morrow is the anniversary of the death of my poor father, whom you knew and who was very fond of you. He is buried there, with his violin, in the graveyard of the little church, at the bottom of the slope where we used to play as children, beside the road where, when we were a little bigger, we said good-bye for the last time.'

The Vicomte de Chagny hurriedly consulted a railway guide, dressed as quickly as he could, wrote a few lines for his valet to take to his brother and jumped into a cab which brought him to the Gare Montparnasse just in time to miss the morning train. He spent a dismal day in town and did not recover his spirits until the evening, when seated in his compartment in the Brittany express. He read Christine's note over and over again, smelling its perfume, recalling the sweet pictures of his childhood, and spent the rest of that tedious night journey in feverish dreams that began and ended with Christine Daaé. Day was breaking when he alighted at Lannion. He hurried to the diligence for Perros-Guirec. He was the only passenger. He questioned the driver and learnt that, on the evening of the previous day, a young lady who looked like a Parisian had gone to Perros and put up at the inn known as the Setting Sun.

The nearer he drew to her, the more fondly he remembered the story of the little Swedish singer. Most of the details are still unknown to the public.

There was once, in a little market-town not far from Upsala, a peasant who lived with his family, tilling the earth during the week and singing in the choir on Sundays. This peasant had a little daughter to whom he taught the musical alphabet before she learnt how to read. Daaé's father was a great musician, perhaps without knowing it. Not a fiddler throughout the length and breadth of Scandinavia played as he did. His reputation was widespread; and he was always invited to set the couples dancing at weddings and other festivals. His wife died when Christine was entering upon her sixth year. Then the father, who cared only for his daughter and his music, sold his patch of ground and went to Upsala in search of fame and fortune. He found nothing but poverty.

He returned to the country, wandering from fair to fair, strumming his Scandinavian melodies, while his child, who never left his side, listened to him in ecstasy or sang to his playing. One day, Professor Valerius heard them, at Limby Fair, and took them to Gothenburg. He maintained that the father was the first violinist in the world and that the daughter had the makings of a great artist. Her education and instruction were provided for. She made rapid progress and charmed everybody with her prettiness, her grace of manner and her eagerness to please.

When Valerius and his wife went to settle in France, they took Daaé and Christine with them. 'Mamma' Valerius treated Christine as her daughter. As for Daaé, he began to pine away with home-sickness. He never went out of doors in Paris, but lived in a sort of dream which he kept up with his violin. For hours at a time, he remained locked up in his bedroom with his daughter, fiddling and singing very, very softly. Sometimes, Mamma Valerius would come and listen behind the door, wipe away a tear and go downstairs again on tiptoe, sighing for her Scandinavian skies.

Daaé seemed not to recover his strength until the summer, when the whole family went to stay at Perros-Guirec, in a faraway corner of Brittany, where the sea was of the same colour as in his own country. Often he would play his saddest tunes on the beach and pretend that the sea stopped its roaring to listen to them. And then he induced Mamma Valerius to indulge a queer whim of his. At the time of the 'pardons,' or Breton pilgrimages, the village festivals and dances, he went off with his fiddle, as in the old days, and was allowed to take his daughter with him for a week. They provided the smallest hamlets with music enough to last them for a year and slept at night in a barn, refusing a bed at the inn, lying close together on the straw, as when they were so poor in Sweden. At the same time, they were very neatly dressed, made no collection, refused the halfpence offered them; and the country-folk could not understand the conduct of this rustic fiddler, who tramped the roads with that pretty child who sang like an angel from Heaven. The people followed them from village to village.

One day, a little boy, who was out with his governess, made her take a longer walk than she intended, for he could not tear himself from the little girl whose pure, sweet voice seemed to bind him to her. They came to the shore of a creek which is still called Trestraou, but which now, I believe, boasts a casino or something of the sort. At that time there was nothing there but sky and sea and a stretch of golden beach. Only there was also a high wind, which blew Christine's scarf out to sea. Christine gave a cry and put out her arms, but the scarf was already far on the waves. Then she heard a voice say:

'It's all right; I'll go and fetch your scarf out of the sea.'

And she saw a little boy running fast, in spite of the outcries and indignant protests of a respectable lady in black. The little boy ran into the sea, dressed as he was, and brought her back her scarf. Boy and scarf were both soaked through. The lady in black made a great fuss, but Christine laughed merrily and kissed the little boy, who was none other than the Vicomte Raoul de Chagny, staying at Lannion with his aunt.

During the season, they saw each other and played together almost every day. At the aunt's request, seconded by Professor Valerius, Daaé consented to give the young viscount some violin-lessons. In this way, Raoul learnt to love the same airs that had charmed Christine's childhood. They also both had the same calm and dreamy little souls. They delighted in stories, in old Breton legends; and their favourite sport was to go and ask for them at the cottage-doors, like beggars:

'Ma'am . . .' or 'Kind gentleman . . . have you a little story to tell us, please?'

And it seldom happened that they did not have one 'given' them; for nearly every old Breton grandame has, at least once in her life, seen the 'korrigans' dance by moonlight on the heather.

But their great treat was, in the twilight, in the great silence of the evening, after the sun had set in the sea, when Daaé came and sat down by them on the roadside and, in a low voice, as though fearing lest he should frighten the ghosts whom he evoked, told them the legends of the land of the North. And, the moment he stopped, the children would ask for more.

There was one story that began:

'A king sat in a little boat on one of those deep, still lakes which open like a bright eye in the midst of the Norwegian mountains . . .'

And another:

'Little Lotte thought of everything and nothing. Her hair was gold as the sun's rays and her soul as clear and blue as her eyes. She wheedled her mother, was kind to her doll, took great care of her frock and her little red shoes and her fiddle, but most of all loved, when she went to sleep, to hear the Angel of Music . . .'

While the old man told this story, Raoul looked at Christine's blue eyes and golden hair; and Christine thought that Lotte was very lucky to hear the Angel of Music when she went to sleep. The Angel of Music played a part in all Daddy Daaé's tales; and he maintained that every great musician, every great artist received a visit from the Angel at least once in his life. Sometimes, the Angel leans over their cradle, as happened to Lotte; and that is how there are little prodigies who play the fiddle at six better than men of fifty, which, you must admit, is very wonderful. Sometimes, the Angel comes much later, because the children are naughty and won't learn their lessons or practise their scales. And sometimes, he does not come at all, because the children have a wicked heart or a bad conscience.

No one ever sees the Angel; but he is heard by those who are meant to hear him. He often comes when they least expect him, when they feel sad and discouraged. Then their ears suddenly perceive celestial harmonies, a divine voice, which they remember all their lives long. Persons who are visited by the Angel quiver with a thrill unknown to the rest of mankind. And they cannot touch an instrument or open their mouths to sing, without producing sounds that put all other human sounds to shame. Then people who do not know that the Angel has visited these persons say that they have 'genius.'

Little Christine asked her father if he had heard the Angel of Music. But Daddy Daaé shook his head sadly; and then his eyes lit up, as he said:

'You will hear him one day, my child! When I am in Heaven, I will send him to you!'

Daddy was beginning to cough at that time. Autumn came and parted Raoul and Christine.

Three years later, they met again at Perros. Professor Valerius was dead, but his widow remained in France with Daddy Daaé and his daughter, who continued to play the violin and sing, wrapping in their dream of harmony their kind patroness, who seemed henceforth to live on music alone. The youth, as he now was, had come to Perros on the chance of finding them and went straight to the house in which they used to stay. He first saw the old man; and then Christine entered, carrying the tea-tray. She flushed at the sight of Raoul, who went up to her and kissed her. She asked him a few questions, performed her duties as hostess prettily, took up the tray again and left the room. Then she ran into the garden and took refuge on a bench, a prey to feelings that stirred her young heart for the first time. Raoul followed her and they talked until evening, very shyly. They were quite changed, were as cautious as two diplomatists and told each other things that had nothing to do with their budding sentiments. When they took leave of each other by the roadside, Raoul, pressing a kiss on Christine's trembling lips, said:

'Mademoiselle, I shall never forget you!'

And he went away regretting his words, for he knew that Christine could not be the wife of the Vicomte de Chagny.

As for Christine, she tried not to think of him and devoted herself wholly to her art. She made wonderful progress and those who heard her prophesied that she would be the greatest singer in the world. Meanwhile, the father died; and, suddenly, she seemed to have lost with him her voice, her soul and her genius. She retained just, but only just enough of all this to enter the Conservatoire, where she did not distinguish herself at all, attending the classes without enthusiasm and taking a prize only to please old Mamma Valerius, with whom she continued to live.

The first time that Raoul saw Christine at the Opera, he was charmed by the girl's beauty and by the sweet images of the past which it evoked, but was rather surprised at the negative side of her art. She seemed to have lost touch of things. He returned to listen to her. He followed her in the wings. He would wait for her behind a Jacob's ladder. He tried to attract her attention. More than once, he walked after her to the door of her box, but she did not see him. She appeared, for that matter, to see nobody. She was all indifference. Raoul suffered, for she was very beautiful, while he was shy and dared not confess his love, even to himself. And then came the relevation of that gala performance: the heavens torn asunder and an angel's voice heard upon earth for the delight of mankind and the utter conquest of his heart. . . .

And then . . . and then there was that man's voice behind the door – 'You must love me!' – and no one in the room. . . .

Why did she laugh when he reminded her of the incident of the scarf? Why did she not recognize him? And why had she now written to him? . . .

Perros was reached at last. Raoul walked into the smoky parlour of the Setting Sun and saw Christine standing before him, smiling and showing no astonishment:

'So you have come,' she said. 'I felt that I should find you here when I came back from mass. Some one told me so at the church.'

'Who?' asked Raoul, taking her little hand in his.

'Why, my poor dead father!'

There was a silence; and then Raoul asked:

'Did your father tell you that I love you, Christine, and that I cannot live without you?'

Christine blushed to the eyes and turned away her head. In a trembling voice she said:

'Me? You are dreaming, my friend!'

And she burst out laughing to put herself in countenance.

'Don't laugh, Christine; I am quite serious.'

And she replied gravely:

'I did not send for you to tell me such things as that.'

'You "sent for me," Christine; you knew that your letter would not leave me indifferent and that I was hastening to Perros. How can you have thought that, if you did not think I loved you?'

'I thought you would remember our games here, as children, in which my father so often joined. I really don't know what I thought. . . . Perhaps I was wrong to write to you. . . . This anniversary and your sudden appearance in my room at the Opera, the other evening, reminded me of the time long past and made me write to you as the little girl that I then was. . . .'

There was something in Christine's attitude that struck Raoul as not quite natural. He did not feel any hostility in her; far from it: the sad tenderness shining in her eyes told him that. But why was this tenderness so sad? That was what he wished to know and what was irritating him. . . .

'When you saw me in your dressing-room, was that the first time you noticed me, Christine?'

She was incapable of lying:

'No,' she said, 'I had often seen you in your brother's box. And also on the stage.'

'I thought so!' said Raoul, compressing his lips. 'But then why, when you saw me in your room, at your feet, reminding you that I had rescued your scarf from the sea, why did you answer me as though you did not know me and also why did you laugh?'

The tone of these questions was so rough that Christine stared at Raoul without replying. The young man himself was aghast at the sudden quarrel which he had dared to raise at the very moment when he had resolved to speak words of gentleness, love and submission to Christine. A husband, a lover with all rights would talk no differently to a wife, a mistress who had offended him. But he had gone too far and saw no other way out of the ridiculous position than to behave odiously:

'You don't answer!' he said, angrily and unhappily. 'Well, I will answer for you. It was because there was some one in the room who was in your way, Christine, some one whom you did not wish to know that you could be interested in any one else!'

'If any one was in my way, my friend,' Christine broke in, coldly, 'if any one was in my way that evening it was yourself, because I told you to leave the room!'

'Yes . . . so that you might remain with the other!'

'What are you saying, monsieur?' asked the girl, excitedly. 'And what other do you refer to?'

'To the man to whom you said, "I sing only for you! . . . To-night, I gave you my soul and I am dead!" '

Christine seized Raoul's arm and clutched it with a strength which one would not have suspected in so frail a creature:

'Then you were listening behind the door?'

'Yes, because I love you. . . . And I heard everything. . . .'

'You heard what?'

And the young girl, becoming strangely calm, released Raoul's arm.

'He said to you, "Christine, you must love me!" '

At these words, a deathly pallor spread over Christine's face, dark rings formed round her eyes, she staggered and seemed on the point of swooning. Raoul darted forward with arms out-stretched, but Christine had overcome her passing faintness and, in a low, almost dying voice:

'Go on!' she said. 'Go on! Tell me all you heard!'

At an utter loss to understand, Raoul answered:

'I heard him reply, when you said that you had given him your soul, "Your soul is a beautiful thing, child, and I thank you. No emperor ever received so fair a gift. The angels wept to-night." '

Christine carried her hand to her heart, a prey to indescribable emotion. Her eyes stared before her like a madwoman's. Raoul was terror-stricken. But suddenly Christine's eyes moistened and two great tears trickled, like two pearls, down her ivory cheeks. . . .

'Christine!'

'Raoul!'

The young man tried to take her in his arms, but she escaped and fled in great disorder.

While Christine remained locked in her room, Raoul was at his wits' end what to do. He refused to take lunch. He was terribly concerned and bitterly grieved to see the hours, which he had hoped to find so sweet, slip past without the presence of the young Swedish girl. Why did she not come to roam with him through the country where they had so many memories in common? And, as she seemed to have nothing more to do at Perros and, in fact, was doing nothing there, why did she not go back to Paris at once? He heard that she had had a mass said that morning for the repose of her father's soul and that she had spent a long time praying in the little church and on the fiddler's tomb.

Raoul walked away, dejectedly, to the churchyard and wandered alone among the graves, reading the inscriptions; but, suddenly, as he turned behind the apse, he was struck by the dazzling note of the flowers that sighed upon the granite tombstones, straggled over the white ground and made fragrant all that frozen corner of the Breton winter. They were marvellous red roses that had blossomed in the morning, in the snow, giving a glimpse of life among the dead, for death was all around him. It also, like the flowers, issued from the ground, which had rejected a number of its corpses. Skeletons and skulls by the hundred were heaped against the wall of the church, held in position by a wire that left the whole gruesome stack visible. Dead men's bones arranged in rows, like so many bricks, seemed to form the first course upon which the sacristy-walls were built. The door of the sacristy opened in the middle of that bony structure, which is often seen beside old Breton churches.

Raoul said a prayer for Daaé and then, painfully impressed by the eternal smiles on the mouths of all those skulls, he climbed the slope and sat down on the edge of the moor overlooking the sea. The wind fell with the evening. Raoul was surrounded by icy darkness, but he did not feel the cold. It was here, he remembered, that he used to come with little Christine to see the korrigans dance at the rising of the moon. He had never seen any, though his eyes were good, whereas Christine, who was a little short-sighted, pretended that she had seen many. He smiled at the thought and then suddenly gave a start. A voice behind him said:

'Do you think the korrigans will come this evening?'

It was Christine. He tried to speak. She put her gloved hand on his mouth;

'Listen, Raoul. I have decided to tell you something serious, very serious. . . . Do you remember the legend of the Angel of Music?'

'I do indeed,' he said. 'I believe it was here that your father first told it to us.'

'And it was here that he said, "When I am in Heaven, my child, I will send him to you." Well, Raoul, my father is in Heaven; and I have been visited by the Angel of Music.'

'I have no doubt of it,' replied the young man, gravely, for it seemed to him that his friend, in obedience to a pious thought, was connecting the memory of her father with the brilliancy of her last triumph.

Christine appeared astonished at the Vicomte de Chagny's coolness:

'How do you understand it, Raoul?' she asked, bringing her pale face so close to his that he might have thought that Christine intended to give him a kiss; but she only wanted to read his eyes, in spite of the dark.

'I understand,' he said, 'that no human being can sing as you sang the other evening without the intervention of some miracle. No professor on earth can teach you such accents as those. You have heard the Angel of Music, Christine.'

'Yes,' she said, solemnly, *'in my dressing-room.* That is where he comes to give me my daily lesson.'

'In your dressing-room?' he echoed, stupidly.

'Yes, that is where I have heard him; and I have not been the only one to hear him. . . .'

'Who else heard him, Christine?'

'You, my friend.'

'I? I heard the Angel of Music?'

'Yes, the other evening, it was he who was talking when you were listening behind the door. It was he who said, "You must love me!" But I then thought that I was the only one to hear his voice. Imagine my astonishment when you told me, this morning, that you could hear him too. . . .'

Raoul burst out laughing. The first rays of the moon came and shrouded the two young people in their light. Christine turned on Raoul with a hostile air. Her eyes, usually so gentle, flashed fire:

'What are you laughing at? *You* think you heard a man's voice, I suppose?'

'Well! . . .' replied the young man, whose ideas began to grow confused in the face of Christine's determined attitude.

'You, Raoul, say that? You, my old play-fellow? You, my father's friend? How you have changed since those days! What are you thinking of? I am an honest girl, M le Vicomte de Chagny, and I don't lock myself up in my dressing-room with men's voices. If you had opened the door, you would have seen that there was no one there!'

'That's true! I did open the door when you were gone, and I found no one in the room. . . .'

'So you see! . . . Well?'

The viscount summoned all his courage:

'Well, Christine, I think that somebody is making game of you.'

She gave a cry and ran away. He ran after her, but, in a tone of fierce anger, she called out:

'Leave me! Leave me!'

And she disappeared.

Raoul returned to the inn, feeling very weary, very low spirited and very sad. He was told that Christine had gone to her bedroom saying that she would not be down to dinner. Raoul dined alone, in a very gloomy mood. Then he went to his room and tried to read, went to bed and tried to sleep. There was no sound in the next room.

The hours passed slowly. It was about half-past eleven when he distinctly heard some one moving, with a light, stealthy step, in the room next to his. Then Christine had not gone to bed! Without troubling for a reason, Raoul dressed, taking care not to make a sound, and waited. Waited for what? How could he tell? But his heart thumped in his chest when he heard Christine's door turn slowly on its hinges. Where could she be going, at this hour, when every one at Perros was fast asleep? Softly opening the door, he saw Christine's white form, in the moonlight, slip along the passage. She went down the stairs and he leant over the baluster above her. Suddenly, he heard two voices in rapid conversation. He caught one sentence:

'Don't lose the key.'

It was the landlady's voice. The door facing the sea was opened and locked again. Then all was still.

Raoul ran back to his room and threw open the window. Christine's white form stood on the deserted quay.

The first floor of the Setting Sun was at no great height and a tree growing against the wall held out its branches to Raoul's impatient arms and enabled him to climb down, unknown to the landlady. Her amazement, therefore, was great when, the next morning, the young man was brought back to her half-frozen, more dead than alive, and when she learnt that he had been found stretched at full length on the steps of the high altar of the little church. She ran at once to tell Christine, who hurried down and, with the help of the landlady, did her best to revive him. He soon opened his eyes and was not long in recovering when he saw his friend's charming face bent over him.

A few weeks later, when the tragedy at the Opera compelled the intervention of the public prosecutor, M Mifroid, the commissary of police, examined the Vicomte de Chagny, touching the events of the night at Perros. I quote the questions and answers as given in the official report (pp. 150 *et seq.*):

'*Q*. Did Mlle Daaé not see you come down from your room by the curious road which you selected?

'*R*. No, monsieur, no, although, when walking behind her, I took no pains to deaden the sound of my footsteps. In fact, I was anxious that she should turn round and see me. I realized that I had no excuse for following her and that this sort of spying on her was unworthy of me. But she seemed not to hear me and acted exactly as though I were not there. She quietly left the quay and then suddenly walked quickly up the road. The church clock had struck a quarter to twelve and I thought that this must have made her hurry, for she began almost to run and continued at this pace till she came to the churchyard.

'*Q*. Was the gate open?

'*R*. Yes, monsieur, and this surprised me, but did not seem to surprise Mlle Daaé.

'*Q*. Was there no one in the churchyard?

'*R*. I did not see any one; and, if there had been, I must have seen him. The moon was shining on the snow and made the night quite light.

'*Q*. Was it not possible for a person to hide behind the tombstones?

'*R*. No, monsieur. They were quite small, poor tombstones, partly hidden under the snow, with their crosses just above the level of the ground. The only shadows were those of the crosses and ourselves. The church stood out quite brightly. I never saw so clear a night. It was very fine and very cold; and one could see everything.

'*Q*. Are you superstitious?

'*R*. No, monsieur, I am a practising Catholic.

'*Q*. In what condition of mind were you?

'*R*. Very sane and peaceful, I assure you. Mlle Daaé's curious action in going out at this hour had worried me at first; but, as soon as I saw her go to the churchyard, I thought that she meant to fulfil some pious duty on her father's grave and I considered this so natural that I recovered all my calmness. I was only surprised that she had not heard me walking behind her, for my footsteps were quite audible on the hard snow. But she must have been taken up with her intentions and I resolved not to disturb her. She knelt down by her father's grave, made the sign of the cross and began to pray. At that moment, it struck midnight. At the last stroke, I saw Mlle Daaé lift her eyes to the sky and stretch out her arms as though in ecstasy. I was wondering what the reason could be, when I myself raised my head and everything within me seemed drawn towards the Unseen, *which was playing the most perfect music!* Christine and I knew that music: we had heard it as children. But it had never been executed with such divine art, not even by M Daaé. I remembered all that Christine had told me of the Angel of Music. The air was the *Resurrection of Lazarus*, which old M Daaé used to play to us in his hours of melancholy and of faith. If Christine's Angel had existed, he could not have played better, that night, on the late musician's violin. When the music stopped, I seemed to hear a noise from the skulls in the heap of bones: it was as though they were chuckling; and I could not help shuddering.

'*Q*. Did it not occur to you that the musician might be hiding behind that very heap of bones?

'*R*. It was the one thought that did occur to me, monsieur, so much so that I omitted to follow Mlle Daaé when she stood up and walked slowly to the gate. She was so much absorbed just then that I am not surprised that she did not see me.

'*Q*. Then what happened, that you were found in the morning lying half-dead on the steps of the high altar?

'*R*. First a skull rolled to my feet . . . then another . . . then another. . . . It was as if I were the jack of that ghastly game of bowls. And I had an idea that a false step must have destroyed the balance of the structure behind which our musician was concealed. This surmise seemed to be confirmed when I saw a shadow suddenly glide along the sacristy-wall. I ran up. The shadow had already pushed open the door and entered the church. But I was quicker than the shadow and caught hold of a corner of its cloak. At that moment, we were just in front of the high altar; and the moonbeams fell straight upon us through the stained-glass windows of the apse. As I did not let go of the cloak, the shadow turned round; and I saw a terrible death's-head, which darted a look at me from a pair of scorching eyes. I felt as if I were face to face with Satan; and, in the presence of this unearthly apparition, my heart gave way, my courage failed me . . . and I remember nothing more until I recovered consciousness at the Setting Sun.'

CHAPTER VI

A Visit To Box 5

WE LEFT M FIRMIN RICHARD and M Armand Moncharmin at the moment when they were deciding to 'look into that little matter of Box 5.'

Leaving behind them the broad staircase which leads from the lobby outside the managers' offices to the stage and its dependencies, they crossed the 'tray,' went out by the subscribers' door and entered the house through the first little passage on the left. Then they made their way through the front rows of stalls and looked at Box 5 on the grand tier. They could not see it clearly, because it was half in darkness and there were covers flung over the red-velvet ledges of all the boxes.

They were almost alone in the huge, gloomy house; and a great silence surrounded them. It was the time when most of the stage-hands go out for a drink. The staff had deserted the boards for the moment, leaving a scene half set. A few rays of light, a wan, sinister light, that seemed stolen from an expiring luminary, fell through some opening or other upon an old tower that raised its pasteboard battlements on the stage. Everything, in this deceptive light, adopted a fantastic shape. In the orchestra-stalls, the drugget covering them looked like an angry sea, whose bluey-grey waves had been suddenly rendered stationary by a secret order from the storm phantom, whose name, as we know, is Adamastor. MM Moncharmin and Richard were the shipwrecked mariners amid this motionless turmoil of a calico sea. They made for the left-hand boxes, ploughing their way like sailors who leave their ship and try to struggle to the shore. The eight great polished columns loomed in the dusk like so many tall piles supporting the threatening, crumbling, big-bellied cliffs whose layers were represented by the circular, parallel, waving lines of the balconies of the grand, first and second tiers of boxes. At the top, right on top of the cliff, lost in M Lenepveu's copper ceiling, figures grinned and grimaced, laughed and jeered at MM Richard and Moncharmin's distress And yet these figures were usually very serious. Their names were Isis, Amphitrite, Hebe, Pandora, Psyche, Thetis, Pomona, Daphne, Clytie, Galatea and Arethusa. Yes, Arethusa herself and Pandora, whom we all know by her box, looked down upon the two new managers of the Opera, who ended by clutching at some piece of wreckage and from there stared silently at Box 5 on the grand tier.

I had said that they were distressed. At least, I presume so. M Moncharmin, in any case, admits that he was impressed. To quote his own words, in his *Memoirs:*

'This moonshine about the Opera ghost, in which, since we first took over the duties of MM Poligny and Debienne, we had been so nicely steeped' – Moncharmin's style is not always above reproach – 'had no doubt ended by blinding my imaginative and also my visual faculties. It may be that the exceptional surroundings in which we found ourselves, in the midst of an incredible silence, impressed us to an unusual extent. It may be that we were the sport of some kind of hallucination, produced by the semidarkness of the theatre and the partial gloom that filled Box 5. At any rate, I saw and Richard also saw a shape in the box. Richard said nothing, nor did I. But we spontaneously seized each other's hand. We stood like that for some minutes, without moving, with our eyes fixed on the same point; but the figure had disappeared. Then we went out and, in the lobby, communicated our impressions to each other and talked about "the shape." The misfortune was that my shape was not in the least like Richard's. I had seen a thing like a death's-head resting on the ledge of the box, whereas Richard saw the shape of an old woman who looked like Mother Giry. We soon discovered that we had really been the victims of an illusion, whereupon, without further delay and laughing like madmen, we ran to Box 5 on the grand tier, went inside and found no shape of any kind.'

Box 5 is just like all the grand-tier boxes. There is nothing to distinguish it from any of the others. M Moncharmin and M Richard, ostensibly highly amused and laughing at each other, moved the furniture of the box, lifted the covers and the chairs and particularly examined the arm-chair in which 'the man's voice' used to sit. But they saw that it was a respectable armchair, with no magic about it. Altogether, the box was the most ordinary box in the world, with its red hangings, its chairs, its carpet and its ledge covered in red velvet. After feeling the carpet in the most serious manner possible and discovering nothing here or anywhere else, they went down to the corresponding box on the pit tier below. In Box 5 on the pit tier, which is just inside the first entrance from the stalls on the left, they found nothing worth mentioning either:

'Those people are all making fools of us!' Firmin Richard ended by exclaiming. 'It will be *Faust* on Saturday: let us both watch the performance from Box 5 on the grand tier!'

CHAPTER VII

The Fatal Performance

ON THE SATURDAY MORNING, on reaching their office, the joint managers found a letter from O.G., worded in these terms:

'MY DEAR MANAGERS,

'So it is to be war between us?

'If you still care for peace, here is my ultimatum. It consists of the care of the four following conditions:

'1. You must give me back my private box; and I shall expect to have it at my free disposal from this day forward.

'2. The part of Margarita shall be sung to-night by Christine Daaé. Never mind about Carlotta: she will be ill.

'3. I absolutely insist upon the good and loyal services of Mme Giry, my box-keeper, whom you will reinstate in her functions forthwith.

'4. Let me know by a letter handed to Mme Giry, who will see that it reaches me, that you accept, as did your predecessors, the terms of the lease relating to my monthly allowance. I will inform you later how you are to pay it to me.

'*If you refuse, you will give* Faust *to-night in a house with a curse upon it.*

'Take my advice and be warned in time.

O.G.'

'Look here, I'm sick of him, dead-sick of him!' shouted Richard, bringing his fists down on his office-table.

Just then, Mercier, the acting-manager, entered:

'Lachenel would like to see one of you gentlemen,' he said. 'He says that his business is urgent; the chap seems quite upset.'

'Who is Lachenel?' asked Richard.

'He's your stud-groom.'

'What do you mean, my stud-groom?'

'Yes, sir,' explained Mercier, 'there are several grooms at the Opera and M Lachenel is at the head of them.'

'And what does this groom do?'

'He has the chief management of the stable.'

'What stable?'

'Why, yours, sir, the stable of the Opera.'

'Is there a stable at the Opera? Upon my word, I didn't know. Where is it?'

'In the cellars, on the Rotunda side. It's a very important department: we have twelve horses.'

'Twelve horses! And what for, in heaven's name?'

'Why, we want trained horses for the processions in the *Juive*, the *Prophète* and so on; horses used to the boards. It is the grooms' business to teach them. M Lachenel is very clever at it. He used to manage Franconi's stables.'

'Very well . . . but what does he want?'

'I don't know; I never saw him in such a state.'

'He can come in.'

M Lachenel came in, carrying a riding-whip, with which he lashed his right boot in an irritable manner.

'Good-morning, M Lachenel,' said Richard, somewhat impressed. 'To what do we owe the honour of your visit?'

'Mr Manager, I have come to ask you to get rid of the whole stable.'

'What, you want to get rid of our horses?'

'I'm not talking of the horses, but of the stablemen.'

'How many stablemen have you, M Lachenel?'

'Six.'

'Six stablemen! That's at least two too many.'

'These are "places," ' interposed Mercier, 'created and forced upon us by the under-secretary for fine-arts. They are filled by protégés of the government;' and, if I may venture to . . .'

'I don't care a hang for the government! ' roared Richard. 'We don't need more than four stablemen for twelve horses.'

'Eleven,' said the stud-groom, correcting him.

'Twelve,' repeated Richard.

'Eleven,' repeated Lachenel.

'Oh, the acting-manager told me that you had twelve horses!'

'I did have twelve, but I have only eleven since César was stolen.'

And M Lachenel caught himself a great smack on the boot with his whip.

'Has César been stolen?' cried the acting-manager. 'César, the white horse in the *Prophète?*'

'There are not two Césars,' said the stud-groom, dryly. 'I was ten years at Franconi's and I have seen plenty of horses in my time. Well, there are not two Césars. And he's been stolen.'

'How?'

'I don't know. Nobody knows. That's why I have come to ask you to sack the whole stable.'

'What do your stablemen say?'

'All sorts of nonsense. . . . Some of them accuse the supers. . . . Others pretend that it's the acting-manager's doorkeeper. . . .'

'My door-keeper? I'll answer for him as I would for myself!' protested Mercier.

'But, after all, M Lachenel,' cried Richard, 'you must have some idea. . . .'

'Yes, I have,' M Lachenel declared. 'I have an idea and I'll tell you what it is. There's no doubt about it in my mind.' He walked up to the two managers and whispered, 'It's the ghost that did the trick!'

Richard gave a jump:

'What, you too! You too!'

'How do you mean, I too? Isn't it natural, after what I saw. . .?'

'What did you see?'

'I saw, as clearly as I now see you, a black shadow riding a white horse that was as like César as one pea is to another!'

'And didn't you run after them?'

'I did and I shouted, but they were too fast for me and disappeared in the darkness of the underground gallery. . . .'

M Richard rose:

'That will do, M Lachenel. You can go. . . . We will lodge a complaint against "the ghost." '

'And sack my stable . . .?'

'Oh, of course! Good-morning.'

M Lachenel bowed and withdrew. Richard foamed at the mouth:

'Settle that idiot's account at once, please.'

'He is a friend of the government's representative!' Mercier ventured to say.

'And he takes his vermouth at Tortoni's with Lagréné, Scholl and Pertuiset, the lion-hunter,' added Moncharmin. 'We shall have the whole press against us! He'll tell the story of the ghost; and everybody will be laughing at our expense! We may as well be dead as make ourselves ridiculous!'

'All right, say no more about it. . . .'

At that moment the door opened. It must have been deserted by its usual Cerberus, for Mame Giry entered without ceremony, holding a letter in her hand, and said, hurriedly:

'I beg your pardon, excuse me, gentlemen, but I had a letter this morning from the Opera ghost. He told me to come to you, that you had something to . . .'

She did not complete the sentence. She saw Firmin Richard's face; and a terrible sight it was. He seemed ready to burst. He said nothing, he could not speak. But suddenly he acted. First, his left arm seized upon the quaint person of Mame Giry and made her describe so unexpected a semi-circle that she uttered a despairing cry. Next, his right foot imprinted its sole on the black taffeta of a skirt which certainly had never before undergone a similar outrage in a similar place. The thing happened so quickly that Mame Giry, when she found herself outside, in the passage, was still quite bewildered and seemed not to understand. Then, suddenly, she understood; and the Opera rang with her indignant yells, her violent protests and threats.

About the same time, Carlotta, who had a small house of her own in the Rue du Faubourg Saint-Honoré, rang for her maid, who brought her letters to her in bed. Among them was an anonymous missive, written in red ink, in a hesitating, clumsy hand, which ran:

'If you appear to-night, you must be prepared for a great misfortune at the moment when you open your mouth to sing . . . a misfortune worse than death.'

The letter took away Carlotta's appetite for breakfast. She pushed back her chocolate, sat up in bed and thought hard. It was not the first letter of the kind which she had received, but she had never had one couched in such threatening terms.

She thought herself, at that time, the victim of a thousand jealous attempts and went about saying that she had a secret enemy who had sworn to ruin her. She pretended that a wicked plot was being hatched against her, a cabal which would come to a head one of those days; but she added that she was not the woman to be intimidated.

The truth is that, if there was a cabal, it was led by Carlotta herself against poor Christine, who had no suspicion of it. Carlotta had never forgiven Christine for the triumph which she had achieved in taking her place at a moment's notice. When Carlotta heard of the astounding reception bestowed upon her understudy, she was at once cured of an incipient attack of bronchitis and a bad fit of sulking against the management and lost the slightest inclination to shirk her duties. From that time, she worked with all her might to 'smother' her rival, enlisting the services of influential friends to persuade the managers not to give Christine an opportunity for a fresh triumph. Certain newspapers which had begun to extol the talent of Christine now interested themselves only in the fame of Carlotta. Lastly, in the theatre itself, the celebrated but heartless and soulless diva made the most scandalous remarks about Christine and tried to cause her endless minor unpleasantnesses.

When Carlotta had finished thinking over the threat contained in the strange letter, she got up:

'We shall see,' she said, adding a few oaths in her native Spanish with a very determined air.

The first thing she saw, when looking out of her window, was a hearse. She was very superstitious; and the hearse and the letter convinced her that she was running the most serious risk that night. She collected all her supporters, told them that she was threatened at that evening's performance with a plot organized by Christine Daaé and declared that they must play a trick upon the chit by filling the house with her, Carlotta's, admirers. She had no lack of them, had she? She relied upon them to hold themselves prepared for any eventuality and to silence the adversaries, if, as she feared, they created a disturbance.

M Richard's private secretary called to ask after the diva's health and returned with the assurance that she was perfectly well and that, 'were she dying,' she would sing the part of Margarita that evening. The secretary urged her, in his chief's name, to commit no imprudence, to stay at home all day and to be careful of draughts; and Carlotta could not help, after he had gone, comparing this unusual and unexpected advice with the threats contained in that letter.

It was five o'clock when the post brought her a second anonymous letter in the same hand as the first. It was short, and said simply;

'You have a bad cold. If you are wise, you will see that it is madness to try to sing to-night.'

Carlotta sneered, shrugged her handsome shoulders and sang two or three notes to reassure herself.

Her friends were faithful to their promise. They were all at the Opera that night, but looked round in vain for the fierce conspirators whom they were instructed to suppress. The only unusual thing was the presence of M Richard and M Moncharmin in Box 5. Carlotta's friends thought that, perhaps, the managers had wind, on their side, of the proposed disturbance and that they had determined to be in the house, so as to stop it then and there; but this was an unjustifiable supposition, as the reader knows. M Richard and M Moncharmin were thinking of nothing but their ghost.

> Vain! In vain do I call, through my vigil weary,
> On creation and its Lord!
> Never reply will break the silence dreary!
> No sign! No single words!

The famous tenor, Carolus Fonta, had hardly finished Dr Faust's first appeal to the powers of darkness, when M Firmin Richard, who was sitting in the ghost's own chair, the front chair on the right, leant over to his partner and asked him, chaffingly:

'Well, has the ghost whispered a word in your ear yet?'

'Wait, don't be in such a hurry!' replied M Armand Moncharmin, in the same gay tone. 'The performance has only begun;

and you know that the ghost does not usually come until the middle of the first act.'

The first act passed without incident, which did not surprise Carlotta's friends, because Margarita does not sing in this act. As for the managers, they looked at each other when the curtain fell:

'That's one!' said Moncharmin.

'Yes, the ghost is late,' said Firmin Richard.

'It's not a bad house,' said Moncharmin, 'for "a house with a curse upon it." '

M Richard smiled and pointed to a fat, rather vulgar woman, dressed in black, sitting in a stall in the middle of the auditorium, with a man in a broadcloth frock-coat on either side of her:

'Who on earth are "those"?' asked Moncharmin.

' "Those," my dear fellow, are my concierge, her husband and her brother.'

'Did you give them their tickets?'

'I did. . . . My concierge had never been to the Opera – this is the first time – and, as she is now going to come every night, I wanted her to have a good seat, before spending her time showing other people to theirs.'

Moncharmin asked what he meant; and Richard answered that he had persuaded his concierge, in whom he had the greatest confidence, to come and take Mame Giry's place for a time. Yes, he would like to see if, with that woman, instead of the old lunatic, to look after it Box 5 would continue to astonish the nations.

'By the way,' said Moncharmin, 'you know that Mother Giry is going to lodge a complaint against you.'

'With whom? The ghost?'

The ghost! Moncharmin had almost forgotten the ghost! However, that mysterious person did nothing to recall himself to the managers' memory; and they were just saying so to each other for the second time, when the door of the box suddenly opened to admit the startled stage-manager.

'What's the matter?' they both asked, amazed at seeing him there at such a time.

'It seems there's a plot got up by Christine Daaé's friends against Carlotta. Carlotta's furious.'

'What on earth . . .?' said Richard, knitting his brows.

But the curtain rose on the kermesse scene and Richard made a sign to the stage-manager to go away. When the two were alone again, Moncharmin leant over to Richard:

'Then Daaé has friends?' he asked.

'Yes, she has.'

'Whom?'

Richard glanced across at a box on the grand tier containing no one but two men.

'The Comte de Chagny?'

'Yes, he spoke to me on her behalf with such warmth, that, if I had not known him to be Sorelli's friend . . .'

'Really? . . . Really?' . . . said Moncharmin.

'And who is that pale young man beside him?'

'That's his brother, the viscount.'

'He ought to be in his bed. He looks ill.'

The stage rang with gay song:

> , Red or white liquor,
> Coarse or fine!
> What can it matter,
> So we have wine?

Students, citizens, soldiers, girls and matrons whirled light-heartedly outside the inn with the figure of Bacchus for a sign. Siebel made her entrance. Christine Daaé looked charming in her boy's clothes; and Carlotta's partisans expected to hear her greeted with an ovation which would have enlightened them as to the intentions of her friends. But nothing happened.

On the other hand, when Margarita crossed the stage and sang the only two lines allotted her in this second act:

> Not my lord, not a lady am I, nor yet a beauty,
> And do not need an arm to help me on my way.

Carlotta was received with enthusiastic applause. It was so unexpected and so uncalled-for that those who knew nothing about the rumours looked at one another and asked what was happening. And this act also finished without incident.

Then everybody said:

'Of course, it will be during the next act.'

Some, who seemed better-informed than the rest, declared that the 'row' would begin with the ballad of the *King of Thule* and rushed to the subscribers' entrance to warn Carlotta. The managers left the box during the entr'acte to find out more about the 'plot' of which the stage-manager had spoken; but they soon returned to their seats, shrugging their shoulders and treating the whole affair as silly.

The first thing they saw, on entering, was a box of English sweets on the little shelf of the ledge. Who had put it there? They asked the box-keepers, but none of them knew. Then they went back to the shelf and, next to the box of sweets, found an opera-glass. They looked at each other. They had no inclination to laugh. All that Mame Giry had told them returned to their memory . . . and besides . . . besides . . . they seemed to feel a curious kind of draught around them. . . . They sat down in silence.

The scene represented Margarita's garden:

> Gentle flow'rs in the dew,
> Be message from me . . .

As she sang these first two lines, with her bunch of roses and lilac in her hand, Christine, raising her head, saw the Vicomte de Chagny in his box: and, from that moment, her voice seemed less sure, less crystal-clear than usual. Something seemed to deaden and dull her singing. . . .

'What a queer girl she is!' said one of Carlotta's friends in the stalls, almost aloud. 'The other day, she was divine; and tonight she's simply bleating. She has no experience, no training.'

> Gentle flow'rs, lie ye there
> And tell her from me . . .

The viscount put his head in his hands and wept. The count, behind him, gnawed his moustache, viciously shrugged his shoulders and frowned. For him, usually so cool and correct, to betray his inner feelings like that, by outward signs, the count must be very angry. He was. He had seen his brother return from a rapid and mysterious journey in an alarming state of health. The explanation that followed was unsatisfactory and the count asked Christine Daaé for an appointment. She had the audacity to reply that she could not see either him or his brother . . .

> Would she but deign to hear me
> And with one smile to cheer me . . .

'The little baggage!' growled the count.

And he wondered what she wanted, what she was hoping for. . . . She was a virtuous girl, she was said to have no friend, no protector of any sort. . . . That angel from the North must be very artful!

Raoul, behind the curtain of his hands that veiled his boyish tears, thought only of the letter which he received on his return to Paris, where Christine, fleeing from Perros like a thief in the night, had arrived before him:

'MY DEAR OLD LITTLE PLAYFELLOW'

'You must have the courage not to see me again, not to speak to me again. If you love me just a little, do this for me, for me who will never forget you, my dear Raoul. My life depends upon it. Your life depends upon it.

'Your little CHRISTINE.'

Thunders of applause. Carlotta made her entrance:

> I wish I could but know who was he
>> That addressed me,
>> If he was noble, or, at least, what his name is . . .

When Margaret had finished singing the ballad of the *King of Thule*, she was loudly cheered and again when she came to the end of the jewel song:

> Ah, the joy past compare
> These jewels bright to wear! . . .

Thenceforth, certain of herself, certain of her friends in the house, certain of her voice and her success, fearing nothing, Carlotta flung herself into her part without the least modesty or self-restraint. . . . She was no longer Margarita, she was Carmen. She was applauded all the more; and her duet with Faust seemed about to bring her a new success, when suddenly . . . a terrible thing happened

Faust had knelt on one knee:

> Let me gaze on the form before me,
>> While from yonder ether blue
> Look how the star of eve, bright and tender, lingers o'er me.
>> To love thy beauty too!

And Margarita replied:

> Oh, how strange!
>   Like a spell does the evening bind me!
> And a deep languid charm
> I feel without alarm
>   With its melody enwind me
> And all my heart subdue.

At that moment, at that identical moment, the terrible thing happened . . . Carlotta croaked like a toad:

'Co-ack!'

There was consternation on Carlotta's face and consternation on the faces of all the audience. The two managers in their boxes could not suppress an exclamation of horror. Every one felt that the thing was not natural, that there was witchcraft behind it. That toad smelt of brimstone. Poor, wretched, despairing, crushed Carlotta!

The uproar in the house was indescribable. If the thing had happened to any one but Carlotta, she would have been hooted. But everybody knew how perfect an instrument her voice was; and there was no display of anger, but only of horror and dismay, the sort of dismay which men would have felt if they had witnessed the catastrophe that broke the arms of the Venus de Milo! . . . And even then they would have seen . . . and understood . . .

But here this toad was incomprehensible! So much so that, after some seconds spent in asking herself if she had really heard that note, that sound, that infernal noise issue from her throat, she tried to persuade herself that it was not so, that she was the victim of an illusion, an illusion of the ear, and not of treachery on the part of her voice. . . .

Meanwhile, in Box 5, Moncharmin and Richard had turned very pale. This extraordinary and inexplicable incident filled them with a dread which was the more awful inasmuch, as for some little time, they had been within the direct influence of the ghost. They had felt his breath. Moncharmin's hair stood on end. Richard wiped the perspiration from his forehead. Yes, the ghost was there, around them, behind them, beside them: they felt his presence without seeing him, they heard his breath, close, close, close to them! . . . They were sure that there were three people in the box. . . . They trembled. . . . They thought of running away. . . . They dared not. . . . They dared not make a movement or exchange a word which might have told the ghost that they knew that he was there! . . . What was going to happen?

This happened:

'Co-ack!'

Their joint exclamation of horror was heard all over the house. *They felt that they were smarting under the ghost's attacks.* Leaning over the ledge of their box, they stared at Carlotta as though they did not recognize her. That infernal girl, with her 'Co-ack,' must have given the signal for some catastrophe. Ah, they were waiting for the catastrophe! The ghost had told them it would come! The house had a curse upon it! The two managers gasped and panted under the weight of the catastrophe. Richard was heard calling to Carlotta, in a smothered voice:

'Well, go on!'

No, Carlotta did not go on. . . . Bravely, heroically, she started afresh on the fatal line at the end of which the toad had appeared.

An awful silence succeeded the uproar. Again, Carlotta's voice alone filled the resounding house:

I feel without alarm . . .

The audience felt also, but not without alarm. . .

I feel without alarm – Co-ack!
With its melody enwind me – Co-ack!
And all my heart sub – Co-ack!

The toad also had started afresh!

The house broke into a wild tumult. The two managers collapsed in their chairs and dared not even turn round: they had not the strength; the ghost was chuckling behind their backs! And, at last, they distinctly heard his voice in their right ears, the impossible voice, the mouthless voice, saying:

'*She is singing to-night to bring the chandelier down!*'

With one accord, they raised their eyes to the ceiling and uttered a terrible cry. The chandelier, the immense mass of the chandelier was slipping down, coming towards them, at the call of that fiendish voice. Released from its hook, it plunged from the ceiling and came smashing into the middle of the stalls, amid a thousand shouts of terror. A wild rush for the doors followed.

The papers of the day state that there were numbers wounded and one killed. The chandelier had crashed down upon the head of the wretched woman who had come to the Opera for the first time in her life, the woman whom M Richard had appointed to succeed Mame Giry, the ghost's box-keeper, in her functions! She was killed on the spot and, the next morning, a newspaper appeared with this heading:

TWO HUNDRED THOUSAND KILOS ON THE HEAD OF A CONCIERGE!

That was her sole epitaph!

CHAPTER VIII

The Mysterious Brougham

THAT TRAGIC EVENING was a bad one for all concerned. Carlotta fell ill. As for Christine Daaé, she disappeared after the performance. A fortnight elapsed during which she was seen neither at the Opera nor outside the Opera.

Raoul, of course, was the first to be astonished at the young diva's absence. He wrote to her at Mme Valerius' flat and received no reply. His grief increased and he ended by being seriously alarmed at never seeing her name on the programme. *Faust* was played without her.

One afternoon, he went to the managers' office to ask the reason of Christine's disappearance. He found both of them looking extremely worried. Their own friends did not recognize them: they had lost all their gaiety and spirits. They were seen crossing the stage with hanging heads, careworn brows, pale cheeks, as though pursued by some abominable thought or the sport of some persistent fate.

The fall of the chandelier had involved them in no little responsibility; but it was difficult to make them speak about it. The inquest had ended in a verdict of accidental death, caused by the wear and tear of the chains with which the chandelier was hung from the ceiling; but it was the duty of both the old and the new managers to discover this wear and tear and have it remedied in time. And I feel bound to say that MM Richard and Moncharmin at this time appeared so changed, so absentminded, so mysterious, so incomprehensible that many of the subscribers thought that some event even more horrible than the fall of the chandelier must have affected their state of mind.

In their daily intercourse, they showed themselves very impatient, except with Mme Giry, who had been reinstated in her functions. And their reception of the Vicomte de Chagny, when he came to ask about Christine, was anything but cordial.

They merely told him that she was taking a holiday. He asked how long the holiday was for; and they replied, curtly, that it was for an unlimited period, as Mlle Daaé had requested leave of absence for reasons of health.

'Then she is ill!' he cried. 'What is the matter with her?'

'We don't know.'

'Didn't you send the doctor of the Opera to see her?'

'No, she did not ask for him; and, as we trust her, we took her word.'

Raoul left the building a prey to the gloomiest thoughts. He resolved, come what might, to go and enquire at Mamma Valerius'. He remembered the strong phrases in Christine's letter, forbidding him to make any attempt to see her. But what he had seen at Perros, what he had heard behind the dressing-room door, his conversation with Christine at the edge of the moor made him suspect some machination which, devilish though it might be, was none the less human.

The girl's highly strung imagination, her affectionate and credulous mind, the primitive education which had surrounded her childhood with a circle of legends, the constant brooding over her dead father and, above all, the state of sublime ecstasy into which music threw her from the moment that this art was made manifest to her under exceptional conditions, as in the churchyard at Perros: all this seemed to him to constitute a moral ground only too favourable for the malevolent designs of some mysterious and unscrupulous person. Of whom was Christine Daaé the victim? This was the very sensible question which Raoul put to himself as he hurried off to Mamma Valerius'.

He trembled as he rang at a little flat in the Rue Notre-Dame-des-Victoires. The door was opened by the maid whom he had seen coming out of Christine's dressing-room one evening. He asked if he could speak to Mme Valerius and was told that she was ill in bed and was not receiving visitors.

'Take in my card, please,' he said.

The maid soon returned and showed him into a small and scant-ily-furnished drawing-room, in which portraits of Professor Valerius and old Daaé faced each other on the walls.

'Madame begs monsieur le vicomte to excuse her,' said the ser-vant. 'She can only see him in her bedroom; the poor lady has lost the use of her legs.'

Five minutes later, Raoul was ushered into an ill-lit room, where he recognised the good, kind face of Christine's benefac-tress in the semi-darkness of an alcove. Mamma Valerius' hair was quite white now, but her eyes had grown no older: never, indeed, had their expression been so bright, so pure, so childlike.

'M de Chagny!' she cried, gaily, putting out both her hands to her visitor. 'Ah, it's heaven that sends you here! . . . We can talk of *her*.'

This last sentence sounded very gloomily in the young man's ears. He at once asked:

'Madame . . . where is Christine?'

And the old lady replied, calmly:

'She is with her good genius!'

'What good genius?' exclaimed poor Raoul.

'Why, the Angel of Music!'

The viscount dropped into a chair. Really? Christine was with the Angel of Music? And there lay Mamma Valerius in bed, smil-ing to him and putting her finger to her lips, to warn him to be silent! And she added:

'You must not tell anybody!'

'You can rely on me,' said Raoul.

He hardly knew what he was saying, for his ideas about Chris-tine, already greatly confused, were becoming more and more tan-gled; and it seemed as if everything was beginning to turn around him, around the room, around that extraordinary good lady with the white hair and the forget-me-not eyes.

'I know! I know I can!' she said, with a happy laugh. 'But why don't you come near me, as you used to when you were a little boy? Give me your hands, as when you brought me the story of little Lotte, which Daddy Daaé had told you. I am very fond of you, M Raoul, you know. And so is Christine very fond of you!'

'She is fond of me!' sighed the young man.

He found a difficulty in collecting his thoughts and bringing them to bear on Mamma Valerius' 'good genius,' on the Angel of Music, of whom Christine had spoken to him so strangely, on the death's-head which he had seen in a sort of nightmare on the high altar at Perros and also on the Opera ghost, whose fame had come to his ears one evening when he was standing behind the scenes, within hearing of a group of scene-shifters who were repeating the ghastly description which the hanged man, Joseph Buquet, had given of the ghost before his mysterious death.

He asked, in a low voice:

'What makes you think that Christine is fond of me, madame?'

'She used to speak of you every day.'

'Really? . . . And what did she tell you?'

'She told me that you had made her a proposal!'

And the good old lady began laughing whole-heartedly. Raoul sprang from his chair, flushing to the temples, suffering agonies.

'What's this? Where are you going? . . . Sit down again at once, will you? . . . Do you think I will let you go like that? . . . If you're angry with me for laughing, I beg your pardon. . . . After all, what has happened isn't your fault. . . . Didn't you know? . . . Did you think that Christine was free? . . .'

'Is Christine engaged to be married?' asked the wretched Raoul, in a choking voice.

'Why, no! Why, no! . . . You know as well as I do that Christine couldn't marry, even if she wanted to! . . .'

'But I don't know anything about it! . . . And why can't Christine marry?'

'Because of the Angel of Music, of course! . . .'

'I don't follow. . . .'

'Yes, he forbids her to! . . .'

'He forbids her! . . . The Angel of Music forbids her to marry! . . .'

'Oh, he forbids her . . . without forbidding her. It's like this: he tells her that, if she got married, she would never hear him again. That's all! . . . And that he would go away for ever! . . . So, you understand, she can't let the Angel of Music go. It's quite natural.'

'Yes, yes,' echoed Raoul, submissively, 'it's quite natural.'

'Besides, I thought Christine had told you all that, when she met you at Perros, where she went with her good genius.'

'Oh, she went to Perros with her good genius, did she?'

'That is to say, he arranged to meet her down there, in the churchyard at Perros, by Daaé's grave. He promised to play her the *Resurrection of Lazarus* on her father's violin!'

Raoul de Chagny rose and, with a very masterful air, pronounced these peremptory words:

'Madame, you will have the goodness to tell me where that genius lives.'

The old lady did not seem surprised at this indiscreet command. She raised her eyes and said:

'In Heaven!'

Such simplicity baffled him. He did not know what to say in the presence of this candid and perfect faith in a genius who came down nightly from Heaven to haunt the dressing-rooms at the Opera.

He now realized the possible state of mind of a girl brought up between a superstitious fiddler and a visionary old woman and he shuddered when he thought of the consequences of it all:

'Is Christine still good?' he asked, suddenly, in spite of himself.

'I swear it, as I hope to be saved!' exclaimed the old woman, who, this time, seemed incensed. 'And, if you doubt it, sir I don't know what you are here for!'

Raoul tore at his gloves:

'How long has she known this "genius"?'

'About three months. . . . Yes, it's quite three months since he began to give her lessons.'

The viscount threw up his arms with a gesture of despair:

'The genius gives her lessons! . . . And where, pray?'

'Now that she has gone away with him, I can't say; but up to a fortnight ago, it was in Christine's dressing-room. It would be impossible in this little flat. The whole house would hear them. Whereas, at the Opera, at eight o'clock in the morning, there is no one about, you see!'

'Yes, I see! I see!' cried the viscount.

And he hurriedly took leave of Mme Valerius, who asked herself if the young nobleman was not a little off his head.

He walked home to his brother's house in a pitiful state. He could have struck himself, banged his head against the walls! To think that he had believed in her innocence, in her purity! The Angel of Music! He knew him now! He saw him! It was, no doubt, some frightful tenor, a good-looking popinjay, who mouthed and simpered as he sang! He thought himself as absurd and wretched as could be. Oh, what a miserable little insignificant, silly young man was M le Vicomte de Chagny, thought Raoul, furiously! And she, what a bold and damnably sly creature!

His brother was waiting for him and Raoul fell into his arms, like a child. The count consoled him, without asking for explanations; and Raoul certainly would have hesitated before telling him the story of the Angel of Music. His brother suggested taking him out to dinner. Overcome as he was with despair, Raoul would probably have refused any invitation that evening, if the count had not, as an inducement, told him that the lady of his thoughts had been seen, the night before, in the company of some one of the other sex in the Bois. At first, the viscount refused to believe it; but he received such exact details that he ceased protesting. She had been seen, it appeared, driving in a brougham, with the window down. She seemed to be slowly breathing the cold night air. There was a glorious moon shining. She was recognized beyond a doubt. As for her companion, only his shadowy outline was seen, leaning back in the dark. The carriage was going at a walking pace, down a lonely drive, behind the grandstand at Longchamp.

Raoul dressed in frantic haste, prepared to forget his distress by flinging himself, as people say, into 'the vortex of pleasure.' Alas, he was but a dull guest and, leaving his brother early, found himself, by ten o'clock in the evening, in a cab, behind the Longchamp race-course.

It was freezing hard. The road lay deserted and very bright under the moonlight. He told the driver to wait for him at the corner of an avenue and, hiding as best he could, stood stamping his feet to keep warm. He had been indulging in this healthy exercise for half an hour or so, when a carriage turned into the road and came quietly in his direction, at a walking pace.

As it approached, he saw that a woman was leaning her head from the window. And, suddenly, the moon shed a pale gleam over her features.

'Christine!'

The sacred name of his love had sprung from his heart and his lips. He could not keep it back. . . . He would have given anything to withdraw it, for that name, proclaimed in the stillness of the night, had acted as though it was the preconcerted signal for a furious rush on the part of the whole turn-out, which dashed past him before he could put into execution his plan of leaping at the horses' heads. The carriage-window was raised and the girl's face had disappeared. And the brougham, behind which he was running, was now no more than a black spot on the white road.

He called out again:

'Christine!'

No reply. And he stopped in the midst of the silence.

With lack-lustre eyes, he stared down that cold, desolate road and into the pale, dead night. Nothing was colder than his heart, nothing was half so dead: he had loved an angel and now he despised a woman!

Raoul, how that little fairy of the North has tricked you! Was it really, was it really necessary to have so fresh and young a face, a forehead so shy and always ready to cover itself with the pink blush of modesty in order to pass in the lonely night, in a carriage and pair, accompanied by a mysterious lover? Surely there should be some limit to hypocrisy and lying! . . .

She had passed without answering his cry. . . . And he was thinking of dying; and he was twenty years old!

His valet found him in the morning sitting on his bed. He had not undressed and the servant feared, at the sight of his face, that some disaster had occurred. Raoul snatched his letters from the man's hands. He had recognized Christine's paper and handwriting. She said:

'DEAR,

'Go to the masked ball at the Opera on the night after to-morrow. At twelve o'clock, be in the little room behind the chimney-piece of the big crush-room. Stand near the door that leads to the Rotunda. Don't mention this appointment to a living soul. Wear a white domino and see that you are well masked. As you love me, do not let yourself be recognized.

'CHRISTINE'

CHAPTER IX

At The Masked Ball

THE ENVELOPE WAS COVERED WITH MUD and unstamped. It bore the words 'To be handed to M le Vicomte Raoul de Chagny,' followed by his address, in pencil. It must have been flung out in the hope that a passer-by would find the note and deliver it, which was what happened. The note had been picked up on the pavement of the Place de l'Opéra.

Raoul read it over again with fevered eyes. No more was needed to revive his hope. The sombre picture, which he had for a moment imagined, of a Christine forgetting her duty to herself made way for his original conception of an unfortunate, innocent child, the victim of imprudence and exaggerated sensibility. To what extent, this time, was she really a victim? Whose prisoner was she? Into what whirlpool had she been dragged? He asked himself these questions with a cruel anguish; but even this pain seemed endurable beside the frenzy into which he was thrown at the thought of a lying and deceitful Christine. What had happened? What influence had she undergone? What monster had carried her off and by what means? . . .

By what means indeed but that of music? He knew Christine's story. After her father's death, she acquired a distaste for everything in life, including her art. She went through the Conservatoire like a poor, soulless singing-machine. And suddenly, she awoke as though through the intervention of a god. The Angel of Music appeared upon the scene! She sang Margarita in *Faust* and triumphed! . . .

The Angel of Music! . . . For three months, the Angel of Music had been giving Christine lessons. . . . Ah, he was a punctilious singing-master! . . . And now he was taking her for drives in the Bois! . . .

Raoul's fingers clutched at his flesh, above his jealous heart. In his inexperience, he now asked himself with terror what game the girl was playing? Up to what point could an opera singer make a fool of a fond young man, quite new to love? O misery! . . .

Thus did Raoul's thoughts fly from one extreme to the other. He no longer knew whether to pity Christine or curse her; and he pitied and cursed her turn and turn about. At all events, he bought a white domino.

The hour of the appointment came at last. With his face in a mask trimmed with long, thick lace, looking a very pierrot in his white wrap, the viscount thought himself most ridiculous. Men of the world do not go to the Opera ball in fancy-dress! It was laughable. One thought, however, consoled the viscount: he would certainly never be recognized!

This ball was an exceptional affair, given some time before Shrovetide, in honour of the anniversary of the birth of a famous draughtsman; and it was expected to be much gayer, noisier, more Bohemian than the ordinary masked ball. Numbers of artists had arranged to go, accompanied by a whole cohort of models and pupils, who by midnight, began to create a tremendous din. Raoul arrived at five minutes to twelve, did not linger to look at the motley dresses displayed all the way up the marble staircase – one of the richest settings in the world – allowed no facetious mask to draw him into a contest of wits, replied to no jests and shook off the bold familiarity of a number of couples who had already become a trifle too gay. Crossing the big crush-room and escaping from a mad whirl of dancers in which he was momentarily caught, he at last entered the room mentioned in Christine's letter. He found it crammed; for this small space was the point where all those who were going to supper in the Rotunda met those who were returning from taking a glass of champagne. The fun, here, waxed fast and furious.

Raoul leant against a door-post and waited. He did not wait long. A black domino passed and gave a quick squeeze to the tips of his fingers. He understood that it was she and followed her:

'Is that you, Christine?' he asked, between his teeth.

The black domino turned round promptly and raised her finger to her lips, no doubt to warn him not to mention her name again. Raoul continued to follow her in silence.

He was afraid of losing her, after meeting her again in such strange circumstances. His grudge against her was gone. He was even sure, now, that she had 'nothing to reproach herself with,' however peculiar and inexplicable her conduct might seem. He was ready to make any display of clemency, forgiveness or cowardice. He was in love. And, no doubt, he would soon receive a very natural explanation of her curious absence.

The black domino turned back from time to time to see if the white domino were still following.

As Raoul once more passed through the great crush-room, this time in the wake of his guide, he could not help noticing a group crowding round a person whose disguise, eccentric air and cadaverous appearance were causing a sensation. It was a man dressed all in scarlet, with a huge hat and feathers on the top of a wonderful death's-head. From his shoulders hung an immense red-velvet cloak, which trailed along the floor like a king's train; and on this cloak was embroidered, in gold letters, which every one read and repeated aloud:

'Touch me not! I am Red Death stalking abroad!'

Then one, greatly daring, did try to touch him . . . but a skeleton hand shot out of a crimson sleeve and violently seized the rash one's wrist; and he, feeling the clutch of the knucklebones, the furious grasp of Death, uttered a cry of pain and terror. When Red Death released him at last, he ran away like a madman, pursued by the jeers of the bystanders.

It was at this moment that Raoul passed in front of the funereal masquerader, who had just happened to turn in his direction. And he nearly exclaimed:

'The death's-head of Perros-Guirec!'

He had recognized him! . . . He wanted to dart forwards, forgetting Christine; but the black domino, who also seemed a prey to some strange excitement, caught him by the arm and dragged him from the crush-room far from the mad crowd through which Red Death was stalking. . . .

The black domino kept on turning back and, apparently, on two occasions, saw something that startled her, for she hurried her pace and Raoul's as though they were being pursued.

They went up two floors. Here, the stairs and corridors were almost deserted. The black domino opened the door of a private box and beckoned to the white domino to follow her. Then Christine, whom he now knew by the sound of her voice, closed the door behind them and warned him, in a whisper, to remain at the back of the box and on no account to show himself. Raoul took off his mask. Christine kept on hers. And, when Raoul was about to ask her to remove it, he was surprised to see her put her ear to the partition and listen eagerly for a sound outside. Then she opened the door ajar, looked out into the corridor, and, in a low voice, said:

'He must have gone up higher.'

Suddenly she exclaimed:

'He is coming down again!'

She tried to close the door, but Raoul prevented her; for he had seen, on the top step of the staircase that led to the floor above, a *red foot*, followed by another . . . and slowly, majestically, the whole scarlet dress of Red Death met his eyes. And he once more saw the death's-head of Perros-Guirec:

'It's he!' he exclaimed. 'This time, he shall not escape me! . . .'

But Christine had slammed the door at the moment when Raoul was on the point of rushing out. He tried to push her aside.

'Whom do you mean?' she asked, in a changed voice. 'Who shall not escape you?'

Raoul tried to overcome the girl's resistance by force, but she repelled him with a strength which he would not have suspected in her. He understood, or thought he understood, and at once lost his temper:

'Who?' he repeated, angrily. 'Why, he, the man who hides behind that hideous mask of death! . . . The evil genius of the churchyard at Perros! . . . Red Death! . . . In a word, madam, your friend . . . your Angel of Music! . . . But I shall snatch off his mask, as I shall snatch off my own; and, this time, we shall look each other in the face, he and I, with no veil and no lies between us; and I shall know whom you love and who loves you!'

He burst into a mad laugh, while Christine gave a disconsolate moan behind her velvet mask. With a tragic gesture, she flung out her two arms, fixing a barrier of white flesh against the door:

'In the name of our love, Raoul, you shall not pass! . . .'

He stopped. What had she said? . . . In the name of their love? . . . Never before had she confessed that she loved him. And yet she had had opportunities enough! . . . Pooh, her only object was to gain a few seconds! . . . She wished to give Red Death time to escape. . . . And, in accents of childish hatred, he said:

'You lie, madam, for you do not love me and you have never loved me! What a poor fellow I must be to let you mock and flout me as you have done! Why did you give me every reason for hope, at Perros . . . for honest hope, madam, for I am an honest man and I believed you to be an honest woman, when your only intention was to deceive me! Alas, you have deceived us all! You have taken a shameful advantage of the candid affection of your benefactress herself, who continues to believe in your sincerity, while you go about the Opera ball with Red Death! . . . I despise you! . . .'

And he burst into tears. She allowed him to insult her. She thought of but one thing, to prevent him from leaving the box:

'You will beg my pardon, one day, for all those ugly words, Raoul, and I shall forgive you! . . .'

He shook his head:

'No, no, you have driven me mad! . . . When I think that I had only one object in life: to give my name to an Opera wench! . . .'

'Raoul! . . . How can you? . . .'

'I shall die of shame!'

'No, dear, live!' said Christine, in a grave and breaking voice. 'And . . . good-bye. Good-bye, Raoul! . . .'

The boy stepped forward, staggering as he went. He risked one more sarcasm:

'Oh, but you must let me come and applaud you from time to time!'

'I shall never sing again, Raoul! . . .'

'Really?' he replied, still more satirically. 'So he is taking you off the stage: I congratulate you! . . . But we shall meet in the Bois, one of these evenings?'

'Not in the Bois nor anywhere, Raoul: you shall not see me again. . . .'

'May one at least ask to what darkness you are returning? . . .

For what hell are you leaving, mysterious lady . . . or for what paradise? . . .'

'I came to tell you . . . dear . . . but I cannot tell you now . . . you would not believe me! You have lost faith in me, Raoul; it is finished! . . .'

She spoke in such a despairing voice that the lad began to feel remorse for his cruelty:

'But look here,' he cried, 'can't you tell me what all this means? . . . You are free; there is no one to interfere with you. . . . You go about Paris. . . . You put on a domino to come to the ball . . . . Why do you not go home? . . . What have you been doing this past fortnight? . . . What is this tale, about the Angel of Music, which you have been telling Mamma Valerius? . . . Some one may have taken you in, played upon your innocence. . . . I was a witness of it myself, at Perros . . . but you know what to believe now! . . . You seem to me quite sensible, Christine. . . . You know what you are doing. . . . And meanwhile Mamma Valerius lies waiting for you at home and appealing to your "good genius"! . . . Explain yourself, Christine, I beg of you! . . . Any one might have been deceived as I was. . . . What is this farce? . . .'

Christine simply took off her mask and said:

'Dear, it is a tragedy! . . .'

Raoul now saw her face and could not restrain an exclamation of surprise and terror. The fresh complexion of former days was gone. A mortal pallor covered those features, which he had known so charming and so gentle, and sorrow had furrowed them with pitiless lines and traced dark and unspeakably sad shadows under her eyes.

'My dearest! My dearest!' he moaned, holding out his arms. 'You promised to forgive me. . . .'

'Perhaps! . . . Some day, perhaps!' she said, resuming her mask; and she went away, forbidding him, with a gesture, to follow her. . . .

He tried to disobey her; but she turned round and repeated her gesture of farewell with such authority that he dared not move a step.

He watched her till she was out of sight. Then he also went down among the crowd, hardly knowing what he was doing, with throbbing temples and an aching heart; and, as he crossed the dance-floor, he asked if anybody had seen Red Death. Yes, every one had seen Red Death; but Raoul could not find him and, at two o'clock in the morning, he turned down the passage, behind the scenes, that led to Christine Daaé's dressing-room.

His footsteps took him to that room where he had first known suffering. He tapped at the door. There was no answer. He entered, as he had entered when he looked everywhere for 'the man's voice.' The room was empty. A gas-jet was burning, turned down low. He saw some letter-paper on a little desk. He thought of writing to Christine, but he heard steps in the passage. He had only time to hide in the inner room, which was separated from the dressing-room by a curtain. . . .

Christine entered, took off her mask with a weary movement and flung it on the table. She sighed and let her pretty head fall into her two hands. What was she thinking of? . . . Of Raoul? . . . No, for Raoul heard her murmur:

'Poor Erik!'

At first, he thought that he must be mistaken. To begin with, he was persuaded that, if any one was to be pitied, it was he, Raoul. It would have been quite natural if she had said, 'Poor Raoul,' after what had happened between them. But, shaking her head, she repeated:

'Poor Erik!'

What had this Erik to do with Christine's sighs and why was she pitying Erik when Raoul was so unhappy?

Christine began to write, deliberately, calmly and so placidly that Raoul, who was still trembling from the effects of the tragedy that separated them, was painfully impressed:

'What coolness!' he said to himself.

She wrote on, filling two, three, four sheets. Suddenly she raised her head and hid the sheets in her bodice. . . . She seemed to be listening. . . . Raoul also listened. . . . Whence came that strange sound, that distant rhythm? . . . A faint singing seemed to issue from the walls . . . yes, it was as though the walls themselves were singing! . . . The song became plainer . . . the words were now distinguishable . . . he heard a voice, a very beautiful, very soft, very captivating voice . . . but, for all its softness, it remained a male voice. . . . The voice came nearer and nearer . . . it came through the wall . . . it approached . . . and now the voice was *in the room*, in front of Christine. Christine rose and addressed the voice, as though speaking to some one beside her:

'Here I am, Erik,' she said. 'I am ready. But you are late.'

Raoul, peeping from behind the curtain, could not believe his eyes, which showed him nothing. Christine's face lit up. A smile of happiness appeared upon her bloodless lips, a smile like that of sick people when they receive the first hope of recovery.

The voice without a body went on singing; and certainly Raoul had never in his life heard anything more absolutely and heroically sweet, more gloriously suggestive, more delicate, more powerful, in short, more irresistibly triumphant. He listened to it in a fever and he now began to understand how Christine Daaé was able to appear one evening, before the stupefied audience, with accents of a beauty hitherto unknown, of a superhuman exaltation, while doubtless still under the influence of the mysterious and invisible master.

The voice was singing the Wedding-night Song from *Romeo and Juliet*. Raoul saw Christine stretch out her arms to the voice as she had done, in the churchyard at Perros, to the invisible violin playing the *Resurrection of Lazarus*. And nothing could describe the passion with which the voice sang:

Fate links thee to me for ever and a day!

The strains went through Raoul's heart. Struggling against the charm that seemed to deprive him of all his will and all his energy and almost all his lucidity, at the moment when he needed them most, he succeeded in drawing back the curtain that hid him and he walked to where Christine stood. She herself was moving to the back of the room, the whole wall of which was occupied by a great mirror that reflected her image, but not his, for he was just behind and entirely covered by her.

Fate links thee to me for ever and a day!

Christine walked towards her image in the glass and the image came towards her. The two Christines – the real one and the reflection – ended by touching; and Raoul put out his arms to clasp the two in one embrace. But, by a sort of dazzling miracle that sent him staggering, Raoul was suddenly flung back, while an icy blast swept across his face; he saw not two, but four, eight, twenty Christines spinning round him, laughing at him and fleeing so swiftly that he could not touch one of them. At last, everything stood still again; and he saw himself in the glass. But Christine had disappeared.

He rushed up to the glass. He struck at the walls. Nobody! And meanwhile the room still echoed with a distant passionate singing:

Fate links thee to me for ever and a day!

Which way, which way had Christine gone? . . . Which way would she return? . . .

Would she return? . . . Alas, had she not declared to him that everything was finished? . . . And was the voice not repeating:

Fate links thee to me for ever and a day!

To me? To whom? . . .

Then, worn-out, beaten, empty-brained, he sat down on the chair which Christine had just left. Like her, he let his head fall into his hands. When he raised it, the tears were streaming down his young cheeks, real, heavy tears like those which jealous children shed, tears that wept for a sorrow which was in no way fanciful, but which was common to all the lovers on earth and which he expressed aloud:

'Who is this Erik?' he said.

CHAPTER X

'Forget The Man's Voice!'

THE DAY AFTER CHRISTINE HAD VANISHED before his eyes in a sort of dazzling whirl that still made him doubt the evidence of his senses, M le Vicomte de Chagny called to enquire at Mamma Valerius'. He came upon a charming picture. Christine herself was seated by the bedside of the old lady, who was sitting up against her pillows, knitting. The pink and white had returned to the young girl's cheeks. The dark rings round her eyes had disappeared. Raoul no longer recognized the tragic face of the day before. If a veil of a melancholy had not lingered over those adorable features as the last trace of the weird drama in whose toils that mysterious child was struggling, he could have believed that Christine was not its heroine at all.

She rose, without showing any emotion, and offered him her hand. But Raoul's stupefaction was so great that he stood there dumfounded, without a gesture, without a word.

'Well, M de Chagny,' exclaimed Mamma Valerius, 'don't you know our Christine? Her good genius has sent her back to us!'

'Mamma!' the girl broke in promptly, while a deep blush mantled to her eyes. 'I thought, mamma, that there was to be no more question of that! . . . You know there is no such thing as the Angel of Music!'

'But, child, he gave you lessons for three months!'

'Mamma, I promised to explain everything to you one of these days; and I hope to do so . . . but you promised me, until that day, to be silent and to ask me no more questions ever!'

'Provided that you promised never to leave me again! But have you promised that, Christine?'

'Mamma, all this cannot interest M de Chagny. . . .'

'On the contrary, mademoiselle,' said the young man, in a voice which he tried to make firm and brave, but which still trembled. 'Anything that concerns you interests me to an extent which perhaps you will one day understand. I do not deny that my surprise equals my pleasure at finding you with your adopted mother and that, after what happened between us yesterday, after what you said and what I was able to guess, I hardly expected to see you here so soon. I should be the first to delight at your return, if you were not so bent upon preserving a secrecy that may be fatal to you . . . And I have been your friend too long not to be alarmed, with Mme Valerius, at a disastrous adventure which will remain dangerous until we have unravelled its threads and which will certainly end by making you its victim, Christine.'

At these words Mamma Valerius tossed about in her bed:

'What does this mean?' she cried. 'Is Christine in danger?'

'Yes, madame,' said Raoul, courageously, notwithstanding the signs which Christine made to him.

'Great God!' exclaimed the good, simple old woman, gasping for breath. 'You must tell me everything, Christine! Why did you try to reassure me? And what danger is it, M de Chagny?'

'An impostor is abusing her good faith.'

'Is the Angel of Music an impostor?'

'She told you herself that there was no Angel of Music.'

'But then what is it, in heaven's name? You will be the death of me!'

'There is a terrible mystery around us, madame, around you, around Christine, a mystery much more dreadful than any number of ghosts or genii!'

Mamma Valerius turned a terrified face to Christine, who had already run to her adopted mother and was holding her in her arms:

'Don't believe him, Mummy, don't believe him,' she repeated.

'Then tell me that you will never leave me again,' implored the widow.

Christine was silent and Raoul resumed:

'That is what you must promise, Christine. . . . It is the only thing that can reassure your mother and me. We will undertake not to ask you a single question about the past, if you promise us to remain under our protection in future. . . .'

'That is an undertaking which I have not asked of you and a promise which I refuse to make you!' said the young girl, haughtily. 'I am mistress of my own actions, M de Chagny: you have no right to control them; and I will beg you to desist henceforth. As to what I have done during the last fortnight, there is only one man in the world who has the right to demand an account of me: my husband! Well, I have no husband and I never mean to marry!'

She threw out her hands to emphasize her words and Raoul turned pale, not only because of the words which he had heard, but because he had caught sight of a plain gold ring on Christine's finger:

'You have no husband and yet you wear a wedding-ring!'

He tried to seize her hand, but she swiftly drew it back:

'That's a present!' she said, blushing once more and vainly striving to hide her embarrassment.

'Christine! As you have no husband, that ring can only have been given by one who hopes to make you his wife! Why deceive us further? Why torture me still more? That ring is a promise; and that promise has been accepted!'

'That's what I said!' exclaimed the old lady.

'And what did she answer, madame?'

'What I chose,' said Christine, driven to exasperation. 'Don't you think, monsieur, that this cross-examination has lasted long enough? As far as I am concerned . . .'

Raoul was afraid to let her finish her speech. He interrupted her:

'I beg your pardon for speaking as I did, mademoiselle. . . . You know the good intentions that make me meddle, just now, in matters which, no doubt, do not concern me. But allow me to tell you what I have seen – and I have seen more than you suspect, Christine – or what I thought I saw, for, to tell you the truth, I have sometimes been inclined to doubt the evidence of my eyes. . . .'

'Well, what did you see, sir, or think you saw?'

'I saw your ecstasy *at the sound of the voice*, Christine: the voice that came from the wall or the next room to yours . . . yes, *your ecstasy!* . . . And that is what makes me alarmed on your behalf. . . . You are under a very dangerous spell. . . . And yet it seems that you are aware of the imposture, because you say to-day *that there is no Angel of Music!* . . . If that be so, Christine, why did you follow him then? Why did you stand up, with radiant features, as though you were really hearing angels? . . . Ah, it is a very dangerous voice, Christine, for I myself, when I heard it, was so much fascinated that I let you vanish before my eyes without seeing which way you passed! . . . Christine, Christine, in the name of Heaven, in the name of your father who is himself in Heaven now and who loved you so dearly and who loved me too, Christine, tell us, tell your benefactress and me, to whom does that voice belong? If you do, we will save you in spite of yourself. . . . Come, Christine, the name of the man! The name of the man who had the audacity to put a ring on your finger!'

'M de Chagny,' the girl declared, coldly, 'you shall never know! . . .'

Thereupon, seeing the hostile manner in which her ward addressed the viscount, Mamma Valerius suddenly took Christine's part:

'And, if she does love that man, monsieur le vicomte, even then it is no business of yours!'

'Alas, madame,' Raoul humbly replied, unable to restrain his tears, 'alas, I believe that Christine really does love him! . . . But it is not only that which drives me to despair; for what I am not certain of, madame, is that the man whom Christine loves is worthy of her love!'

'It is for me to be the judge of that, monsieur!' said Christine, looking Raoul angrily in the face.

'When a man,' continued Raoul, 'adopts such romantic methods to entice a young girl's affections . . .'

'The man must be either a villain, or the girl a fool: is that it?'

'Christine!'

'Raoul, why do you condemn a man whom you have never seen, whom no one knows and about whom you yourself know nothing? . . .'

'Yes, Christine. . . . Yes. . . . I at least know the name which you thought to keep from me for ever. . . . The name of your Angel of Music, mademoiselle, is Erik! . . .'

Christine at once betrayed herself. She turned as white as a sheet and stammered:

'Who told you?'

'You yourself!'

'How do you mean?'

'By pitying him, the other night, the night of the masked ball. When you went to your dressing-room, did you not say, "Poor Erik"? Well, Christine, there was a poor Raoul who overheard you.'

'This is the second time that you have listened behind the door, M de Chagny!'

'I was not behind the door.... I was in the dressing-room ... in the inner room, mademoiselle.'

'Oh, unhappy man!' moaned the girl, showing every sign of unspeakable terror. 'Unhappy man! Do you want to be killed?'

'Perhaps.'

Raoul uttered this 'perhaps' with so much love and despair in his voice that Christine could not keep back a sob. She took his hands and looked at him with all the pure affection of which she was capable:

'Raoul,' she said, 'forget *the man's voice* and do not even remember its name.... You must never try to fathom the mystery of *the man's voice.*'

'Is the mystery so very terrible?'

'There is no more awful mystery on this earth. Swear to me that you will make no attempt to find out,' she insisted. 'Swear to me that you will never come to my dressing-room again, unless I send for you.'

'Then you promise to send for me sometimes, Christine?'

'I promise.'

'When?'

'To-morrow.'

'Then I swear to do as you ask.'

He kissed her hands and went away, cursing Erik and resolving to be patient.

CHAPTER XI

Above The Trap-Doors

THE NEXT DAY HE SAW HER at the Opera. She was still wearing the plain gold ring. She was gentle and kind to him. She talked to him of the plans which he was forming, of his future, of his career.

He told her that the date of the Polar expedition had been put forward and that he would leave France in three weeks, or a month at latest. She suggested, almost gaily, that he must look upon the voyage with delight, as a stage towards his coming fame. And, when he replied that fame without love was no attraction in his eyes, she treated him as a child whose sorrows were but short-lived.

'How can you speak so lightly of such serious things?' he asked. 'Perhaps we shall never see each other again! . . . I may die during that expedition. . . .'

'Or I,' she said, simply.

She no longer smiled or jested. She seemed to be thinking of some new thing that had entered her mind for the first time. Her eyes were all aglow with it.

'What are you thinking of, Christine?'

'I am thinking that we shall not see each other again. . . .'

'And does that make you so radiant?'

'And that, in a month, we shall have to say goodbye . . . for ever! . . .'

'Unless, Christine, we pledge our faith and wait for each other for ever.'

She put her hand on his mouth:

'Hush, Raoul! . . . You know there is no question of that. : . . And we shall never be married: that is understood!'

She seemed suddenly almost unable to contain an overpowering gaiety. She clapped her hands with childish glee. Raoul stared at her in amazement.

'But . . . but,' she continued, holding out her two hands to Raoul, or rather giving them to him, as though she had suddenly resolved to make him a present of them, 'but, if we cannot be married, we can . . . we can be engaged! . . . Nobody will know but ourselves, Raoul. . . . There have been plenty of secret marriages: why not a secret engagement? . . . We are engaged, dear, for a month! . . . In a month, you will go away; and I can be happy at the thought of that month all my life long!'

She was enchanted with her inspiration. Then she became serious again:

'This,' she said, '*is a happiness that will harm no one.*'

Raoul jumped at the idea. He bowed to Christine and said:

'Mademoiselle, I have the honour to ask for your hand.'

'Why, you have both of them already, my dear betrothed! . . . Oh, Raoul, how happy we shall be! . . . We must play at being engaged from morning till night.'

It was the prettiest game in the world and they enjoyed it like the children that they were. Oh, the wonderful speeches they made to each other and the eternal vows they exchanged! They played at hearts as other children might play at ball; only, as it was really their two hearts that they flung to and fro, they had to be very, very handy to catch them, each time, without hurting them.

One day, about a week after the game began, Raoul's heart was badly hurt and he stopped playing and uttered these wild words:

'I sha'n't go to the North Pole!'

Christine, who, in her innocence, had not dreamt of such a possibility, suddenly discovered the danger of the game and reproached herself bitterly. She did not say a word in reply to Raoul's remark and went straight home.

This happened in the afternoon, in the singer's dressing-room, where they met every day and amused themselves by dining off three biscuits, two glasses of port and a bunch of violets. In the evening, she did not sing and he did not receive his usual letter, though they had arranged to write to each other daily during that month. The next morning, he ran off to Mamma Valerius, who told him that Christine had gone away for two days. She had left at five o'clock the day before.

Raoul was distracted. He hated Mamma Valerius for giving him such news as that with such stupefying calmness. He tried to sound her, but the old lady obviously knew nothing.

Christine returned on the following day. She returned in triumph. She renewed her extraordinary success of the gala performance. Since the adventure of the 'toad,' Carlotta had not been able to appear on the stage. The terror of a fresh 'co-ack' filled her heart and deprived her of all her power of singing; and the theatre that had witnessed her incomprehensible disgrace had become odious to her. She contrived to cancel her contract. Daaé was offered the vacant place for the time. She received thunders of applause in the *Juive*.

The viscount, who, of course, was present, was the only one to suffer on hearing the thousand echoes of this fresh triumph; for Christine still wore her plain gold ring. A distant voice whispered in the young man's ear:

'She is wearing the ring again to-night; and you did not give it to her. She gave her soul again to-night and did not give it to you. . . . If she will not tell you what she has been doing, these last two days . . . you must go and ask Erik!'

He ran behind the scenes and placed himself in her way. She saw him, for her eyes were looking for him. She said:

'Quick! Quick! . . . Come!'

And she dragged him to her dressing-room.

Raoul at once threw himself on his knees before her. He swore that he would go and he entreated her never again to withhold a single hour of the ideal happiness which she had promised him. She let her tears flow. They kissed like a despairing brother and sister who have been smitten with a common loss and who meet to mourn a dead parent.

Suddenly, she snatched herself from the young man's soft and timid embrace, seemed to listen to something . . . and, with a quick gesture, pointed to the door. When he was on the threshold, she said, in so low a voice that the viscount guessed rather than heard her words:

'To-morrow, my dear betrothed! And be happy, Raoul: I sang for you to-night!'

He returned the next day. But those two days of absence had broken the charm of their delightful make-believe. They looked at each other, in the dressing-room, with their sad eyes, without exchanging a word. Raoul had to restrain himself not to cry out:

'I am jealous! I am jealous! I am jealous!'

But she heard him all the same. Then she said:

'Come for a walk, dear. The air will do you good.'

Raoul thought that she would propose a stroll in the country, far from that building which he detested as a prison whose gaoler he could feel walking within the walls . . . the gaoler Erik. . . . But she took him to the stage and made him sit on the wooden curb of a well, in the doubtful peace and coolness of a first scene set for the evening's performance.

On another day, she wandered with him, hand in hand, along the deserted paths of a garden whose creepers had been cut out by a decorator's skilful hands. It was as though the real sky, the real flowers, the real earth were forbidden her for all time and she condemned to breathe no other air than that of the theatre. An occasional fireman passed, watching over their melancholy idyll from afar. And she would drag Raoul up above the clouds, in the magnificent disorder of the grid, where she loved to make him giddy by running in front of him along the frail bridges, among the thousands of ropes fastened to the pulleys, the windlasses, the rollers, in the midst of a regular forest of yards and masts. If he hesitated, she said, with an adorable pout of her lips:

'You, a sailor!'

And then they returned to *terrafirma*, that is to say, to some passage that led them to the little girls' dancing-school, where brats between six and ten were practising their steps, in the hope of becoming great dancers one day, 'covered with diamonds.' . . . Meanwhile, Christine gave them sweets instead.

She took him to the wardrobe- and property-rooms, took him all over her empire, which was artificial, but immense, covering seventeen storeys from the ground floor to the roof and inhabited by an army of subjects. She moved among them like a popular queen, encouraging them in their labours, sitting down in the workshops, giving words of advice to the workwomen whose hands hesitated to cut into the rich stuffs that were to clothe heroes. They were inhabitants of that country who practised every trade. There were cobblers, there were goldsmiths. All had learnt to love her, for she interested herself in all their troubles and all their little hobbies.

She knew unsuspected corners that were secretly occupied by little old couples. She knocked at their door and introduced Raoul to them as a Prince Charming who had asked for her hand; and the two of them, sitting on some worm-eaten 'property,' would listen to the legends of the Opera even as, in their childhood, they had listened to the Breton folk-tales. Those old people remembered nothing outside the Opera. They had lived there for years without number. Past managements had forgotten them; palace revolutions had taken no notice of them; the history of France had run its course unknown to them; and nobody recollected their existence.

The precious days sped in this way; and Raoul and Christine, by affecting excessive interest in outside matters, strove awkwardly to hide from each other the one thought of their hearts. One fact was certain, that Christine, who until then had shown herself the stronger of the two, suddenly became inexpressibly nervous. When on their expeditions, she would start running without reason, or else suddenly stop; and her hand, turning ice-cold in a moment, would hold the young man back. Sometimes her eyes seemed to pursue imaginary shadows. She cried, 'This way,' and, 'This way,' and, 'This way,' laughing a breathless laugh that often ended in tears. Then Raoul tried to speak, to question her, in spite of his promises. But, even before he had worded his question, she answered, feverishly:

'Nothing! . . . I swear it is nothing.'

Once, when they were passing before an open trap-door on the stage, Raoul stopped over the dark cavity and said:

'You have shown me over the upper part of your empire, Christine . . . but there are strange stories told of the lower part. . . . Shall we go down?'

She caught him in her arms, as though she feared to see him disappear down the black hole, and, in a trembling voice, whispered:

'Never! . . . I will not have you go there! . . . Besides, it's not mine . . . *everything that is underground belongs to him!*'

Raoul looked her in the eyes and said, roughly:

'So he lives down there, does he?'

'I never said so. . . . Who told you a thing like that? Come away! I sometimes wonder if you are quite sane, Raoul. . . . You always take things in such an impossible way! . . . Come along! Come!'

And she literally dragged him away, for he was obstinate and wanted to remain by the trap-door; that hole attracted him.

Suddenly, the trap-door was closed, and so quickly that they did not even see the hand that worked it; and they remained quite dazed.

'Perhaps *he* was there,' Raoul said, at last.

She shrugged her shoulders, but did not seem very easy:

'No, no, it was the "trap-door shutters." They must do something, you know. . . . They open and shut the trap-doors without any particular reason. . . . It's like the "door-shutters": they must spend their time somehow.'

'But suppose it were *he*, Christine?'

'No, no! He has shut himself up, he is working.'

'Oh, really! He's working, is he?'

'Yes, he can't open and shut trap-doors and work at the same time.'

She shivered.

'What is he working at?'

'Oh, something terrible! . . . But it's all the better for us. . . . When he's working at that, he sees nothing; he does not eat, drink or breathe for days and nights at a time . . . he becomes a living dead man and has no time to amuse himself with the trap-doors.'

She shivered again. She was still holding him in her arms. Then she sighed and said, in her turn:

'Suppose it were *he!*'

'Are you afraid of him?'

'No, no, of course not,' she said.

For all that, on the next day and the following days, Christine was careful to avoid the trap-doors. Her agitation increased as the hours passed. At last, one afternoon, she arrived very late, with her face so desperately pale and her eyes so desperately red that Raoul resolved to go to all lengths, including that which he foreshadowed when he blurted out that he would not go on the North Pole expedition unless she first told him the secret of the man's voice.

'Hush! Hush, in heaven's name! Suppose *he* heard you, you unfortunate Raoul!'

And Christine's eyes stared wildly at everything around her.

'I will remove you from his power, Christine, I swear it. And you shall not think of him any more.'

'Is it possible?'

She allowed herself this doubt, which was an encouragement, while dragging the young man up to the topmost floor of the theatre, far, far from the trap-doors.

'I shall hide you in some unknown corner of the world, where *he* cannot come to look for you. You will be safe; and then I shall go away . . . as you have sworn never to marry.'

Christine seized Raoul's hands and squeezed them with incredible rapture. But, suddenly alarmed, she turned away her head:

'Higher!' was all she said. 'Higher still!'

And she dragged him up towards the summit of the building.

He had a difficulty in following her. They were soon under the very roof, in the maze of timberwork. They slipped through the buttresses, the rafters, the joists; they ran from beam to beam as they might have run from tree to tree in a forest.

And, despite the care which she took to look behind her at every moment, she failed to see a shadow which followed her like her own shadow, which stopped when she stopped, which started again when she did and which made no more noise than a well-conducted shadow should. As for Raoul, he saw nothing either; for, when he had Christine in front of him, nothing interested him that happened behind.

CHAPTER XII

Apollo's Lyre

IN THIS WAY they reached the roof. Christine tripped over it as lightly as a swallow. Their eyes swept the empty space between the three domes and the triangular pediment. She breathed freely over Paris, the whole valley of which was seen at work below. She called to Raoul to come close to her, and they walked side by side along the zinc streets, in the leaden avenues; they looked at their twin shapes in the huge tanks, full of stagnant water, where, in the hot weather, the little boys of the ballet, a score or so, learn to swim and dive.

The shadow had followed behind them, clinging to their steps; and the two children little suspected its presence when they at last sat down, trustingly, under the mighty protection of Apollo, who, with a great bronze gesture, lifted his huge lyre to the heart of a crimson sky.

It was a gorgeous spring evening. Clouds, which had just received their gossamer robe of gold and purple from the setting sun, drifted slowly by; and Christine said to Raoul:

'Soon we shall go farther and faster than the clouds, to the end of the world; and then you will leave me, Raoul. But, if, when the moment comes for you to take me away, I refuse to go with you, well then, Raoul, you must carry me off by force!'

'Are you afraid that you will change your mind, Christine?'

'I don't know,' she said, shaking her head in an odd fashion. 'He is a demon!' And she shivered and nestled in his arms with a moan. 'I am afraid now of going back to live with him . . . in the ground!'

'What compels you to go back, Christine?'

'If I do not go back to him, terrible misfortunes may happen! . . . But I can't do it, I can't do it! . . . I know one ought to be sorry for people who live underground. . . . But he is too horrible! And yet the time is at hand; I have only a day left; and, if I do not go, he will come and fetch me with his voice. And he will drag me with him, underground, and go on his knees before me, with his death's-head. And he will tell me that he loves me! And he will cry! Oh, those tears. Raoul, those tears in the two black eye-sockets of the death's-head! I cannot see those tears flow again!'

She wrung her hands in anguish, while Raoul pressed her to his heart:

'No, no, you shall never again hear him tell you that he loves you! You shall not see his tears! Let us fly, Christine, let us fly at once!'

And he tried to drag her away, then and there. But she stopped him:

'No, no,' she said, shaking her head sadly. 'Not now! . . . It would be too cruel. . . . Let him hear me sing to-morrow evening . . . and then we will go away. You must come and fetch me in my dressing-room at midnight exactly. He will be waiting for me in the dining-room by the lake: we shall be free and you shall take me away. . . . You must promise me that, Raoul, even if I refuse; for I feel that, if I go back this time, I shall perhaps never return. . . .'

And she gave a sigh to which it seemed to her that another sigh, behind her, replied.

'Didn't you hear?'

Her teeth chattered.

'No,' said Raoul, 'I heard nothing. . . .'

'It is too terrible,' she confessed, 'to be always trembling like this! . . . And yet we run no danger here; we are at home, in the sky, in the open air, in the light. The sun is flaming; and night-birds cannot bear to look at the sun. I have never seen *him* by day-light . . . it must be awful! . . . Oh, the first time I saw him! . . . I thought that he was going to die.'

'Why?' asked Raoul, really frightened at the aspect which this strange confidence was taking.

'*Because I had seen him!*'

This time, Raoul and Christine turned round at the same time:

'There is some one in pain,' said Raoul. 'Perhaps some one has been hurt. . . . Did you hear?'

'I can't say,' Christine confessed. 'Even when he is not there, my ears are full of his sighs. . . . Still, if you heard. . . .'

They stood up and looked around them. They were quite alone on the immense lead roof. They sat down again and Raoul said:

'Tell me how you saw him first.'

'I had heard him for three months without seeing him. The first time I heard it, I thought, as you did, that that adorable voice was singing in another room. I went out and looked everywhere; but, as you know, Raoul, my dressing-room is a long way from the others; and I could not find the voice outside my room, whereas it went on steadily inside. And it not only sang, but it spoke to me and answered my questions, like a real man's voice, with this difference, that it was as beautiful as the voice of an angel. . . . I had never forgotten the Angel of Music whom my poor father had promised to send to me as soon as he was dead. . . . I really think that Mamma Valerius was a little bit to blame. I told her about it; and she at once said, "It must be the Angel; at any rate, you can do no harm by asking him." I did so; and the man's voice replied that yes, it was the Angel's voice, the voice which I was expecting and which my father had promised me. . . . From that time onward, the voice and I became great friends. It asked leave to give me lessons every day. I agreed and never failed to keep the appointments which it gave me in my dressing-room. You have no idea, though you have heard the voice, of what those lessons were like.'

'No, I have no idea,' said Raoul. 'What was your accompaniment?'

'We were accompanied by a music which I do not know: it was behind the wall and wonderfully accurate. The voice seemed to understand mine exactly, to know precisely where my father had left off teaching me. In a few weeks' time, I hardly knew myself when I sang. I was even frightened . . . I feared a sort of witchcraft behind it; but Mamma Valerius reassured me. She said she knew I was much too unsophisticated to give the devil a hold on me. . . . My progress, by the voice's own order, was kept a secret between the voice, Mamma Valerius and myself. It was a curious thing, but, outside the dressing-room, I sang with my ordinary, every-day voice and nobody noticed anything. I did all that the voice asked. It said, 'Wait and see: we shall astonish Paris!' And I waited and lived on in a sort of ecstatic dream. . . . It was then that I saw you for the first time, one evening, in the audience. I was so glad that I never thought of concealing my delight when I reached my dressing-room. Unfortunately, the voice was there before me and soon noticed, by my air, that something had happened. It asked "what was the matter" and I saw no reason for keeping our story secret or concealing the place which you filled in my heart. Then the voice was silent: I called to it, but it did not reply; I begged and entreated, but in vain. I was terrified lest it had gone for good. I wish to heaven it had, dear! . . . That night, I went home in a desperate condition. I told Mamma Valerius, who said, "Why, of course, the voice is jealous!" And that, dear, first told me that I loved you. . . .'

Christine stopped and laid her head on Raoul's shoulder. They sat like that for a moment, in silence, and they did not see, did not perceive the movement, at a few steps from them, of the creeping shadow of two great black wings, a shadow that came along the roof so near, so near them that it could have stifled them by closing over them. . . .

'The next day,' Christine continued, with a sigh, 'I went back to my dressing-room in a very pensive frame of mind. The voice was there, spoke to me with great sadness and told me plainly that if I must bestow my heart on earth, there was nothing for the voice to do but to go back to Heaven. And it said this with such an accent of *human* sorrow that I ought then and there to have suspected and begun to believe that I was the victim of my deluded senses. But my faith in the voice, with which the memory of my father was so closely mingled, remained undisturbed. I feared nothing so much as that I might never hear it again; I had thought about my love for you and realized all the useless danger of it; and I did not even know if you remembered me. Whatever happened, your position in society forbade me to contemplate the possibility of ever marrying you; and I swore to the voice that you were no more to me than a brother nor ever would be and that my heart was incapable of any earthly love. And that, dear, was why I refused to recognize or see you, when I met you on the stage or in the passages. . . . Meanwhile, the hours during which the voice taught me were spent in a divine frenzy, until, at last, the voice said to me, "You can now, Christine Daaé, give to men a little of the music of Heaven!" . . . I don't know how it was that Carlotta did not come to the theatre that night nor why I was called upon to sing in her stead; but I sang with a rapture I had never felt before and I felt for a moment as if my soul were leaving my body!'

'Oh, Christine,' said Raoul, 'my heart quivered that night at every accent of your voice. I saw the tears stream down your cheeks and I wept with you. . . . How could you sing, sing like that while crying?'

'I felt myself fainting,' said Christine, 'I closed my eyes. . . . When I opened them, you were by my side. But the voice was there also, Raoul! . . . I was afraid for your sake and again I would not recognize you and began to laugh when you reminded me that you had picked up my scarf in the sea! . . . Alas, there is no deceiving the voice! . . . The voice recognized you and the voice was jealous! . . . It said that, if I did not love you, I would not avoid you, but treat you like any other old friend. . . . It made me scene upon scene. . . . At last, I said to the voice. "That will do! I am going to Perros to-morrow, to pray on my father's grave, and I shall ask M Raoul de Chagny to go with me." "Do as you please," replied the voice, "but I shall be at Perros too, for I am wherever you are, Christine; and, if you are still worthy of me, if you have not lied to me, I will play you the *Resurrection of Lazarus*, at the stroke of midnight, on your father's tomb and on your father's violin." That, dear, was how I came to write you the letter that brought you to Perros. How could I have been so beguiled? How was it, when I saw the personal, the selfish point of view of the voice, that I did not suspect some imposture? Alas, I was no longer mistress of myself: I had become his thing!'

'But, after all,' cried Raoul, 'you soon came to know the truth! Why did you not at once rid yourself of that abominable nightmare?'

'Know the truth, Raoul? Rid myself of that nightmare? But, my poor boy, I was not caught in the nightmare until the day when I learnt the truth! . . . Pity me, Raoul, pity me! . . . You remember the terrible evening when Carlotta thought that she had been turned into a toad on the stage and when the house was suddenly plunged in darkness through the chandelier crashing to the floor? . . . There were killed and wounded that night and the whole theatre rang with terrified screams. . . . My first thought was for you and the voice. . . . I was at once easy, where you were concerned, for I had seen you in your brother's box and I knew that you were not in danger. But the voice had told me that it would be at the performance and I was really afraid for it, just as if it had been an ordinary person who was capable of dying. I thought to myself, "The chandelier may have come down upon the voice." I was then on the stage and was nearly running into the house, to look for the voice among the killed and wounded, when I thought that, if the voice was safe, it would be sure to be in my dressing-room; and I rushed to my room. The voice was not there. I locked my door and, with tears in my eyes, besought it, if it were still alive, to manifest itself to me. The voice did not reply, but suddenly I heard a long, beautiful wail which I knew well. It was the plaint of Lazarus when, at the sound of the Redeemer's voice, he begins to open his eyes and see the light of day. It was the music which you and I, Raoul, heard at Perros. And then the voice began to sing the leading phrase, "Come! And believe in me! Whoso believes in me shall live! Walk! Whoso hath believed in me shall never die! . . ." I cannot tell you the effect which that music had upon me. It seemed to command me, personally, to come, to stand up and come to it. It retreated and I followed. "Come! And believe in me!" I believed in it, I came. . . . I came and – this was the extraordinary thing – my dressing-room, as I moved, seemed to lengthen out . . . to lengthen out. . . . Evidently, it must have been an effect of mirrors . . . for I had the mirror in front of me. . . . And, suddenly, I was outside the room without knowing how!'

'What! Without knowing how! Christine, Christine, you should really stop dreaming!'

'I was not dreaming, dear! I was outside my room without knowing how! You, who saw me disappear from my room one evening, may be able to explain it; but I cannot. . . . I can only tell you that, suddenly, there was no mirror before me and no dressing-room. . . . I was in a dark passage, I was frightened and I cried out. . . . It was quite dark, but for a faint red glimmer in a distant angle of the wall. I cried out. My voice was the only sound, for the singing and the violin had stopped. And, suddenly, a hand was laid on mine . . . or rather a stone-cold, bony thing that seized my wrist and did not let go. I cried out. An arm took me round the waist and supported me. . . . I struggled for a little while and then gave up the attempt. . . . I was dragged towards the little red light and then I saw that I was in the hands of a man wrapped in a large cloak and wearing a mask that hid his whole face. . . . I made one last effort; my limbs stiffened, my mouth opened to scream, but a hand closed it, a hand which I felt on my lips, on my skin . . . a hand that smelt of death. Then I fainted away. . . . When I opened my eyes, we were still surrounded by darkness. A lantern, standing on the ground, showed a bubbling well. The water splashing from the well disappeared, almost at once, under the floor on which I was lying, with my head on the knee of the man in the black cloak and the black mask. He was bathing my temples and his hands smelt of death. I tried to push them away and asked, "Who are you? Where is the voice?" His only answer was a sigh. Suddenly, a hot breath passed over my face and I perceived a white shape, beside the man's black shape, in the darkness. The black shape lifted me on to the white shape, a glad neighing greeted my astounded ears and I whispered, "César!" The animal quivered. Raoul, I was lying half back on a saddle and I had recognized the white horse out of the *Prophète*, which I had so often fed with sugar and sweets. I remembered that, one evening, there was a rumour in the theatre that the horse had disappeared and that it had been stolen by the Opera ghost. I believed in the voice, but had never believed in the ghost. Now, however, I began to wonder, with a shiver, whether I was the ghost's prisoner. I called upon the voice to help me, for I should never have imagined that the voice and the ghost were one. You have heard about the Opera ghost, have you not, Raoul?'

'Yes, but tell me what happened when you were on the white horse out of the *Prophète!*'

'I made no movement and let myself go. The black shape held me up and I made no effort to escape. A curious feeling of peacefulness came over me and I thought that I must be under the influence of some cordial. I had the full command of my senses; and my eyes became used to the darkness, which was lit, here and there, by fitful gleams. I calculated that we were in a narrow circular gallery, probably running all round the Opera, which is immense, underground. I had once been down into those cellars, but had stopped at the third floor, though there are two lower still, large enough to hold a town. But the figures of which I caught sight frightened me away. There are demons down there, quite black, standing in front of boilers, and they wield shovels and pitchforks and poke up fires and stir up flames and, if you come too near them, they terrify you by suddenly opening the red mouths of their furnaces. . . . Well, while César was quietly carrying me on his back, I saw those black demons in the distance, looking quite small, in front of the red fires of their furnaces: they came in sight, disappeared and came in sight again, as we went on our winding way. . . . At last, they disappeared altogether. The shape was still holding me up and César walked on, unled, and sure-footed. . . . I could not tell you, even approximately, how long this ride lasted; I only know that we seemed to turn and turn and often went down a spiral stair into the very heart of the earth. Even then, it may be that my head was turning, but I don't think so: no, my mind was quite clear. . . . At last, César raised his nostrils, sniffed the air and quickened his pace a little. I felt a moistness in the atmosphere and César stopped. The darkness had lifted. A sort of bluey light surrounded us. We were on the edge of a lake, whose leaden waters stretched into the distance, into the darkness; but the blue light lit up the bank and I saw a little boat fastened to an iron on the wharf.'

'A boat!'

'Yes, but I knew that all that existed and that there was nothing supernatural about that underground lake and boat. But think of the exceptional conditions in which I arrived upon that shore! I don't know whether the effects of the cordial had worn off when the man's shape lifted me into the boat, but my terror began all over again. My gruesome escort must have noticed it, for he sent César back and I heard his hoofs trampling up a staircase while the man jumped into the boat, untied the rope that held it and seized the oars. He rowed with a quick, powerful stroke: and his eyes, under the mask, never left me. We slipped across the noiseless water in the bluey light of which I told you; then we were in the dark again and we touched shore. And I was once more taken up in the man's arms. I cried aloud. And then, suddenly, I was silent, dazed by the light. . . . Yes, a dazzling light in the midst of which I had been set down. I sprang to my feet. I was in the middle of a drawing-room that seemed to me to be decorated, adorned and furnished with nothing but flowers, cut flowers, magnificent and stupid, because of the silk ribbons that tied them into baskets, like the wired flowers in the shops on the boulevards. They were much too elegant, like those which I used to find in my dressing-room after a first night. And, in the midst of all these flowers, stood the black shape of the man in the mask, with arms crossed, and said, "Don't be afraid, Christine; you are in no danger." *It was the voice!* . . . My rage equalled my amazement. I rushed at the mask and tried to snatch it away, so as to see the face of the voice. The man said, "You are in no danger, so long as you do not touch the mask." And, taking me gently by the wrists, he forced me into a chair and then went down on his knees before me and said no more! . . . His humility gave me back some of my courage; and the light restored me to the realities of life. However extraordinary the adventure might be, I was now surrounded by mortal, visible, tangible things. The furniture, the hangings, the candles, the vases and the very flowers in their baskets, of which I could almost have told whence they came and what they cost, inevitably confined my imagination within the limits of a drawing-room quite as commonplace as any that, at least, had the excuse of not being in the cellars of the Opera. I felt that I had to do with some terrible, eccentric person, who had mysteriously succeeded in taking up his abode there, under the Opera-house, five storeys below the level of the ground. And the voice, the voice which I had recognized under the mask, was on its knees before me, *was a man*. And I began to cry. . . . The man, still kneeling, must have understood the cause of my tears, for he said, "It is true, Christine! . . . I am not an angel, nor a genius, nor a ghost . . . I am Erik!" '

Christine's narrative was again interrupted. An echo behind them seemed to repeat the word after her:

'Erik!'

What echo? . . . They both turned round and saw that night had fallen. Raoul made a movement as though to rise, but Christine kept him beside her:

'Don't go,' she said. 'I want you to know everything *here!*'

'But why here, Christine? I am afraid of your catching cold.'

'We have nothing to be afraid of except the trap-doors, dear, and here we are miles away from the trap-doors . . . and I am not allowed to see you outside the theatre. . . . This is not the time to annoy him. . . . We must not arouse his suspicions. . . .'

'Christine! Christine! Something tells me that we are wrong to wait till to-morrow evening and that we ought to fly at once.'

'I tell you that, if he does not hear me sing to-morrow, it will cause him infinite pain.'

'It is difficult not to cause him pain and yet to escape from him for good. . . .'

'You are right in that, Raoul . . . for certainly he will die of my flight. . . .' And she added, in a dull voice, 'But then it counts both ways . . . for we risk his killing us.'

'Does he love you so much?'

'He would commit murder for me.'

'But one can find out where he lives. . . . One can go to him. . . . Now that we know that Erik is not a ghost, one can speak to him and even force him to answer!'

Christine shook her head:

'No, no! There is nothing to be done with Erik . . . except to run away!'

'Then why, when you were able to run away, did you go back to him?'

'Because I had to. . . And you will understand that when I tell you how I left him. . . .'

'Oh, I hate him!' cried Raoul. 'And you, Christine, tell me, do you hate him too?'

'No,' said Christine, simply.

'No, of course not. . . . Why, you love him! Your fear, your terror, those are all just love . . . and love of the most exquisite kind, the kind which people do not admit even to themselves,' said

Raoul, bitterly. 'The kind that gives you a thrill, when you think of it. . . . Picture it: a man who lives in a palace underground!'

And he gave a leer.

'Then you want me to go back there?' said the young girl, cruelly. 'Take care, Raoul; I have told you; I should never return!'

There was an appalling silence between the three of them: the two who spoke and the shadow that listened behind them.

'Before answering that,' said Raoul, at last, speaking very slowly, 'I should like to know with what feelings he inspires you, since you do not hate him. . . .'

'With horror!' she said. 'That is the terrible thing about it. . . . He fills me with horror and I do not hate him. How can I hate him, Raoul? Think of Erik at my feet, in the house on the lake, underground. He accuses himself, he curses himself, he implores my forgiveness! He confesses his cheat. He loves me! He lays at my feet an immense and tragic love. . . . He has carried me off for love! He has imprisoned me with him, underground, for love! . . . But he respects me: he crawls, he moans, he weeps! . . . And, when I stood up, Raoul, and told him that I could only despise him if he did not, then and there, give me my liberty . . . he offered it . . . he offered to show me the mysterious road! . . . Only . . . only he rose too . . . and I was made to remember that, though he was not an angel, nor a ghost, nor a genius, he remained the voice . . . for he sang. And I listened . . . and stayed! . . . That night, we did not exchange another word. He sang me to sleep. . . . When I woke up, I was alone, lying on a sofa in a simply-furnished little bedroom, with an ordinary mahogany bedstead, lit by a lamp standing on the marble top of an old Louis-Philippe chest of drawers. . . . I soon discovered that I was a prisoner, and that the only outlet from my room led to a very comfortable bath-room. On returning to the bedroom, I saw on the chest of drawers a note, in red ink, which said, "My dear Christine, you need have no concern as to your fate. You have no better nor more respectful friend in the world than myself. You are alone, at present, in this home which is yours. I am going out shopping to buy you all the things that you can need." I felt sure that I had fallen into the hands of a madman. I ran round my little apartment, looking for a way of escape, but could not find one. I upbraided myself for my absurd superstition, which had caused me to fall into the trap. I felt inclined to laugh and cry at the same time. . . . This was the state of mind in which Erik found me. After giving three taps against the wall, he walked in quietly through a door which I had not noticed and which he left open. He had his arms full of boxes and parcels and arranged them on the bed, in a leisurely fashion, while I loaded him with abuse and called upon him to take off his mask, if it covered the face of an honest man. He replied, serenely, "You shall never see Erik's face." And he reproached me with not having finished dressing at that time of day: he was good enough to tell me that it was two o'clock in the afternoon. He said he would give me half an hour and, while he spoke, wound up my watch and set it for me. After which, he asked me to come to the dining-room, where a nice lunch was waiting for us. I was very hungry. I slammed the door in his face and went to the bath-room. . . . When I came out again, feeling greatly refreshed, Erik said that he loved me, but that he would never tell me so except when I gave him leave and that the rest of the time would be spent in music. "What do you mean by the rest of the time?" I asked. "Five days," he said, with decision. I asked him if I should then be free and he said, "You will be free, Christine, for, when those five days are past, you will have learnt not to fear me; and then, from time to time, you will come back to see your poor Erik!" He pointed to a chair opposite him, at a small table, and I sat down, feeling very uncomfortable. However, I ate a few prawns and the wing of a chicken and drank half a glass of tokay, which he had himself, he told me, brought from the Königsberg cellars. Erik did not eat or drink. I asked him what his nationality was and if that name of Erik did not point to his Scandinavian origin. He said that he had no name and no country and that he had taken the name of Erik by accident. After lunch, he rose and gave me the tips of his fingers, for he said he would like to show me over his flat; but I snatched away my hand and gave a cry. What I had touched was both moist and, at the same time, bony; and I remembered that his hands smelt of death. "Oh, forgive me!" he moaned. And he opened a door before me. "This is my room, if you care to see it. It is rather curious." His manners, his words, his attitude gave me confidence and I went in without hesitation. I felt as if I were entering a mortuary chamber. The walls were all hung with black but, instead of the white tears that usually relieve that funereal upholstery, there was an enormous stave of music with the notes of the *Dies Irae*, many times repeated. In the middle of the room was a canopy, from which hung curtains of red brocaded stuff, and, under the canopy, an open coffin. "That is where I sleep," said Erik. "One has to get used to everything in life, even to eternity." The sight upset me so much that I turned away my head. Then I saw the keyboard of an organ which filled one whole side of the wall. On the desk was a music-book covered with red notes. I asked leave to look at it, and, on the first page, read, *"Don Juan Triumphant."* "Yes," he said, "I compose sometimes. I began that work twenty years ago. When I have finished, I shall take it away with me in that coffin and never wake up again." "You must work at it as seldom as you can," I said. He replied, "I sometimes work at it for fourteen days and nights together, during which I live on music only, and then I rest for years at a time." "Will you play me something out of your *Don Juan Triumphant?*" I asked, thinking to please him. "You must never ask me that," he said, in a gloomy voice. "I will play you Mozart, if you like, which will only make you weep; but my *Duan Juan* burns, Christine; and yet he is not struck by fire from Heaven." Thereupon we returned to the drawing-room. I noticed that there was no mirror in the whole apartment. I was going to remark upon this, but Erik had already sat down to the piano. He said, "You see, Christine, there is some music so terrible that it consumes all who approach it. Fortunately, you have not come to that music yet, for you would lose all your pretty colouring and nobody would know you when you returned to Paris. Let us sing something *operatic*, Christine Daaé!" He spoke these last words as though he was flinging an insult at me.'

'What did you do?'

'I had no time to think about the meaning he put into his words. We at once began the duet in *Othello* and already the catastrophe was upon us. I sang *Desdemona* with a despair, a terror which I had never displayed before. As for him, his voice thundered forth his revengeful soul at every note. Love, jealousy, hatred burst out around us in harrowing cries. Erik's black mask made me think of the natural mask of the Moor of Venice. He was Othello himself. . . . Suddenly, I felt a need to see beneath the mask. I wanted to know the *face* of the voice and, with a movement which I was utterly unable to control, swiftly my fingers tore away the mask. Oh, horror, horror, horror! . . .'

Christine stopped, at the thought of the vision that had scared her, while the echoes of the night, which had repeated the name of Erik, now thrice moaned the cry:

'Horror! . . . Horror! . . . Horror!'

Raoul and Christine, clasping each other closely, raised their eyes to the stars that shone in a clear and peaceful sky. Raoul said:

'Strange, Christine, that this calm, soft night should be so full of plaintive sounds. One would think that it was sorrowing with us.'

'When you know the secret, Raoul, your ears, like mine, will be full of lamentations.'

She took Raoul's protecting hands in hers and, with a long shiver, continued:

'Yes, if I live to be a hundred, I shall always hear the superhuman cry of grief and rage which he uttered when the terrible sight appeared before my eyes. . . . Raoul, you have seen death's-heads, when they have been dried and withered by the ages, and perhaps, if you were not the victim of a nightmare you saw *his* death's-head at Perros. And then you saw Red Death stalking about at the last masked ball. But all those death's-heads were motionless and their dumb horror was not alive. But imagine, if you can, Red Death's mask suddenly coming to life in order to express, with the four black holes of its eyes, its nose and its mouth, the extreme anger, the mighty fury of a demon; *and not a ray of light from the sockets*, for, as I learnt later, you cannot see his blazing eyes except in the dark. . . . I fell back against the wall and he came up to me, grinding his teeth hideously, and, as I fell upon my knees, he hissed mad, incoherent words and curses at me. Leaning over me, he cried, "Look! You want to see? See! Feast your eyes, glut your soul on my cursed ugliness! Look at Erik's face! Now you know the face of the voice! You were not content to hear me, eh? You wanted to know what I looked like? Oh, you women are so inquisitive! Well, are you satisfied? I'm a good-looking fellow, eh? . . . When a woman has seen me, as you have, she belongs to me. She loves me for ever! I am a kind of Don Juan, you know!" And, drawing himself up to his full height, with his hand on his hip, wagging the hideous thing that was his head on his shoulders, he roared, "Look at me! *I am Don Juan triumphant!*" And, when I turned away my head and begged for mercy, he drew my head back to him, brutally, twisting his dead fingers into my hair.'

'Enough! Enough!' cried Raoul. 'I will kill him. In heaven's name, Christine, tell me where the dining-room on the lake is! I must kill him!'

'Oh, be quiet, Raoul, if you want to know!'

'Yes, I want to know how and why you went back; I must know! . . . But, in any case, I will kill him!'

'Oh, Raoul, listen, listen! . . . He dragged me by my hair and then . . . and then. . . . Oh, it is too horrible!'

'Well, what? Out with it!' exclaimed Raoul, fiercely. 'Out with it, quick!'

'Then he hissed at me, "Ah, I frighten you, do I? . . . I daresay!

. . . Perhaps you think that I have another mask, eh, and that this
. . . this . . . my head is a mask? Well," he roared, "tear it off as you
did the other! Come! Come along! I insist! Your hands! Your
hands! Give me your hands!" And he seized my hands and dug
them into his awful face. He tore his flesh with my nails, tore his
terrible dead flesh with my nails! . . . "Know," he shouted, while
his throat throbbed and panted like a furnace, "know that I am
built up of death from head to foot and that it is a corpse that
loves you and adores you and will never, never leave you! . . .
Look, I am not laughing now, I am crying, crying for you, Christine, who have torn off my mask and who therefore can never
leave me again! . . . As long as you thought me handsome, you
could have come back, I know you would have come back . . . but,
now that you know my hideousness, you would run away for good.
. . . So I shall keep you here! . . . Why did you want to see me? Oh,
mad Christine, who wanted to see me! When my own father never
saw me and when my mother, so as not to see me, presented me
with my first mask!" He had let go of me at last and was now dragging himself about on the floor, uttering terrible sobs. And then
he crawled away like a snake, went into his room, closed the door
and left me alone to my reflections. . . . Presently I heard the
sound of the organ; and then I began to understand Erik's con-
temptuous phrase when he spoke about operatic music. What I
now heard was utterly different from what had charmed me up to
then. His *Don Juan Triumphant* (for I had not a doubt but that he
had rushed to his masterpiece to forget the horror of the moment)
seemed to me at first one awful, long, magnificent sob. But, little
by little, it expressed every emotion, every suffering of which
mankind is capable. It intoxicated me; and I opened the door that
separated us. Erik rose, as I entered, but *dared not turn in my direction.* "Erik," I cried, "show me your face without fear! I swear that
you are the most unhappy and sublime of men; and, if ever again I
shiver when I look at you, it will be because I am thinking of the
splendour of your genius!" Then Erik turned round, for he
believed me; and I also – alas! had faith in myself. He fell at my
feet, with words of love . . . With words of love in his dead mouth
. . . and the music had ceased! . . . He kissed the hem of my dress
and did not see that I closed my eyes. . . . What more can I tell
you, dear? You now know the tragedy. . . . It went on for a fortnight . . . a fortnight during which I lied to him. My lies were as
hideous as the monster who inspired them; but they were the price
of my liberty. I burnt his mask; and I managed so well that, even

when he was not singing, he tried to catch my eye, like a dog sitting by its master. He was my faithful slave and paid me endless little attentions. Gradually, I gave him such confidence that he ventured to take me walking on the banks of the lake and to row me in the boat on its leaden waters; towards the end of my captivity, he let me out through the gates that close the underground passages in the Rue Scribe. Here a carriage awaited us and took us to the Bois. The night when we met you was nearly fatal to me, for he is terribly jealous of you and I had to tell him that you were soon going away. . . . Then, at last, after a fortnight of this horrible captivity, during which I was filled with pity, enthusiasm, despair and horror by turns, he believed me when I said, "I *will come back!*" '

'And you went back, Christine,' groaned Raoul.

'Yes, dear, and I must tell you that it was not his frightful threats when setting me free that helped me to keep my word, but the harrowing sob which he gave on the threshold of the tomb. . . . That sob attached me to the unfortunate man more than I myself suspected when taking leave of him. Poor Erik! Poor Erik!'

'Christine,' said Raoul, rising, 'you tell me that you love me; but you had recovered your liberty hardly a few hours before you returned to Erik! . . . Remember the masked ball!'

'Yes; and remember that those few hours I passed with you, Raoul . . . to the great danger of both of us.'

'I doubted your love for me during those hours.'

'Do you doubt it still, Raoul? . . . Then know that each of my visits to Erik increased my horror of him; for each of those visits, instead of calming him, as I hoped, made him mad with love! . . . And I am so frightened, so frightened! . . .'

'You are frightened . . . but do you love me? . . . If Erik were good-looking, would you love me, Christine?'

She rose in her turn, put her two trembling arms round the young man's neck, and said:

'Oh, my betrothed of a day, if I did not love you, I would not give you my lips! Take them, for the first time and the last.'

He kissed her lips; but the night that surrounded them was rent asunder, they fled as at the approach of a storm and their eyes, filled with dread of Erik, showed them, before they disappeared in the forest under the roof, high up above them, an immense night-bird that stared at them with its blazing eyes and seemed to cling to the strings of Apollo's lyre.

CHAPTER XIII

A Masterstroke

RAOUL AND CHRISTINE RAN AND RAN, eager to escape from the roof and the blazing eyes that showed only in the dark; and they did not stop before they came to the eighth floor on the way down.

There was no performance at the Opera that night and the passages were empty. Suddenly, a queer-looking form stood before them and blocked the road:

'No, not this way!'

And the form pointed to another passage by which they were to reach the wings. Raoul wanted to stop and ask for an explanation. But the form, which wore a sort of long frock-coat and a pointed cap, said:

'Quick! Go away quickly!'

Christine was already dragging Raoul along, compelling him to start running again.

'But who is he? Who is that man?' he asked.

Christine replied:

'It's the Persian.'

'What's he doing here? . . .'

'I don't know. . . . He is always in the Opera. . . .'

'You are making me run away, for the first time in my life. . . . If we really saw Erik, what I ought to have done was to nail him to Apollo's lyre, just as we nail the owls to the walls of our Breton farms; and there would have been no more question of him.'

'My dear Raoul, you would first have had to climb up to Apollo's lyre: that is no easy matter.'

'The blazing eyes were there!'

'Oh, you are getting like me now, seeing him everywhere! What we took for blazing eyes was probably a couple of stars shining through the strings of the lyre.'

And Christine went down another floor, with Raoul following her.

'As you have quite made up your mind to go, Christine, I assure you it would be better to go at once. Why wait for to-morrow? He may have heard us to-night!'

'No, no, he is working, I tell you, at his *Don Juan Triumphant* and not thinking of us.'

'You're so sure of that you keep on looking behind you!'

'Come to my dressing-room.'

'Hadn't we better meet outside the Opera?'

'Never, till we go away for good! It would bring us bad luck if I did not keep my word. I promised him to see you nowhere but here.'

'It's a good thing for me that he allowed you to do as much as that. Do you know,' said Raoul, bitterly, 'that it was very plucky of you to let us play at being engaged?'

'Why, my dear, he knows all about it! He said, "I trust you, Christine. M Raoul de Chagny is in love with you and is going abroad. Before he goes, I want him to be as unhappy as I am." Are people so unhappy when they love?'

'Yes, Christine, when they love and are not sure of being loved.'

They came to Christine's dressing-room:

'Why do you think that you are safer in this room than on the stage?' asked Raoul. 'You heard him through the walls; therefore he can hear us.'

'No. He gave me his word not to be behind the walls of my dressing-room again and I believe Erik's word. This room and my bedroom on the lake are for me, exclusively, and not to be approached by him.'

'How can you have gone from this room into the dark passage, Christine? Suppose we try to repeat your movements: shall we?'

'It is dangerous, dear, for the glass might carry me off again; and, instead of running away, I should be obliged to go to the end of the secret passage, to the lake, and there call Erik.'

'Would he hear you?'

'Erik will hear me wherever I call him. He told me so. He is a very curious genius. You must not think, Raoul, that he is simply a man who amuses himself by living underground. He does things that no other man could do; he knows things which nobody in the world knows.'

'Take care, Christine, you are making a ghost of him again!'

'No, he is not a ghost; he is a man of heaven and earth, that is all.'

'A man of heaven and earth . . . that is all! . . . A nice way to speak of him! . . . And are you still resolved to run away from him?'

'Yes, to-morrow.'

'To-morrow, you will have no resolve left!'

'Then, Raoul, you must run away with me in spite of myself: is that understood?'

'I shall be here at twelve to-morrow night; I shall keep my promise, whatever happens. You say that, after listening to the performance, he is to wait for you in the dining-room on the lake?'

'Yes.'

'And how are you to reach him, if you don't know how to go out by the glass?'

'Why, by going straight to the edge of the lake.'

Christine opened a box, took out an enormous key and showed it to Raoul.

'What's that?' he asked.

'The key of the gate to the underground passage in the Rue Scribe.'

'I understand, Christine. It leads straight to the lake. Give it to me, Christine, will you?'

'Never!' she said. 'That would be treachery!'

Suddenly, Christine changed colour. A mortal pallor overspread her features:

'Oh heaven!' she cried. 'Erik! Erik! Have pity on me!'

'Hold your tongue!' said Raoul. 'You told me he could hear you!'

But the singer's attitude became more and more inexplicable. She wrung her fingers, repeating, with a distraught air:

'Oh heaven! Oh heaven!'

'But what is it? What is it?' Raoul implored.

'The ring . . . the gold ring he gave me. . . .'

'Oh, so Erik gave you that ring!'

'You know he did, Raoul! But what you don't know is that, when he gave it to me, he said, "I give you back your liberty, Christine, on condition that this ring is always on your finger. As long as you keep it, you will be protected against all danger and Erik will remain your friend. But woe to you if ever you part with it, for Erik will have his revenge!" . . . My dear, my dear, the ring is gone! . . . Woe upon us!'

They both looked for the ring, but could not find it. Christine refused to be pacified:

'It was while I gave you that kiss, up above, under Apollo's lyre,' she said. 'The ring must have slipped from my finger and dropped into the street! We can never find it. And what misfortunes are in store for us now! Oh, to run away!'

'Let us run away at once,' Raoul insisted, once more.

She hesitated. He thought that she was going to say yes. . . . Then her bright pupils became dimmed and she said:

'No! To-morrow!'

And she left him hurriedly, still wringing and rubbing her fingers, as though she hoped to bring the ring back like that.

Raoul went home, greatly perturbed at all that he had heard:

'If I don't save her from the hands of that humbug,' he said, aloud, as he went to bed, 'she is lost. But I will save her.'

He put out his lamp and felt a need to insult Erik in the dark. Thrice over, he shouted:

'Humbug! . . . Humbug! . . . Humbug! . . .'

But suddenly, he raised himself on his elbow. A cold sweat poured from his temples. Two eyes, like blazing coals, had appeared at the foot of his bed. They stared at him fixedly, terribly, in the darkness of the night.

Raoul was no coward; and yet he trembled. He put out a groping, hesitating, uncertain hand towards the table by his bedside. He found the matches and lit his candle. The eyes disappeared.

Still uneasy in his mind, he thought to himself:

'She told me that *his* eyes only showed in the dark. His eyes have disappeared in the light, but *he* may be there still.'

And he rose, hunted about, went round the room. He looked under his bed, like a child. Then he thought himself absurd, got into bed again and blew out the candle. The eyes reappeared.

He sat up and stared back at them with all the courage he possessed. Then he cried:

'Is that you, Erik? Man, genius or ghost, is it you?'

He reflected:

'If it's he, he's on the balcony!'

Then he ran to the chest of drawers and groped for his revolver. He opened the balcony-window, looked out, saw nothing and closed the window again. He went back to bed, shivering, for the night was cold, and put the revolver on the table within his reach.

The eyes were still there, at the foot of the bed. Were they between the bed and the window-pane or behind the pane, that is to say, on the balcony? That was what Raoul wanted to know. He also wanted to know if those eyes belonged to a human being. . . . He wanted to know everything. . . .

Then, patiently, calmly, he seized his revolver and took aim. He aimed a little above the two eyes. Surely, if they were eyes and if above those two eyes there was a forehead and if Raoul was not too clumsy . . .

The shot made a terrible noise amid the silence of the slumbering house. . . . And, wild footsteps came hurrying along the passages, Raoul sat up with outstretched arm, ready to fire again, if need be. . . .

This time, the two eyes had disappeared.

. Servants appeared, carrying lights; Count Philippe, terribly anxious:

'What is it?'

'I think I have been dreaming,' replied the younger man. 'I fired at two stars that kept me from sleeping.'

'You're raving! . . . Are you ill? . . . For God's sake, tell me, Raoul: what happened?'

And the count seized hold of the revolver.

'No, no, I'm not raving. . . . Besides, we shall soon see. . . .'

He got out of bed, put on a dressing-gown and slippers, took a light from the hands of a servant and, opening the window, stepped out on the balcony.

The count saw that the window had been pierced by a bullet at a man's height. Raoul was leaning over the balcony with his candle:

'Aha!' he said. 'Blood! . . . Blood! . . . Here, there, more blood! . . . That's a good thing! A ghost who bleeds is less dangerous!' he grinned.

'Raoul! Raoul! Raoul!'

The count was shaking him as though he were trying to waken a sleep-walker.

'But, my dear brother, I'm not asleep!' Raoul protested, impatiently. 'You can see the blood for yourself. I thought I had been dreaming and firing at two stars. It was Erik's eyes . . . and here is his blood! . . . After all, perhaps I was wrong to shoot; and Christine is quite capable of never forgiving me. . . . All this would not have happened if I had drawn the curtains before going to bed. . . .'

'Raoul, have you suddenly gone mad? Wake up!'

'What, again? You would do better to help me find Erik . . . for, after all, a ghost who bleeds can always be found. . . .'

The count's valet said:

'That is so, sir; there is blood on the balcony.'

The other man-servant brought a lamp, by the light of which they examined the balcony carefully. The marks of blood followed the rail till they reached a gutter-spout; then they went up the gutter-spout.

'My dear fellow,' said Count Philippe, 'you have fired at a cat.'

'The misfortune is,' said Raoul, with a grin, 'that it's quite possible. With Erik, you never know. Is it Erik? Is it the cat? Is it the ghost? No, with Erik, you can't tell!'

Raoul went on making these strange remarks, which corresponded so intimately and logically with the distractions of his brain and which, at the same time, tended to persuade many people that his mind was unhinged. The count himself was seized with this idea; and later, the examining magistrate, on receiving the report of the commissary of police, came to the same conclusion.

'Who is Erik?' asked the count, pressing his brother's hand.

'He is my rival. And if he's not dead, it's a pity.'

He dismissed the servants with a wave of the hand and the two Chagnys were left alone. But the men were not out of earshot before the count's valet heard Raoul say, distinctly and emphatically:

'I shall carry off Christine Daaé to-night.'

This phrase was afterwards repeated to M Faure, the examining magistrate. But no one ever knew exactly what passed between the two brothers at this interview. The servants declared that this was not their first quarrel. Their voices penetrated the wall; and it was always an actress called Christine Daaé that was in question.

At breakfast – the early morning breakfast, which the count took in his study – Philippe sent for his brother. Raoul arrived silent and gloomy. The scene was a very short one. Philip handed his brother a copy of the *Epoque* and said:

'Read that!'

The viscount read:

'The latest news in the Faubourg is that there is a promise of marriage between Mlle Christine Daaé, the opera-singer, and M le Vicomte Raoul de Chagny. If the gossips are to be believed, Count Philippe has sworn that, for the first time on record, the Chagnys shall not keep their promise. But, as love is all-powerful, at the Opera as – and even more than – elsewhere, we wonder how Count Philippe intends to prevent the viscount, his brother, from leading the new Margarita to the altar. The two brothers are said to adore each other; but the count is curiously mistaken if he imagines that brotherly love will triumph over love pure and simple.'

'You see, Raoul,' said the count, 'you are making us ridiculous!
. . . That little girl has turned your head with her ghost stories.'

The viscount had evidently repeated Christine's narrative to his
brother during the night. All that he now said was:

'Good-bye, Philippe.'

'Have you quite made up your mind? You are going to-night?
With her?'

No reply.

'Surely you will not do anything so foolish? Mind you, I shall
know how to prevent you!'

'Good-bye, Philippe,' the viscount repeated and left the room.

This scene was described to the examining-magistrate by the
count himself, who did not see Raoul again until that evening, at
the Opera, a few minutes before Christine's disappearance.

Raoul, in fact, devoted the whole day to his preparations for
flight. The horses, the carriage, the coachman, the provisions, the
luggage, the money required for the journey, the road to be taken
(he had resolved not to go by train, so as to throw the ghost off the
scent): all this had to be settled and provided for; and it occupied
him until nine o'clock at night.

At nine o'clock, a sort of travelling-barouche, with the curtains
of its windows close-drawn, took its place in the rank on the
Rotunda side. It was drawn by two powerful horses driven by a
coachman whose face was almost concealed in the long folds of a
muffler. In front of this travelling-carriage were three broughams,
belonging respectively to Carlotta, who had suddenly returned to
Paris, to Sorelli, and, at the head of the rank, to the Comte
Philippe de Chagny. No one left the barouche. The coachman
remained on his box. And the three other coachmen remained on
theirs.

A shadow in a long black cloak and a soft black felt hat passed
along the pavement between the Rotunda and the carriages, examined the barouche carefully, went up to the horses and the coachman and then moved away without saying a word. The magistrate
afterwards believed that this shadow was that of the Vicomte
Raoul de Chagny; but I do not agree, seeing that that evening, as
every evening, the Vicomte de Chagny was wearing a tall hat,
which hat, besides, was subsequently found. I am more inclined to
think that the shadow was that of the ghost, who knew all about
the business, as the reader will soon learn.

They were giving *Faust*, as it happened, to a splendid house.
The Faubourg was magnificently represented; and the paragraph

in that morning's *Epoque* had already produced its effect, for all eyes were turned to the box in which Count Philippe sat alone, apparently in a very indifferent and careless frame of mind. The feminine element in the brilliant audience seemed curiously puzzled; and the viscount's absence gave rise to any amount of whispering behind the fans. Christine Daaé met with a rather cold reception. That very special audience could not forgive her for aiming so high.

The singer noticed this unfavourable attitude of a portion of the house and was confused by it.

The regular frequenters of the Opera, who pretended to know the truth about the viscount's love-story exchanged significant smiles at certain passages in Margarita's part; and they made a show of turning and looking at Philippe de Chagny's box when Christine sang:

> I wish I could but know who was he
> That addressed me,
> If he was noble, or, at least, what his name is. . .

The count sat with his chin on his hand and seemed to pay no attention to these manifestations. He kept his eyes fixed on the stage; but his thoughts appeared to be far away. . . .

Christine lost her self-assurance more and more. She trembled. She felt on the verge of a breakdown. . . . Carolus Fonta wondered if she was ill, if she could keep the stage until the end of the Garden Act. In the front of the house, people remembered the catastrophe that had befallen Carlotta at the end of that act and the historic 'co-ack' which had momentarily interrupted her career in Paris.

Just then, Carlotta made her entrance in a box facing the stage, a sensational entrance. Poor Christine raised her eyes upon this fresh subject of excitement. She recognized her rival. She thought she saw a sneer on her lips. That saved her. She forgot everything, in order to triumph once more.

From that moment, the prima donna sang with all her heart and soul. She tried to surpass all that she had done till then; and she succeeded. In the last act, when she began the invocation to the angels, she made all the members of the audience feel as though they too had wings.

In the centre of the amphitheatre, a man stood up and remained standing, facing the singer. It was Raoul.

Holy angel, in Heaven blessed. . . .

And Christine, her arms outstretched, her throat filled with music, the glory of her hair falling over her bare shoulders, uttered the divine cry:

My spirit longs with thee to rest!

It was at this moment that the stage was suddenly plunged into darkness. It happened so quickly that the spectators hardly had time to utter a sound of stupefaction, for the gas at once lit the stage again. . . . But Christine Daaé was no longer there! . . .

What had become of her? What was the miracle? All exchanged glances, without understanding, and the excitement at once reached its height. Nor was the tension any less great on the stage itself. Men rushed from the wings to the spot where Christine had been singing that very instant. The performance was interrupted amid the greatest disorder.

Where had Christine gone? What witchcraft had snatched her away before the eyes of thousands of enthusiastic onlookers and from the arms of Carolus Fonta himself? It was as though the angels had really carried her up 'to rest.'

Raoul, still standing up in the amphitheatre, had given a cry. Count Philippe had sprung to his feet in his box. People looked at the stage, at the count, at Raoul and wondered if this curious event were connected in any way with the paragraph in that morning's paper. But Raoul hurriedly left his seat, the count disappeared from his box and, while the curtain was lowered, the subscribers rushed to the door that led behind the scenes. The rest of the audience waited amid an indescribable hubbub. Every one spoke at once. Every one tried to suggest an explanation of the extraordinary incident.

At last, the curtain rose slowly and Carolus Fonta stepped to the conductor's desk and, in a sad and serious voice, said:

'Ladies and gentleman, an unprecedented event has taken place and thrown us into a state of the greatest alarm. Our sister-artist, Christine Daaé, has disappeared before our eyes and nobody can tell us how!'

CHAPTER XIV

The Safety-Pin

BEHIND THE CURTAIN there was an indescribable crowd. Artists, scene-shifters, dancers, supers, choristers, subscribers were all asking questions, shouting and hustling one another:

'What became of her?'

'She's run away.'

'With the Vicomte de Chagny, of course!'

'No, with the count!'

'Ah, here's Carlotta! Carlotta did the trick!'

'No, it was the ghost!'

And a few laughed, especially as a careful examination of the trap-doors and boards had put the idea of an accident out of the question.

Amid this noisy throng, three men stood talking in a low voice and with despairing gestures. They were Gabriel, the chorus-master; Mercier, the acting-manager; and Rémy, the secretary. They retired to a corner of the lobby by which the stage communicates with the wide passage leading to the foyer of the ballet. Here they stood and argued behind some enormous 'properties:'

'I knocked at the door,' said Rémy. 'They did not answer. Perhaps they are not in their office. In any case, it's impossible to find out, for they took the keys with them.'

'They' were obviously the managers, who had given orders, during the last entr'acte, that they were not to be disturbed on any pretext whatever. They were not in to anybody.

'All the same,' exclaimed Gabriel, 'a singer isn't run away with, from the middle of the stage, every day!'

'Did you shout that to them?' asked Mercier.

'I'll go back again,' said Rémy and disappeared, at a run. Thereupon, the stage-manager arrived, in a great state of flurry:

'Well, M Mercier, are you coming? What are you two doing here? You're wanted, Mr Acting-Manager.'

'I refuse to do anything or to know anything before the commissary arrives,' declared Mercier. 'I have sent for Mifroid. We shall see, when he comes!'

'And I tell you that you ought to go down to the organ at once.'

'Not before the commissary comes. . . .'

'I've been down to the organ myself.'

'Ah! And what did you see?'

'Well, I saw nobody! Do you hear? Nobody!'

'What do you want me to do down there?'

'You're right!' said the stage-manager, frantically pushing his hands through his rebellious hair. 'You're right! But there might be some one at the organ who could tell us how the stage came to be suddenly darkened. Now Mauclair is not to be found: do you understand that?'

Mauclair was the gas-man, who dispensed light and darkness on the Opera stage.

'Mauclair is not to be found!' repeated Mercier, taken aback. 'Well, what about his assistants?'

'There's no Mauclair and no assistants! No one at the lights, I tell you! You can imagine,' roared the stage-manager, 'that that little woman must have been carried off by somebody: she didn't run away by herself! It was a thought-out piece of "business" and we've got to find out about it. . . . And what are the managers doing all this time? . . . I say, I gave orders that no one was to go down to the lights and I posted a fireman in front of the gas-man's box beside the organ. Wasn't that right?'

'Yes, yes, quite right, quite right. . . . And now let's wait for the commissary.'

The stage-manager walked away, shrugging his shoulders, fuming, muttering insults at those milk-sops who remained quietly squatting in a corner while the whole theatre was topsy-turvy.

Gabriel and Mercier were not so quiet as all that. Only they had received an order that paralyzed them. The managers were not to be disturbed on any account. Rémy had violated that order and met with no success.

At that moment, he returned from his new expedition, wearing a curiously startled air.

'Well, have you seen them?' asked Mercier.

'Moncharmin opened the door at last. His eyes were starting out of his head. I thought he meant to strike me. I could not get a word in; and what do you think he shouted to me? "Have you a safety-pin?" "No!" "Well, then, clear out!" I tried to tell him that an extraordinary thing had happened on the stage, but he roared,

"A safety-pin! Give me a safety-pin at once!" A boy heard him –
he was bellowing like a bull – ran up with a safety-pin and gave it
to him; whereupon Moncharmin slammed the door in my face and
there you are!'

'And couldn't you have said, "Christine Daaé . . ."'

'I should like to have seen you in my place! . . . He was foaming
at the mouth. . . . He thought of nothing but his safety-pin. . . . I
believe, if they hadn't brought him one, he would have fallen
down in a fit! . . . Oh, all that isn't normal; and our managers are
going mad! . . . Besides, it can't go on like this! I'm not used to
being treated in that fashion!'

Suddenly, Gabriel whispered:

'It's another trick of O.G.'s.'

Rémy gave a grin, Mercier a sigh and seemed about to speak . . .
but, meeting Gabriel's eye, said nothing.

However, Mercier felt his responsibility increase as the minutes
passed without the managers appearing; and, at last, he could
stand it no longer:

'Look here, I'll go and hunt them out myself!'

Gabriel, turning very gloomy and serious, stopped him:

'Be careful what you're doing, Mercier! If they're staying in
their office, it's probably because they've got to! O.G. has more
than one trick up his sleeve!'

But Mercier shook his head:

'That's their look-out! I 'm going! If people had listened to me,
the police would have known everything long ago!'

And he went.

'What's everything?' asked Rémy. 'What was there to tell the
police? Why don't you answer, Gabriel? . . . Ah, so you know
something, do you? Well, you'd do better to tell me too, if you
don't want me to shout out that you are all going mad! . . . Yes,
that's what you are: mad!'

Gabriel put on a stupid look and pretended not to understand
the private secretary's unseemly outburst:

'What "something" am I supposed to know?' he said. 'I don't
know what you mean.'

Rémy began to lose his temper:

'This evening, Richard and Moncharmin were behaving like
lunatics, here, between the acts.'

'I never noticed it,' growled Gabriel, very much annoyed.

'Then you're the only one! . . . Do you think that I didn't see
them? . . . And that M Parabise, the manager of the Crédit Cen-

tral, noticed nothing? . . . And that M de la Borderie, the ambassador, has no eyes to see with? . . . Why, all the subscribers were pointing at our managers!'

'But what were our managers doing?' asked Gabriel, putting on his most innocent air.

'What were they doing? You know better than any one what they were doing! . . . You were there! . . . And you were watching them, you and Mercier! . . . And you were the only two who didn't laugh. . . .'

'I don't understand!'

Gabriel raised his arms and dropped them to his side again, which gesture was meant to convey that the question did not interest him. Rémy continued:

'What is the sense of this new mania of theirs? . . . *Why won't they have any one come near them now?*'

'What? *Won't they have any one come near them?*'

'*And they won't let any one touch them!*'

'Really? Have you noticed *that they won't let any one touch them?* That is certainly odd!'

'Oh, so you admit it! And high time too! And *then they walk backwards!*'

'*Backwards?* You have seen our managers *walk backwards?* Why, I thought that only crabs walked backwards!'

'Don't laugh, Gabriel, don't laugh!'

'I'm not laughing,' protested Gabriel, looking as solemn as a judge.

'Perhaps you can tell me this, Gabriel, as you're an intimate friend of the management: when I went up to M Richard, outside the foyer, during the Garden interval, with my hand out before me, why did M Moncharmin whisper to me, "Go away! Go away! Whatever you do, don't touch M le directeur"? . . . Am I supposed to have an infectious disease?'

'It's incredible!'

'And, a little later, when M de la Borderie went up to M Richard, didn't you see M Moncharmin fling himself between them and hear him exclaim, "M l'ambassadeur, I entreat you not to touch M le directeur"?'

'It's terrible! . . . And what was Richard doing meanwhile?'

'What was he doing? Why, you saw him! He turned about, *bowed in front of him, though there was nobody in front of him,* and withdrew *backwards.*'

'*Backwards?*'

'And Moncharmin, behind Richard, also turned about, that is, he described a semi-circle behind Richard and also *walked backwards!* . . . And they went *like that* to the staircase leading to the manager's office: *backwards, backwards, backwards!* . . . Well, if they are not mad, will you explain what it means?'

'Perhaps they were practising a figure in the ballet,' suggested Gabriel, without much conviction in his voice.

The secretary was furious at this wretched joke, made at so dramatic a moment. He knit his brows and compressed his lips. Then he put his mouth to Gabriel's ear:

'Don't be so sly, Gabriel. There are things going on for which you and Mercier are partly responsible.'

'What do you mean?' asked Gabriel.

'Christine Daaé is not the only one who suddenly disappeared to-night.'

'Oh, nonsense!'

'There's no nonsense about it. Perhaps you can tell me why, when Mother Giry came down to the foyer just now, Mercier took her by the hand and hurried her away with him?'

'Really?' said Gabriel. 'I never saw it.'

'You did see it, Gabriel, for you went with Mercier and Mother Giry to Mercier's office. Since then, you and Mercier have been seen, but no one has seen Mother Giry. . . .'

'Do you think we've eaten her?'

'No, but you've locked her up in the office; and anyone passing the office can hear her yelling, "Oh, the scoundrels! Oh, the scoundrels" '

At this point of that singular conversation, Mercier arrived, all out of breath:

'There!' he said, in a gloomy voice. 'It's worse than ever! . . . I shouted, "It's a serious matter! Open the door! It's I, Mercier." I heard footsteps. The door opened and Moncharmin appeared. He was very pale. He said, "What do you want?" I answered, "Some one has run off with Christine Daaé." What do you think he said? "And a good job too!" And he shut the door, after putting this in my hand.'

Mercier opened his hand; Rémy and Gabriel looked:

'The safety-pin!' cried Rémy.

'Strange! Strange!' muttered Gabriel, who could not help shivering.

Suddenly, a voice made them all three turn round:

'I beg your pardon, gentlemen. But could you tell me where Christine Daaé is?'

In spite of the serious circumstances, the absurdity of the question would have made them roar with laughter, if they had not caught sight of a face so sorrow-stricken that they were at once seized with pity. It was the Vicomte Raoul de Chagny.

CHAPTER XV

'Christine! Christine!'

RAOUL'S FIRST THOUGHT after Christine Daaé's fantastic disappearance, was to accuse Erik. He no longer doubted the almost supernatural powers of the Angel of Music, in this domain of the Opera where he had set up his empire. And Raoul rushed onto the stage, in a mad fit of love and despair:

'Christine! Christine!' he moaned, calling to her as he felt that she must be calling to him from the depths of that dark pit to which the monster had carried her. 'Christine! Christine!'

And he seemed to hear the girl's screams through the frail boards that separated him from her. He bent forward, he listened . . . he wandered over the stage like a madman. Ah, to descend, to descend into that pit of darkness, every entrance to which was closed to him . . . for the stairs that led below the stage were forbidden to everybody that night. . . .

'Christine! Christine! . . .'

People pushed him aside, laughing. . . . They made fun of him. . . . They thought the poor lover's brain was gone! . . .

By what mad road, through what black, mysterious passages known to himself alone had Erik dragged that pure-souled child to the awful haunt, with the Louis-Philippe room, opening on the lake?

'Christine! Christine! . . . Why don't you answer? . . . Are you alive? . . .'

Hideous thoughts flashed through Raoul's congested brain. Of course, Erik must have discovered their secret, must have known that Christine had played him false. What a vengeance would be his!

And Raoul thought again of the yellow stars that had come, the night before, and roamed over his balcony. Why had he not put them out for good? There were some men's eyes that dilated in the dark and shone like stars or like cats' eyes. Certain albinos, who seemed to have rabbits' eyes by day, had cats' eyes at night: everybody knew that! . . . Yes, yes, he had undoubtedly fired at Erik. Why had he not killed him? The monster had fled up the gutter-spout like a cat or a convict who – everybody knew that also – would scale the very skies with the help of a gutter-spout. . . . No doubt, Erik was at that moment contemplating some decisive step against Raoul; but he had been wounded and had escaped, only to turn against poor Christine instead. . . .

Such were the cruel thoughts that haunted Raoul as he ran to the singer's dressing-room:

'Christine! Christine!'

Bitter tears scorched the boy's eyelids as he saw scattered over the furniture the clothes which his beautiful bride was to have worn at the hour of their flight. . . . Oh, oh, why had she refused to leave earlier? Why had she delayed?

Why had she toyed with the threatening catastrophe? Why toyed with the monster's heart? Why, in a final access of pity, had she insisted on flinging, as a last sop to that demon's soul, her divine song:

> Holy angel, in Heaven blessed,
> My spirit longs with thee to rest!

Raoul, his throat filled with sobs, oaths and insults, fumbled awkwardly at the great mirror that had opened one night, before his eyes, to let Christine pass to the murky dwelling below. He pushed, pressed, groped about . . . but the glass apparently obeyed no one but Erik. . . . Perhaps actions were not enough with a glass of that kind? . . . Perhaps he was expected to utter certain words? . . . When he was a little boy, he had heard that there were things that obeyed the spoken word! . . .

Suddenly, Raoul remembered something about a gate opening into the Rue Scribe, an underground passage running straight from the Rue Scribe to the lake. . . . Yes, Christine had told him about that. . . And, when he found that the key was no longer in the box, he nevertheless ran to the Rue Scribe.

Outside, in the streets, he passed his trembling hands over the huge stones, felt for openings . . . came upon iron bars . . . were those they? . . . Or these? . . . Or could it be that air-hole? . . . He plunged his useless eyes through the bars . . . How dark it was in there! . . . He listened. . . . All was silence! . . . He went round the building . . . and came to bigger bars, immense gates! . . . It was the entrance to the Cour de l'Administration.

Raoul rushed into the door-keeper's lodge:

'I beg your pardon, madame, but could you tell me where to find a gate, or a door, made of bars, iron bars, opening in the Rue Scribe . . . and leading to the lake? . . . You know the lake I mean? . . . The lake . . . the underground lake . . . under the Opera.'

'Yes, sir, I know there is a lake under the Opera, but I don't know which door leads to it. . . . I have never been there!'

'And the Rue Scribe, madame, the Rue Scribe? . . . Have you never been to the Rue Scribe?'

The woman laughed, screamed with laughter! Raoul darted away, roaring with anger, ran upstairs, four steps at a time, ran downstairs, rushed through the whole of the business side of the Opera-house, found himself once more in the light of the 'tray.'

He stopped, with his heart thumping in his chest: suppose Christine Daaé had been found? He saw a group of men and asked:

'I beg your pardon, gentlemen. But could you tell me where Christine Daaé is?'

And somebody laughed.

At the same moment, the stage buzzed with a new sound and, amid a crowd of men in evening-dress, all talking and gesticulating together, appeared a man who seemed very calm and displayed a pleasant face, all pink and chubby, crowned with curly hair and lit up with a pair of wonderfully clear blue eyes. Mercier, the acting-manager, drew the Vicomte de Chagny's attention to him and said:

'This is the gentleman to whom you should put your question, monsieur. Let me introduce M Mifroid, the commissary of police.'

'Ah, M le Vicomte de Chagny! Delighted to meet you, monsieur,' said the commissary. 'Would you mind coming with me? . . . And now where are the managers? . . . Where are the managers? . . .'

Mercier did not answer and Rémy, the secretary, volunteered the information that the managers were locked up in their office and knew nothing of what had happened.

'You don't mean to say so! . . . Let us go to the office!'

And M Mifroid, followed by an ever-increasing crowd, turned towards the business side of the building. Mercier took advantage of the confusion to slip a key into Gabriel's hand:

'This is all going very badly,' he whispered. 'You had better let Mother Giry out. . . .'

And Gabriel moved away.

They soon came to the managers' door. Mercier stormed in vain: the door remained closed.

'Open in the name of the law!' commanded M Mifroid, in a loud and rather anxious voice.

At last, the door opened. All rushed into the office, on the commissary's heels.

Raoul was the last to enter. As he was following the others into the room, a hand was laid on his shoulder and he heard these words spoken in his ear:

'Erik's secrets concern no one but himself!'

He turned round, with a stifled exclamation. The hand that had been laid on his shoulder was now placed on the lips of a person with an ebony skin, with eyes of jade and with an astrakhan cap on his head: the Persian!

The stranger continued the gesture recommending discretion and then, at the moment when the astonished viscount was about to ask the reason of his mysterious interventions, bowed and disappeared.

CHAPTER XVI

Mame Giry And The Ghost

BEFORE FOLLOWING THE COMMISSARY into the managers' office, I must describe some extraordinary events that took place in that office, where Rémy and Mercier had vainly tried to obtain admission and where MM Richard and Moncharmin had locked themselves in for a reason which the reader does not yet know, but which it is my duty, as an historian, to reveal without further delay.

I have had occasion to say that the managers' mood had undergone a change for the worse for some time past and to convey the fact that this change was due not only to the fall of the chandelier on the famous night of the gala performance.

The reader must know that the ghost had calmly received his first twenty-thousand francs. Oh, there had been wailing and gnashing of teeth indeed! And yet the thing had happened as simply as could be.

One morning, the managers found on their table an envelope ready addressed to 'Monsieur O.G. – *Private*' and accompanied by a note from O.G. himself:

'The time has come to carry out the clause in the lease. Please put twenty notes of a thousand francs each into this envelope, seal it with your own seal and hand it to Mme Giry, who has my instructions.'

The managers did not hesitate: without wasting time in enquiring how those confounded communications came to be delivered in an office which they were careful to keep locked, they seized this opportunity of laying hands on the mysterious blackmailer. And, after telling the whole story, under promise of secrecy, to Gabriel and Mercier, they put the twenty-thousand francs into the envelope and, without asking for explanations, handed it to Mame Giry, who had been reinstated in her functions. The box-keeper displayed no astonishment. I need hardly say that she was well watched. She went straight to the ghost's box and placed the precious envelope on the little shelf attached to the ledge. The two managers, as well as Gabriel and Mercier, were hidden in such a way that they did not lose sight of the envelope for a second during the performance and even afterwards, for, as the envelope had not been moved, those who watched it did not move either. The theatre emptied; and Mame Giry went away while the managers, Gabriel and Mercier were still there. At last, they became tired of waiting and opened the envelope, after ascertaining that the seals had not been broken.

At first sight, Richard and Moncharmin thought that the notes were still there; but soon they perceived that they were not the same. The twenty real notes were gone and had been replaced by twenty notes of the 'Bank of St Farce'![1]

The managers' rage and fright were unspeakable. Moncharmin wanted to send for the commissary of police, but Richard objected. He no doubt had a plan of his own, for he said:

'Don't let us make ourselves ridiculous! All Paris would laugh at us. O.G. has won the first game: we will win the second.'

He was evidently thinking of the next month's allowance.

Nevertheless, they had been so absolutely tricked that they were bound to feel a certain dejection. And, upon my word, it was not

[1] Flash notes drawn on the 'Bank of St Farce' in France correspond with those drawn on the 'Bank of Engraving' in England. – *Editor's Note.*

difficult to understand. We must not forget that the managers had an idea at the back of their minds that this strange incident might, all the time, be only an unpleasant practical joke on the part of their predecessors and that it would not do to divulge it prematurely. On the other hand, Moncharmin was sometimes troubled with suspicion of Richard himself, who occasionally had queer ideas. And so they were content to await events, while keeping an eye on Mother Giry. Richard would not have her spoken to:

'If she is a confederate,' he said, 'the notes are gone long ago. But, in my opinion, she is merely an idiot.'

'She's not the only idiot in this business,' said Moncharmin, pensively.

'Well, who could have expected it?' moaned Richard. 'But don't be afraid . . . next time, I shall have taken my precautions.'

The next time fell on the very day that witnessed the disappearance of Christine Daaé. In the morning, a note from the ghost reminded the managers that the money was due:

'Do just as you did last time,' said O.G., amiably. 'It worked very well. Put the twenty-thousand francs in the envelope and hand it to our excellent Mme Giry.'

And the note was accompanied by the usual envelope. They had only to insert the notes.

This was done about half an hour before the curtain rose on the first act of *Faust*. Richard showed the envelope to Moncharmin. Then he counted the twenty thousand-franc notes in front of him and put the notes into the envelope, but without closing it:

'And now,' he said, 'let's have Mother Giry in.'

The old woman was sent for. She entered with a sweeping curtsey. She still wore her black taffeta dress, the colour of which was rapidly turning to rust and lilac, to say nothing of the dingy bonnet. She seemed in a good temper. She at once said:

'Good-evening, gentlemen! It's for the envelope, I suppose.'

'Yes, Mme Giry,' said Richard, most amiably. 'For the envelope . . . and something else besides.'

'At your service, M Richard, at your service. . . . And what is the something else, please?'

'First of all, Mme Giry, I have a little question to put to you.'

'By all means, M Richard: Mame Giry is here to answer you.'

'Are you still on good terms with the ghost?'

'Couldn't be better, sir, couldn't be better.'

'Ah, we are delighted. . . . Look here, Mme Giry,' said Richard, in the tone of one making an important confidence. 'We may just as well tell you, among ourselves . . . you're no fool!'

'Why, sir,' exclaimed the box-keeper, stopping the pleasant nodding of the two black feathers on her dingy bonnet, 'I assure you no one has ever doubted that!'

'We are quite agreed and we shall soon understand one another. The story of the ghost is just a good joke, is it not? . . . Well, still between ourselves . . . it has lasted long enough.'

Mame Giry looked at the managers as though they were talking Chinese. She walked up to Richard's table and asked, rather anxiously:

'What do you mean? . . . I don't understand.'

'Oh, you understand quite well! In any case, you've got to understand. . . . And, first of all, tell us his name.'

'Whose name?'

'The name of the man whose accomplice you are, Mame Giry!'

'I am the ghost's accomplice? I? . . . His accomplice in what, pray?'

'You do all he wishes.'

'Oh! . . . He's not very troublesome, you know.'

'And does he still tip you?'

'I can't complain.'

'How much does he give you for bringing him that envelope?'

'Ten francs.'

'You poor thing! That's not much, is it?'

'Why?'

'I'll tell you why presently, Mame Giry. Just now, we should like to know for what . . . extraordinary . . . reason you have given yourself body and soul to this ghost. . . . Mame Giry's friendship and devotion are not to be bought for five francs or ten francs.'

'That's true enough. . . . And I can tell you the reason, sir. There's no disgrace about it . . . on the contrary.'

'We're quite sure of that, Mame Giry!'

'Well, it's like this . . . only the ghost doesn't like me to talk about his business.'

'Indeed?' sneered Richard.

'But this is a matter that concerns myself alone. . . . Well, it was in Box 5 . . . one evening. I found a letter addressed to myself, a sort of note written in red ink. . . . I needn't read the letter to you, sir, I know it by heart and I shall never forget it if I live to be a hundred!'

And Mame Giry, drawing herself up, recited the letter with touching eloquence:

MADAME

'1825. Mlle Ménétrier, a dancer, became Marquise de Cussy.

'1832. Mlle Marie Taglioni, a dancer, became Comtesse Gilbert des Voisins.

'1846. La Sota, a dancer, married a brother of the King of Spain.

'1847. Lola Montes, a dancer, became the morganatic wife of King Louis of Bavaria and was created Countess of Landsfeld.

'1848. Mlle Maria, a dancer, became Baronne d'Herneville.

'1870. Thérèse Hessler, a dancer, married Dom Fernando, brother to the King of Portugal. . . .'

Richard and Moncharmin listened to the old woman, who, as she proceeded with the enumeration of these glorious nuptials, swelled out, drew herself up, took courage and, at last, in a voice bursting with pride, flung out the last sentence of the prophetic letter:

'1885. *Meg Giry, Empress*!'

Exhausted by this supreme effort, the box-keeper fell into a chair, saying:

'Gentlemen, the letter was signed, "Opera Ghost." I had heard speak of the ghost, but only half believed in him. From the day when he declared that my little Meg, the flesh of my flesh, the fruit of my womb, would be empress, I believed in him altogether.'

And really it was not necessary to make a long study of Mame Giry's hysterical features to understand what could be got out of that fine intellect with the two words 'ghost' and 'empress.'

But who pulled the strings of that extraordinary puppet? That was the question.

'You have never seen him, he speaks to you and you believe all he says?' asked Moncharmin.

'Yes. To begin with, I owe it to him that my little Meg was promoted to be the leader of a row. I said to the ghost, " If she is to be empress in 1885, there is no time to lose; she must become a leader at once." He said, "Look upon it as done." And he had only a word to say to M Poligny and the thing *was* done.'

'So you see that M Poligny saw him!'

'No, not any more than I did; but he heard him. The ghost said a word in his ear, you know, on the evening when he left Box 5, looking so pale.'

Moncharmin heaved a sigh:

'What a business!' he groaned.

'Ah!' said Mame Giry. 'I always thought there were secrets between the ghost and M Poligny. Anything that the ghost asked M Poligny to do, M Poligny did. M Poligny could refuse the ghost nothing.'

'You hear, Richard: Poligny could refuse the ghost nothing.'

'Yes, yes, I hear!' said Richard. 'M Poligny is a friend of the ghost; and, as Mme Giry is a friend of M Poligny, there we are! . . . But I don't care a hang about M Poligny,' he added, roughly. 'The only person whose fate really interests me is Mme Giry. . . . Mme Giry, do you know what is in this envelope?'

'Why, of course not,' she said.

'Well, look.'

Mame Giry looked into the envelope with a lack-lustre eye, which soon recovered its brilliancy, however:

'Thousand-franc notes!' she cried.

'Yes, Mme Giry, thousand-franc notes! . . . And you knew it! . . '

'I sir? I? . . . I swear . . .'

'Don't swear, Mme Giry! . . . And now I will tell you the second reason why I sent for you. . . . Mme Giry, I am going to have you arrested.'

The two black feathers on the dingy bonnet, which usually affected the attitude of two notes of interrogation, changed into two notes of exclamation; as for the bonnet itself, it swayed in menace on the old lady's tempestuous chignon. Surprise, indignation, protest and dismay were furthermore displayed by little Meg's mother in a sort of extravagant movement of offended virtue, half bound, half slide, that brought her right under the nose of M Richard, who could not help pushing back his chair.

'*Have me arrested!!!!*'

The mouth that spoke those words seemed to spit the three teeth that were left to it into Richard's face.

M Richard behaved like a hero. He retreated no further. His menacing forefinger seemed already to point out the keeper of Box 5 to the absent magistrates.

'I am going to have you arrested, Mme Giry, as a thief!'

'Say that again!'

And Mme Giry caught Mr Manager Richard a mighty box on the ear, before Mr Manager Moncharmin had time to intervene. But it was not the withered hand of the angry old beldame that fell on the managerial ear, but the envelope itself, the cause of all the trouble, the magic envelope that opened with the blow, scattering the banknotes, which escaped in a fantastic whirl of giant butter-flies.

The two managers gave a shout; and the same thought made them both go on their knees, feverishly picking up and hurriedly examining the precious scraps of paper.

'Are they still genuine, Moncharmin?'

'Are they still genuine, Richard?'

'Yes, they are still genuine!'

Above their heads, Mame Giry's three teeth were clashing in a noisy contest, full of hideous interjections. But all that could be clearly distinguished was this *leitmotif*:

'I, a thief! . . . I, a thief, I?'

She choked with rage. She shouted:

'I never heard of such a thing!'

And, suddenly, she darted up to Richard again:

'In any case,' she yelped, 'you, M Richard, ought to know better than I where the twenty-thousand francs went to!'

'I?' asked Richard, astounded. 'And how should I know?'

Moncharmin, looking severe and dissatisfied, at once insisted that the good lady should explain herself:

'What does this mean, Mme Giry?' he asked. 'And why do you say that M Richard ought to know better than you where the twenty-thousand francs went to?'

As for Richard, who felt himself turning red under Moncharmin's eyes, he took Mme Giry by the wrist and shook it violently. In a voice growling and rolling like thunder, he roared:

'Why should I know better than you where the twenty-thousand francs went to? Why? Answer me!'

'Because they went into your pocket!' gasped the old woman, looking at him as if he were the devil incarnate.

Richard would have rushed upon Mame Giry, if Moncharmin had not stayed his avenging hand and hastened to ask her, more gently:

'How can you suspect my partner, M Richard, of putting twenty-thousand francs in his pocket?'

'I never said that,' declared Mame Giry, 'seeing that it was I myself who put the twenty-thousand francs into M Richard's pocket.' And she added, under her voice, 'There! It's out! . . . And may the ghost forgive me!'

Richard began bellowing anew, but Moncharmin authoritatively ordered him to be silent:

'Allow me! Allow me! Let the woman explain herself. Let me question her.' And he added, 'It is really astonishing that you should take up such a tone! . . . We are on the verge of clearing up the whole mystery. And you're in a rage! . . . You shouldn't behave like that. . . . I'm enjoying myself immensely.'

Mame Giry, like the martyr that she was, raised her head, which beamed with faith in her own innocence:

'You tell me there were twenty-thousand francs in the envelope which I put into M Richard's pocket; but I tell you again that I knew nothing about it. . . . Nor M Richard either, for that matter!'

'Aha!' said Richard, suddenly assuming a swaggering air which Moncharmin did not like. 'I knew nothing either! You put twenty-thousand francs in my pocket and I knew nothing either! I am very glad to hear it, Mme Giry!'

'Yes,' the terrible dame agreed, 'it's true . . . . We neither of us knew anything. . . . But you, you must have ended by finding out!'

Richard would certainly have swallowed Mame Giry alive, had Moncharmin not been there! But Moncharmin protected her. He resumed his questions:

'What sort of envelope did you put in M Richard's pocket? It was not the one which we gave you, the one which you took to Box 5 before our eyes; and yet that was the one which contained the twenty-thousand francs.'

'I beg your pardon. The envelope which M le directeur gave me was the one which I slipped into M le directeur's pocket,' explained Mame Giry. 'The one which I took to the ghost's box was another envelope, just like it, which the ghost gave me beforehand and which I hid up my sleeve.'

So saying, Mame Giry took from her sleeve an envelope ready prepared and similarly addressed to that containing the twenty-thousand francs. The managers took it from her. They examined it and saw that it was fastened with seals stamped with their own managerial seal. They opened it. It contained twenty Bank of St Farce notes, like those which had so much astounded them the month before.

'How simple!' said Richard.

'How simple!' repeated Moncharmin. And he continued, with

his eyes fixed upon Mame Giry, as though trying to hypnotise her, 'So it was the ghost who gave you this envelope and told you to substitute it for the one which we gave you? And it was the ghost who told you to put the other into M Richard's pocket?'

'Yes, it was the ghost.'

'Then would you mind giving us a specimen of your little talents? Here is the envelope. Act as though we knew nothing.'

'As you please, gentlemen.'

Mame Giry took the envelope with the twenty notes inside it and made for the door. She was on the point of going out, when the two managers rushed at her:

'Oh no! Oh no! We won't be "done" a second time! Once bitten, twice shy!'

'I beg your pardon, gentlemen,' said the old woman, in self-excuse. 'You told me to act as though you knew nothing. . . . Well, if you knew nothing, I should go away with your envelope!'

'And then how would you slip it into my pocket?' argued Richard, whom Moncharmin fixed with his left eye, while keeping his right on Mame Giry: a proceeding likely to strain his sight, but Moncharmin was prepared to go to all lengths to discover the truth.

'I am to slip it into your pocket when you least expect it, sir. You know that I always take a little turn behind the scenes, in the course of the evening, and I often go with my daughter to the ballet-foyer, which I am entitled to do, as her mother; I bring her her shoes, when the ballet is about to begin . . . in fact, I come and go as I please . . . . The subscribers come and go too . . . . So do you, sir. . . . There are lots of people about . . . . I go behind you and slip the envelope into the tail-pocket of your dress-coat. . . . There's no witchcraft about that!'

'No witchcraft!' growled Richard, rolling his eyes like Jupiter Tonans. 'No witchcraft! Why, I've just caught you in a lie, you old witch!'

Mame Giry bristled, with her three teeth sticking out of her mouth:

'And why, may I ask?'

'Because I spent that evening watching Box 5 and the sham envelope which you put there. I was not in the foyer of the ballet for one second. . . .'

'No, sir, I did not give you the envelope that evening, but at the next performance . . . on the evening when the under-secretary of state for fine-arts . . .'

At these words, M Richard suddenly interrupted Mame Giry:

'Yes, that's true, I remember now! The under-secretary went behind the scenes. He asked for me. I went down to the ballet-foyer for a moment. I was on the foyer steps. . . . The under-secretary and his chief clerk were in the foyer itself . . . . I suddenly turned round . . . I had felt you pass behind me, Mme Giry. . . . You seemed to push against me. . . . There was no one else behind me. . . . Oh, I can see you still, I can see you still!'

'Yes, that's it, sir, that's it. I had just finished my little business. That pocket of yours, sir, is very handy!'

And Mame Giry once more suited the action to the word. She passed behind M Richard and, so nimbly that Moncharmin himself was impressed by it, slipped the envelope into one of the tail-pockets of M Richard's dress-coat.

'Of course!' exclaimed Richard, looking a little pale. 'It's very clever of O. G. The problem which he had to solve was this: how to get rid of any dangerous intermediary between the man who gives the twenty-thousand francs and the man who receives it. And by far the best notion he could hit upon was to come and take the money from my pocket without my noticing it, as I myself did not know that it was there. It's wonderful!'

'Oh, wonderful, no doubt!' Moncharmin agreed. 'Only, you forget, Richard, that I provided ten-thousand francs of the twenty and that nobody put anything in *my* pocket!'

CHAPTER XVII

The Safety-Pin Again

MONCHARMIN'S LAST PHRASE so clearly expressed the suspicion in which he now held his partner that it was bound to cause a stormy explanation, at the end of which it was agreed that Richard should yield to all Moncharmin's wishes, with the object of helping him to discover the miscreant who was victimizing them.

This brings us to the interval after the Garden Act, with the strange conduct observed by M Rémy and those curious lapses from the dignity that might be expected of the managers. It was arranged between Richard and Moncharmin, first, that Richard should repeat the exact movements which he made on the night of the disappearance of the first twenty-thousand francs; and, secondly, that Moncharmin should not for an instant lose sight of Richard's coat-tail pocket, into which Mame Giry was to slip the twenty-thousand francs.

M Richard went and placed himself at the identical spot where he had stood when he had bowed to the under-secretary for fine-arts. M Moncharmin took up his position a few steps behind him.

Mame Giry passed, rubbed up against M Richard, got rid of her twenty-thousand francs in the manager's coat-tail pocket and disappeared. . . . Or rather she was conjured away. In accordance with the instructions received from Moncharmin a few minutes earlier, Mercier took the good lady to the acting-manager's office and turned the key on her, thus making it impossible for her to communicate with her ghost.

Meanwhile, M Richard was bending and bowing and scraping and walking backwards, just as if he had that high and mighty minister, the under-secretary for fine-arts, before him. Only, though these marks of politeness would have created no astonishment, if the under-secretary of fine-arts had really been in front of M Richard, they caused an easily-comprehensible amazement to the spectators of this very natural, but quite inexplicable scene, when M Richard had nobody in front of him.

M Richard bowed . . . to nobody; bent his back . . . before nobody; and walked backwards . . . before nobody. . . . And, a few steps behind him, M Moncharmin did exactly the same thing as M Richard was doing, in addition to pushing away M Rémy and begging M de la Borderie, the ambassador, and M Parabise, the manager of the Crédit Central 'not to touch M le directeur.'

Moncharmin, who had his own ideas, did not want Richard to come to him presently, when the twenty-thousand francs were gone, and say:

'Perhaps it was the ambassador . . . or the manager of the Crédit Central . . . or Rémy.'

The more so as, at the time of the first scene, as Richard himself admitted, Richard had met nobody in that part of the theatre after Mame Giry had brushed up against him. . . .

Having begun by walking backwards in order to bow, Richard continued to do so from prudence, until he reached the passage leading to the offices of the management. . . . In this way, he was constantly watched by Moncharmin from behind and himself kept an eye on any one approaching from the front. Once more, this novel method of walking behind the scenes, adopted by the managers of our National Academy of Music, attracted attention; but the managers themselves thought of nothing but their twenty-thousand francs.

On reaching the dark passage, Richard said to Moncharmin, in a low voice:

'I am sure that nobody has touched me. . . . You had now better keep at some distance from me and watch me till I come to the door of the office: it is better not to arouse suspicion and we can see anything that happens.'

But Moncharmin replied:

'No, Richard, no! . . . You walk ahead and I'll walk immediately behind you! I won't leave you by a step!'

'But, in that case,' exclaimed Richard, 'they will never steal our twenty-thousand francs!'

'I should hope not, indeed!' declared Moncharmin.

'Then what we are doing is absurd!'

'We are doing exactly what we did last time. . . . Last time, I joined you as you were leaving the stage and followed close behind you down this passage.'

'That's true!' sighed Richard, shaking his head and passively obeying Moncharmin.

Two minutes later, the joint managers locked themselves into their office. Moncharmin himself put the key in his pocket:

'We remained locked up like this, last time,' he said, 'until you left the Opera to go home.'

'That's so. No one came and disturbed us, I suppose?'

'No one.'

'Then,' said Richard, who was trying to collect his memory, 'then I must certainly have been robbed on my way home from the Opera. . . .'

'No,' said Moncharmin, in a drier tone than ever, 'no, that's impossible . . . . For I dropped you, in my cab . . . . The twenty-thousand francs disappeared at your place: there's not a shadow of a doubt about that.'

'It's incredible!' protested Richard. 'I am sure of my servants . . . and, if one of them had done it, he would have disappeared since.'

Moncharmin shrugged his shoulders, as though to say that he did not wish to enter into details, and Richard began to think that Moncharmin was treating him in a very insupportable fashion:

'Moncharmin, I've had enough of this!'

'Richard, I've had too much of it!'

'Do you dare to suspect me?'

'Yes, of a silly joke.'

'One doesn't joke with twenty-thousand francs.'

'That's what I think,' declared Moncharmin, unfolding a newspaper and ostentatiously studying its contents.

'What are you doing?' asked Richard. 'Are you going to read the paper next?'

'Yes, Richard, until I take you home.'

'Like last time?'

'Yes, like last time!'

Richard snatched the paper from Moncharmin's hands. Moncharmin stood up, more irritated than ever, and found himself faced by an exasperated Richard, who crossing his arms on his chest, said:

'Look here, I'm thinking of this, *I'm thinking of what I might think*, if, like last time, after my spending the evening alone with you, you drove me home, and if, at the moment of parting, I perceived that twenty-thousand francs had disappeared from my coat-pocket . . . like last time.'

'And what might you think?' asked Moncharmin, crimson with rage.

'I might think that, as you hadn't left me by a foot's breadth and as, by your own wish, you were the only one to approach me, like last time, I might think that, if that twenty-thousand francs was no longer in my pocket it stood a very good chance of being in yours!'

Moncharmin leapt up at the suggestion:

'Oh!' he shouted. 'A safety-pin!'

'What do you want a safety-pin for?'

'To fasten you up with! . . . A safety-pin! . . . A safety-pin!'

'You want to fasten me with a safety-pin?'

'Yes, to fasten you to the twenty-thousand francs! . . . Then, whether it's here, or on the drive from here to your place, or *at* your place, you will feel the hand that pulls at your pocket . . . and you will see if it's mine! . . . Ah, so you're suspecting me now, are you? . . . A safety-pin!'

And that was the moment when Moncharmin opened the door on the passage and shouted:

'A safety-pin! . . . Somebody give me a safety-pin!'

And we also know how, at the same moment, Rémy, who had no safety-pin, was received by Moncharmin, while a boy procured the pin so eagerly longed for. And what happened was this: Moncharmin first locked the door again. Then he knelt down behind Richard's back:

'I hope,' he said, 'that the notes are still there?'

'So do I,' said Richard.

'The real ones?' asked Moncharmin, resolved not to be 'had' this time.

'Look for yourself,' said Richard. 'I refuse to touch them.'

Moncharmin took the envelope from Richard's pocket and drew out the banknotes with a trembling hand, for, this time, in order frequently to make sure of the presence of the notes, he had not sealed the envelope nor even fastened it. He felt reassured on finding that they were all there and quite genuine. He put them back in the tail-pocket and pinned them with great care. Then he sat down behind Richard's coat-tails and kept his eyes fixed on them, while Richard, sitting at his writing-table, did not stir.

'A little patience, Richard,' said Moncharmin. 'We have only a few minutes to wait. . . . The clock will soon strike twelve. Last time, we left at the last stroke of twelve.'

'Oh, I shall have all the patience necessary!'

The time passed, slow, heavy, mysterious, stifling. Richard tried to laugh:

'I shall end by believing in the omnipotence of the ghost,' he said. 'Just now, don't you find something uncomfortable, disquieting, alarming in the atmosphere of this room?'

'You're quite right,' said Moncharmin, who was really impressed.

'The ghost!' continued Richard, in a low voice, as though fearing lest he should be overhead by invisible ears. 'The ghost! Suppose, all the same, it were a ghost who puts the magic envelopes on the table . . . who talks in Box 5 . . . who killed Joseph Buquet . . . who unhooked the chandelier . . . and who robs us! For, after all, after all, after all, there is no one here except you and me . . . and, if the notes disappear and neither you nor I have anything to do with it . . . well, we shall have to believe in the ghost . . . in the ghost. . . .'

At that moment, the clock on the mantelpiece gave its warning click and the first stroke of twelve was heard.

The two managers shuddered. The perspiration streamed from their foreheads. The twelfth stroke sounded strangely in their ears.

When the clock stopped, they gave a sigh and rose from their chairs:

'I think we can go now,' said Moncharmin.

'I think so,' Richard agreed.

'Before we go, do you mind if I look in your pocket?'

'But, of course, Moncharmin, you *must!* . . . Well?' he asked, as Moncharmin was feeling at the pocket.

'Well, I can feel the pin.'

'Of course, as you said, we can't be robbed without noticing it.'

But Moncharmin, whose hands were still fumbling, bellowed:

'I can feel the pin, but I can't feel the notes!'

'Come, no joking, Moncharmin! . . . This isn't the time for it.'

'Well, feel for yourself.'

Richard tore off his coat. The two managers turned the pocket inside out. *The pocket was empty.* And the curious thing was that the pin remained, stuck in the same place.

Richard and Moncharmin turned pale. There was no longer any doubt about the witchcraft.

'The ghost' muttered Moncharmin.

But Richard suddenly sprang upon his partner:

'No one but you has touched my pocket! . . . Give me back my twenty-thousand francs! . . . Give me back my twenty-thousand francs! . . .'

'On my soul,' sighed Moncharmin, who was ready to swoon, 'on my soul, I swear I haven't got it! . . .'

Then somebody knocked at the door. Moncharmin opened it automatically, seemed hardly to recognize Mercier, his business-manager, exchanged a few words with him, without knowing what he was saying, and, with an unconscious movement, put the safety-pin, for which he had no further use, into the hands of his bewildered subordinate. . . .

CHAPTER XVIII

The Commissary Of Police

THE FIRST WORDS of the commissary of police, when he entered the managers' office, were to ask after the missing prima donna:

'Is Christine Daaé here?'

'Christine Daaé?' echoed Richard. 'No. Why?'

As for Moncharmin, he had not the strength left to utter a word.

Richard repeated, for the commissary and the compact crowd which had followed him into the office observed an impressive silence:

'Why do you ask if Christine Daaé is here, M le commissaire?'

'Because she must be found,' declared the commissary of police, solemnly.

'How do you mean, she must be found? Has she disappeared?'

'In the middle of the performance!'

'In the middle of the performance? This is extraordinary!'

'Isn't it? And what is quite as extraordinary is that you should first learn it from me!'

'Yes,' agreed Richard, taking his head in his hands and muttering, 'What is this fresh trouble? Oh, it's enough to make a man send in his resignation! . . .'

And he pulled a few hairs out of his moustache without even knowing what he was doing:

'So she . . . so she disappeared in the middle of the performance?' he repeated, as though in a dream.

'Yes, she was carried off in the Prison Act, at the moment when she was invoking the aid of the angels; but I doubt if she was carried off by an angel.'

'And I am sure that she was!'

Everybody looked round. A young man, pale and trembling with excitement, repeated:

'I am sure of it!'

'Sure of what?' asked Mifroid.

'That Christine Daaé was carried off by an angel, M le commissaire, and I can tell you his name.'

'Aha! M le Vicomte de Chagny! So you maintain that Christine Daaé was carried off by an angel: an angel of the Opera, no doubt?'

'Yes, monsieur, by an angel of the Opera; and I will tell you where he lives . . . when we are alone.'

'You are right, monsieur.'

And the commissary of police, inviting Raoul to take a chair, cleared the room of all the rest, excepting the managers.

Then Raoul spoke:

'M le commissaire, the angel is called Erik, he lives in the Opera and he is the Angel of Music!'

'The Angel of Music! Really! That is very curious! . . . The Angel of Music!' And, turning to the managers, M Mifroid asked, 'Have you an Angel of Music on the premises, gentlemen?'

Richard and Moncharmin shook their heads, without even smiling.

'Oh,' said the viscount, 'those gentlemen have heard of the Opera ghost. Well, I am in a position to state that the Opera ghost and the Angel of Music are one and the same person; and his real name is Erik.'

M Mifroid rose and looked at Raoul attentively:

'I beg your pardon, monsieur, but are you trying to make fun of the police? And, if not, what is all this about the Opera ghost?'

'I say that these gentlemen have heard of him.'

'Gentlemen, it appears that you know the Opera ghost?'

Richard rose, with the remaining hairs of his moustache in his hand:

'No, Mr Commissary, no, we do not know him, but we wish we did! For, this very evening, he has robbed us of twenty-thousand francs!'

And Richard turned a terrible look on Moncharmin, which seemed to say:

'Give me back the twenty-thousand francs, or I'll tell the whole story.'

Moncharmin understood what he meant, for, with a distracted gesture, he said:

'Oh, tell everything and have done with it!'

As for Mifroid, he looked at the managers and at Raoul by turns and wondered whether he had strayed into a lunatic asylum. He passed his hand through his hair:

'A ghost,' he said, 'who, on the same evening, carries off an opera-singer and steals twenty-thousand francs is a ghost who must have his hands pretty full! If you don't mind, we will take the questions in order. The singer first, the twenty-thousand francs next. Come, M de Chagny, let us try to talk seriously. You believe that Mlle Christine Daaé has been carried off by an individual called Erik. Do you know this person? Have you seen him?'

'Yes.'

'Where?'

'In a churchyard.'

M Mifroid gave a start, began to scrutinize Raoul again and said:

'Of course! . . . That's where ghosts usually hang out! . . . And what were you doing in that churchyard?'

'Monsieur,' said Raoul, 'I can quite understand how absurd my replies must seem to you. But I beg you to believe that I am in full possession of my faculties. The safety of the person dearest to me in the world is at stake. I should like to convince you in a few words, for time is pressing and every minute is valuable. Unfortunately, if I do not tell you the strangest story that ever was from the very beginning, you will not believe me. I will tell you all I know about the Opera ghost, Mr Commissary. Alas, I do not know much! . . .'

'Never mind, go on, go on!' exclaimed Richard and Moncharmin, suddenly greatly interested.

Unfortunately for their hopes of learning some detail that could put them on the track of their hoaxer, they were soon compelled to accept the fact that M Raoul de Chagny had completely lost his head. All that story about Perros-Guirec, death's-heads and enchanted violins could only have taken birth in the disordered brain of a youth mad with love. It was evident, also, that Mr Commissary Mifroid shared their view; and the magistrate would certainly have cut short the incoherent narrative if the circumstances themselves had not happened to interrupt it.

The door opened and a man entered, curiously dressed in a huge frock-coat and a tall hat, at once shabby and shiny, that came down to his ears. He went up to the commissary and spoke to him in a whisper. He was obviously a detective come to deliver an important communication.

During this colloquy, M Mifroid did not take his eyes off Raoul. At last, addressing him, he said:

'Monsieur, we have talked enough about the ghost. We will now talk a little about yourself if you have no objection: you were to carry off Mlle Christine Daaé to-night?'

'Yes, M le commissaire?'

'After the performance?'

'Yes, M le commissaire.'

'All your arrangements were made?'

'Yes, M le commissaire.'

'The carriage that brought you was to take you both away. There were fresh horses in readiness at every stage. . . .'

'That is true, M le commissaire.'

'And nevertheless your carriage is still outside the Rotunda awaiting your orders, is it not?'

'Yes, M le commissaire.'

'Did you know that there were three other carriages there, in addition to yours?'

'I did not pay the least attention. . . .'

'They were the carriages of Mlle Sorelli, which could not find room in the Cour de l'Administration; of Carlotta; and of your brother, M le Comte de Chagny. . . .'

'Very likely. . . .'

'What is certain is that, though your carriage and Sorelli's and Carlotta's are still there, against the Rotunda pavement, M le Comte de Chagny's carriage is gone.'

'This has nothing to say to . . .'

'I beg your pardon. Was not M le Comte opposed to your marriage with Mlle Daaé?'

'That is a matter that only concerns the family.'

'You have answered my question: he was opposed to it . . . and that was why you were taking Christine Daaé out of your brother's reach . . . . Well, M de Chagny, allow me to inform you that your brother has been smarter than you! . . . It is he who has carried off Christine Daaé!'

'Oh, impossible!' moaned Raoul, pressing his hand to his heart. 'Are you sure?'

'Immediately after the artist's disappearance, which was procured by means which we have still to ascertain, he flung himself into his carriage, which drove straight across Paris at a furious pace.'

'Across Paris?' asked poor Raoul in a hoarse voice. 'What do you mean by across Paris?'

'Across Paris and out of Paris . . . by the Brussels road.'

'Oh,' cried the young man, 'I shall catch them!'

And he rushed out of the office.

'And bring her back to us!' cried the commissary gaily. . . . 'Ah, that's a trick worth two of the Angel of Music's!'

And, turning to his audience, M Mifroid delivered a little lecture on police methods:

'I don't know in the least whether M le Comte de Chagny has really carried off Christine Daaé or not . . . but I want to know; and I believe that, at this moment, no one is more anxious to inform us than his brother. . . . And now he is flying in pursuit of him! He is my chief auxillary! This, gentleman, is the art of the police, which is thought to be so complicated, but which, nevertheless, becomes so simple as soon as you see that it consists in getting your work done by people who have nothing to do with the police.'

But Mr Commissary Mifroid would not have been quite so satisfied with himself if he had known that the rush of his rapid emissary was stopped at the entrance to the very first corridor. A tall figure blocked Raoul's way:

'Where are you going so fast, M de Chagny?' asked a voice.

Raoul impatiently raised his eyes and recognized the astrakhan cap of an hour ago. He stopped:

'It's you!' he cried, in a feverish voice. 'You, who know Erik's secrets and do not wish me to speak of them. Who are you?'

'You know who I am! . . . I am the Persian!'

CHAPTER XIX

The Viscount And The Persian

RAOUL NOW REMEMBERED that his brother had once shown him that mysterious creature, of whom nothing was known except that he was a Persian and that he lived in a little old-fashioned flat in the Rue de Rivoli.

The man with the ebony skin, the eyes of jade and the astrakhan cap bent over Raoul:

'I hope, M de Chagny,' he said, 'that you have not betrayed Erik's secret?'

'And why should I hesitate to betray that monster, sir?' Raoul rejoined, haughtily, trying to shake off the intruder. 'Is he your friend, by any chance?'

'I hope that you said nothing about Erik, sir, because Erik's secret is also Christine Daaé's and to talk about one is to talk about the other!'

'Oh, sir,' said Raoul, becoming more and more impatient, 'you seem to know about many things that interest me; and yet I have no time to listen to you!'

'Once more, M de Chagny, where are you going so fast?'

'Cannot you guess? To Christine Daaé's assistance. . . .'

'Then, sir, stay here . . . for Christine Daaé is here! . . .'

'With Erik?'

'With Erik.'

'How do you know?'

'I was at the performance and no one in the world but Erik could contrive an abduction like that! . . . Oh,' he said, with a deep sigh, 'I recognized the monster's touch! . . .'

'You know him then?'

The Persian did not reply, but heaved a fresh sigh.

'Sir,' said Raoul, 'I do not know what your intentions are . . . but can you do anything to help me? . . . I mean, to help Christine Daaé?'

'I think so, M de Chagny, and that is why I spoke to you.'

'What can you do?'

'Try to take you to her . . . and to him.'

'If you can do me that service, sir, my life is yours! . . . One word more: the commissary of police tells me that Christine Daaé has been carried off by my brother, Count Philippe. . . .'

'Oh, M de Chagny, I don't believe a word of it! . . .'

'It's not possible, is it?'

'I don't know if it is possible or not; but there are ways and ways of carrying people off; and M le Comte Philippe has never, as far as I know, had anything to do with witchcraft.'

'Your arguments are convincing, sir, and I am a fool! . . . Oh, let us be quick! I place myself entirely in your hands! . . . How should I not believe you, when you are the only one to believe me . . . when you are the only one not to smile when Erik's name is mentioned?'

And the young man impetuously seized the Persian's hands. They were ice-cold.

'Silence!' said the Persian, stopping and listening to the distant sounds of the theatre. 'We must not mention that name here. Let us say "he" and "him"; then there will be less danger of attracting his attention. . . .'

'Do you think he is near us?'

'It is quite possible, sir . . . if he is not, at this moment, with his victim, *in the house on the lake.*'

'Ah, so you know that house too?'

'If he is not there, he may be here, in the walls, in the floor, in the ceiling! . . . Come!'

And the Persian, asking Raoul to deaden the sound of his footsteps, led him down passages which Raoul had never seen before, even at the time when Christine used to take him for walks through that labyrinth.

'If only Darius has come!' said the Persian.

'Who is Darius?'

'Darius? My servant.'

They were now in the centre of a regular deserted square, an immense space ill-lit by a small lamp. The Persian stopped Raoul and, in the softest of whispers, asked:

'What did you say to the commissary?'

'I said that Christine Daaé's abductor was the Angel of Music, *alias* the Opera ghost, and that his real name was . . .'

'Hush! . . . And did he believe you?'

'No.'

'He attached no importance to what you said?'

'No.'

'He took you for a bit of a madman?'

'Yes.'

'So much the better!' sighed the Persian.

And they continued their road. After going up and down several staircases which were new to Raoul, the two men found themselves in front of a door which the Persian opened with a master-key. The Persian and Raoul were both, of course, in dress-clothes; but, whereas Raoul had a tall hat, the Persian wore the astrakhan cap which I have already mentioned. It was an infringement of the rule which insists upon the tall hat behind the scenes; but in France foreigners are allowed every licence: the Englishman his travelling-cap, the Persian his cap of astrakhan.

'Sir,' said the Persian, 'your tall hat will be in your way: you would do well to leave it in the dressing-room. . . .'

'Which dressing-room?' asked Raoul.

'Christine Daaé's.'

And the Persian, letting Raoul through the door which he had just opened, showed him the actress's room opposite.

They were at the end of the passage the whole length of which Raoul had been accustomed to traverse before knocking at Christine's door.

'How well you know the Opera, sir!'

'Not so well as "he" does!' said the Persian, modestly.

And he pushed the young man into Christine's dressing-room, which was as Raoul had left it a few minutes earlier.

Closing the door, the Persian went to a very thin partition that separated the dressing-room from a big lumber-room next to it. He listened and then coughed loudly.

There was a sound of some one stirring in the lumber-room; and, a few seconds later, a finger tapped at the door.

'Come in,' said the Persian.

A man entered, also wearing an astrakhan cap and dressed in a long overcoat or frock. He bowed, took a richly-carved case from under his coat, put it on the dressing-table, bowed once again and went to the door.

'Did no one see you come in, Darius?'

'No, master.'

'Let no one see you go out.'

The servant glanced down the passage and swiftly disappeared.

The Persian opened the case. It contained a pair of long pistols.

'When Christine Daaé was carried off, sir, I sent word to my servant to bring me these pistols. I have had them a long time and they can be relied upon.'

'Do you mean to fight a duel?' asked the young man.

'It will certainly be a duel which we shall have to fight,' said the other, examining the priming of his pistols. 'And what a duel!' Handing one of the pistols to Raoul, he added, 'In this duel we shall be two to one; but you must be prepared for everything, for we shall be fighting the most terrible adversary that you can imagine. But you love Christine Daaé, do you not?'

'I worship the ground she walks on! But you, sir, who do not love her, tell me why I find you ready to risk your life for her! . . . You must certainly hate Erik!'

'No, sir,' said the Persian, sadly, 'I do not hate him. If I hated him, he would long ago have ceased to do harm.'

'Has he done you harm?'

'I have forgiven him the harm which he has done me.'

'I do not understand you. You treat him as a monster, you speak of his crimes, he has done you harm and I find in you the same inexplicable pity that drove me to despair when I saw it in Christine! . . .'

The Persian did not reply. He fetched a stool and set it against the wall facing the great mirror that filled the whole of the partition opposite. Then he climbed on the stool and, with his nose to the wall-paper, seemed to be looking for something:

'Ah,' he said, after a long search, 'I have it!'

And, raising his finger above his head, he pressed against a corner in the pattern of the paper. Then he turned round and jumped off the stool:

'In half a minute,' he said, 'we shall be *on his road!*'

And, crossing the whole length of the dressing-room, he felt the great mirror:

'No, it is not yielding yet,' he muttered.

'Oh, are you going out by the mirror?' asked Raoul. 'Like Christine Daaé?'

'So you knew that Christine Daaé went out by the mirror?'

'She did so before my eyes, sir! . . . I was hidden behind the curtain of the inner room and I saw her vanish not by the glass, but in the glass!'

'And what did you do?'

'I thought it was an aberration of my senses, a mad dream. . . .'

'Or some new fancy of the ghost's!' chuckled the Persian. 'Ah, M de Chagny,' he continued, still with his hand on the mirror, 'would that we had to do with a ghost! We could then leave our pistols in their case. . . . Put down your hat, please . . . there . . . and cover your shirt-front as well as you can with your coat . . . as I am doing now. . . . Bring the lapels forward . . . turn up the collar. . . . We must make ourselves as invisible as possible. . . .'

Bearing against the mirror, after a short silence, he said:

'It takes some time to release the counter-balance, when you press on the spring from the inside of the room. It is different when you are behind the wall and can act directly on the counter-balance. Then the mirror turns at once and is moved with incredible rapidity. . . .'

'What counter-balance?' asked Raoul.

'Why, the counter-balance that lifts the whole of this wall on to its pivot. You surely don't expect it to move by itself, by enchantment! . . . If you watch, you will see the mirror rise an inch or two and then shift an inch or two from left to right. It will then be on a pivot and will swing round.'

'It's not turning!' said Raoul, impatiently.

'Oh, wait! You have time enough to be impatient, sir! The mechanism has obviously become rusty, or else the spring isn't working. . . . Unless it is something else,' added the Persian, anxiously.

'What?'

'He may simply have cut the cord of the counter-balance and blocked the whole apparatus. . . .'

'Why should he? He does not know that we are coming this way!'

'I daresay he suspects it, for he knows that I understand the system.'

'It's not turning! . . . And Christine, sir, Christine?'

The Persian said, coldly;

'We shall do all that it is humanly possible to do! . . . But he may stop us at the first step! . . . He commands the walls, the doors and the trap-doors. In my country, he was known by a name which means the "trap-door lover."'

'But why do these walls obey him alone? He did not build them!'

'Yes, sir, that is just what he did do!'

Raoul looked at him in amazement; but the Persian made a sign to him to be silent and pointed to the glass. . . . There was a sort of shivering reflection. Their image was troubled as in a rippling sheet of water and then all became stationary again.

'You see, sir, that it is not turning! Let us take another road!'

'To-night, there is no other!' declared the Persian, in a singularly mournful voice. 'And now, look out! And be ready to fire!'

He himself raised his pistol opposite the glass. Raoul imitated his movement. With his free arm, the Persian drew the young man to his chest and, suddenly, the mirror turned, in a blinding daze of cross-lights: it turned like one of those revolving doors which have lately been fixed to the entrances of most restaurants, it turned, carrying Raoul and the Persian with it and suddenly hurling them from the full light into the deepest darkness.

CHAPTER XX

In The Cellars Of The Opera

'YOUR HAND HIGH, READY TO FIRE!' repeated Raoul's companion, quickly.

The wall, behind them, having completed the circle which it described upon itself, closed again; and the two men stood motionless for a moment, holding their breaths.

At last, the Persian decided to make a movement; and Raoul heard him slip on to his knees and feel for something in the dark with his groping hands. Suddenly, the dimness was made visible by a small dark lantern and Raoul instinctively stepped backwards, as though to escape the scrutiny of a secret enemy. But he soon perceived that the light belonged to the Persian, whose movements he was closely observing. The little red disc was turned in every direction and Raoul saw that the floor, the walls and the ceiling were all formed of planking. It must have been the ordinary road taken by Erik to reach Christine's dressing-room and impose upon her innocence. And Raoul, remembering the Persian's remark, thought that it had been mysteriously constructed by the ghost himself. Later, he learnt that Erik had found, all ready prepared for him, a secret passage, long known to himself alone. It had been contrived at the time of the Paris Commune, to allow the gaolers to convey their prisoners straight to the dungeons constructed for them in the cellars; for the Federates had occupied the Opera-house immediately after the 18th of March and had made a starting-place right at the top for their Mongolfier balloons, which carried their incendiary proclamations to the departments, and a state prison right at the bottom.

The Persian went on his knees again and put his lantern on the ground. He seemed to be working at the floor. Suddenly he turned off his light. Then Raoul heard a faint click and saw a very pale luminous square in the floor of the passage. It was as though a window had opened on the Opera cellars, which were still lit. Raoul no longer saw the Persian, but he felt him by his side and heard his breathing.

'Follow me and do all that I do.'

Raoul turned to the luminous aperture. Then he saw the Persian, who was still on his knees, hang by his hands from the rim of the opening, with his pistol between his teeth, and slide into the cellar below.

Curiously enough, the viscount had absolute confidence in the Persian, though he knew nothing about him. His emotion when speaking of the 'monster' struck Raoul as sincere; and, if the Persian had cherished any sinister designs against him, he would not have armed him with his own hands. Besides, Raoul must reach Christine at all costs. He therefore went on his knees also and hung from the trap with both hands.

'Let go!' said a voice.

And he dropped into the arms of the Persian, who told him to lie down flat, closed the trap-door above him and crouched down beside him. Raoul tried to ask a question, but the Persian's hand was on his mouth and he heard a voice which he recognized as that of the commissary of police.

Raoul and the Persian were completely hidden behind a wooden partition. Near them, a small staircase led to a little room in which the commissary appeared to be walking up and down, asking questions. The faint light was just enough to enable Raoul to distinguish the shape of things around him. And he could not restrain a dull cry: there were three corpses there.

The first lay on the narrow landing of the little staircase; the two others had rolled to the bottom of the staircase. Raoul could have touched one of the two poor wretches by passing his fingers through the partition.

'Silence!' whispered the Persian.

He too had seen the bodies and he gave one word in explanation: '*He!*'

The commissary's voice was now heard more distinctly. He was asking for information about the system of lighting, which the stage-manager supplied. The commissary therefore must be in the 'organ' or its immediate neighbourhood.

Contrary to what one might think, especially in connection with an opera-house, the 'organ' is not a musical instrument. At that time, electricity was employed only for a very few scenic effects and for the bells. The immense building and the stage itself were still lit by gas. Hydrogen gas was used to regulate and modify the lighting of a scene; and this was done by means of a special apparatus which, because of the multiplicity of its pipes, was known as the 'organ.' A box next to the prompter's box was reserved for the gas-man, who from there gave his orders to his assistants and saw that they were executed. Mauclair stayed in this box during all the performances.

But now Mauclair was not in his box and his assistants not in their places.

'Mauclair! Mauclair!'

The stage-manager's voice echoed through the cellars. But Mauclair did not reply.

I have said that a door opened on a little staircase that led to the second cellar. The commissary pushed it, but it resisted.

'I say,' he said to the stage-manager, 'I can't open this door: is it always so difficult?'

The stage-manager forced it open with his shoulder. He saw that, in doing so, he was pushing a human body and he could not restrain an exclamation, for he recognized the body at once:

'Mauclair! Poor devil! He is dead!'

But Mr Commissary Mifroid, whom nothing surprised, was stooping over that big body:

'No,' he said, 'he is dead-drunk, which is not quite the same thing.'

'It's the first time, if so,' said the stage-manager.

'Then some one has given him a narcotic. That is quite possible.'

Mifroid went down a few steps and said:

'Look!'

By the light of a little red lantern, at the foot of the stairs, they saw two other bodies. The stage-manager recognized Mauclair's assistants. Mifroid went down and listened to their breathing:

'They are sound asleep,' he said. 'Very curious business! Some person unknown must have interfered with the gas-man and his staff . . . and that person unknown was obviously working on behalf of the kidnapper. . . . But what a funny idea, to kidnap a performer on the stage! . . . Send for the doctor of the theatre, please.' And Mifroid repeated, 'Curious, very curious business!'

Then he turned to the little room, addressing people whom Raoul and the Persian were unable to see from where they lay:

'What do you say to all this, gentlemen? You are the only ones who have not given your views. And yet you must have an opinion of some sort. . .'

Thereupon, Raoul and the Persian saw the startled faces of the joint managers appear above the landing – only their faces were visible above the landing – and heard Moncharmin's excited voice:

'There are things happening here, M le commissaire, which we are unable to explain.'

And the two faces disappeared.

'Thank you for the information, gentlemen,' jeered Mifroid.

But the stage-manager, holding his chin in the hollow of his right hand, which is the attitude of profound thought, said:

'It is not the first time that Mauclair has fallen asleep in the theatre. I remember finding him, one evening, snoring in his little recess, with his snuff-box beside him.'

'Is that long ago?' asked M Mifroid, carefully wiping his eyeglasses.

'No, not so very long ago. . . . Wait a bit! . . . It was the night . . . of course, yes . . . it was the night when Carlotta – you know, M le commissaire – gave her famous "co-ack"!'

'Really? The night when Carlotta gave her famous "co-ack"?'

And M Mifroid, replacing his gleaming glasses on his nose, fixed the stage-manager with a contemplative stare:

'So Mauclair takes snuff, does he?' he asked, carelessly.

'Yes, M le commissaire. . . . Look, there is his snuff-box, on that little shelf. . . Oh, he's a great snuff-taker!'

'So am I,' said Mifroid, and put the snuff-box in his pocket.

The viscount and the Persian, themselves unseen, watched the removal of the three bodies by a number of scene-shifters, who were followed by the commissary and all the people with him. Their steps were heard for a few minutes on the stage above.

When they were alone, the Persian made a sign to Raoul to stand up. Raoul did so; but, as he did not lift his hand in front of his eyes, ready to fire, the Persian told him to resume that attitude and to continue it, whatever happened.

'But it tires the hand unnecessarily,' whispered Raoul. 'If I do fire, I sha'n't be sure of my aim.'

'Then shift your pistol to the other hand,' said the Persian.

'I can't shoot with my left hand.'

Thereupon, the Persian made this queer reply, which was certainly not calculated to throw light into the young man's dazed brain:

'It's not a question of shooting with the right hand or the left; it's a question of holding one of your hands as though you were going to pull the trigger of a pistol, with your arm bent. As for the pistol itself, when all is said, you can put that in your pocket!' And he added, 'Let this be clearly understood, or I will answer for nothing. It is a matter of life and death. And now, silence! And follow me!'

The cellars of the Opera are enormous and they are five in number. Raoul followed the Persian and wondered what he would have done without his companion in that extraordinary labyrinth. They went down to the third cellar; and their progress was still lit by some distant lamp. . . .

The lower they went, the more precautions the Persian seemed to take. He kept on turning to Raoul to see if he was holding his arm properly, showing him how he himself carried his hand as if always read to fire, though the pistol was in his pocket.

Suddenly, a loud voice made them stop. Some one above them shouted:

'All the door-shutters on the stage! The commissary of police wants them!'

Steps were heard and shadows glided through the darkness. The Persian drew Raoul behind a prop. They saw passing before and above them old men bent by age and the past burden of operatic scenery. Some could hardly drag themselves along; others, from habit, with stooping bodies and outstretched hands, looked for doors to shut.

They were the door-shutters, the old, worn-out scene-shifters on whom a charitable management had taken pity, giving them the job of shutting doors above and below the stage. They went about incessantly, from top to bottom of the building, shutting the doors; and they were also called 'the draught-expellers,' at least at that time, for I have but little doubt that by now they are all dead. Draughts are very bad for the voice, wherever they may come from.[1]

---

[1] M Pedro Gailhard has told me that he himself created a few additional posts as door-shutters for old stage-carpenters whom he was unwilling to dismiss from the service of the Opera.

The Persian and Raoul welcomed this incident, which relieved them of inconvenient witnesses, for some of those door-shutters, having nothing else to do or nowhere to lay their heads, stayed at the Opera, from idleness or necessity, and spent the night there. The two men might have stumbled over them, waking them up and provoking a demand for explanations. For the moment, M Mifroid's enquiry saved them from any such unpleasant encounters.

But they were not left to enjoy their solitude for long. Other shades now came down by the same road by which the door-shutters had gone up. Each of these shades carried a little lantern and moved it about, above, below and all around, as though looking for something or somebody.

'Bother!' muttered the Persian. 'I don't know what they are looking for, but they might easily find us. . . . Let us get away, quick! . . . Your hand up, sir, ready to fire! . . . Bend your arm . . . more . . . that's it! . . . Hand at the level of your eye, as though you were fighting a duel and waiting for the word to fire! . . . Oh, leave your pistol in your pocket! . . . Quick, come along, downstairs!' He dragged Raoul down to the fourth cellar. 'Level of your eye! Question of life and death! . . . Here, this way, these stairs!' They reached the fifth cellar. 'Oh, what a duel, sir, what a duel!'

Once in the fifth cellar, the Persian drew breath. He seemed to enjoy a greater sense of security than he had displayed when they stopped in the third cellar; but he never altered the position of his hand. And Raoul, remembering the Persian's observation – 'I know these pistols can be relied upon' – was more and more astonished, wondering why any one should be so gratified at being able to rely upon a pistol which he did not intend to use!

But the Persian left him no time for reflection. Telling Raoul to stay where he was, he ran up a few steps of the staircase which they had just left and then returned:

'How stupid of us!' he whispered. 'We shall soon have seen the end of those men with their lanterns. . . . It is the firemen going their rounds.'[1]

The two men waited five minutes longer. Then the Persian took Raoul up the stairs again; but suddenly he stopped him with a gesture. Something moved in the darkness before them.

[1] In these days, it was still part of the fireman's duty to watch over the safety of the Opera-house, apart from the performances; but this service has since been suppressed. I asked M Pedro Gailhard the reason; and he replied:

'It was because the management was afraid that, in their utter inexperience of the cellars of the Opera, the firemen *might set fire to the building*.'

'Flat on your stomach!' whispered the Persian.

The two men lay flat on the floor.

They were only just in time. . . . A shade, this time carrying no light, just a shade in the shade, passed. It passed close to them, near enough to touch them.

They felt the warmth of its cloak upon them. For they could distinguish the shade sufficiently to see that it wore a cloak which shrouded it from head to foot. On its head, it had a soft felt hat.

It moved away, dragging its feet along the walls and sometimes giving a kick into a corner.

'Whew!' said the Persian. 'We've had a narrow escape: that shade knows me and has twice taken me to the managers' office.'

'Is it some one belonging to the theatre police?' asked Raoul.

'It's some one worse than that!' replied the Persian, without vouchsafing any further explanation.[1]

'It's not . . . *he?*'

'*He?* . . . If he does not come behind us, we shall always see his yellow eyes! . . . That is more or less our safeguard tonight . . . . But he may come stealing up from behind; and we are dead men if we do not keep our hands as though about to fire, at the level of our eyes, before us!'

The Persian had hardly finished speaking, when a fantastic face came in sight . . . a whole fiery face, not only two yellow eyes!

Yes, a head of fire came towards them, at a man's height, but with no body attached to it. The face shed fire, looked in the darkness like a flame shaped as a man's face.

'Oh!' said the Persian, between his teeth. 'I have never seen this before! . . . Pampin was not mad then, after all: he did see it! . . . What can that flame be? It is not *he*, but he may have sent it! . . . Take care! . . . Take care! . . . Your hand at the level of your eyes, in heaven's name, at the level of your eyes! . . . I know most of his

[1] Like the Persian, I can give no further explanation touching the apparition of this shade. Whereas in this historic narrative, everything else will be normally explained, however abnormal the course of events may seem, I cannot give the reader expressly to understand what the Persian meant by the words, 'It is some one worse than that!' The reader must try to guess for himself, for I promised M Pedro Gailhard, the ex-manager of the Opera, to keep his secret regarding the extremely interesting and useful personality of the wandering, cloaked shade which, while condemning itself to live in the cellars of the Opera, rendered such immense services to those who, on gala evenings, for instance, ventured to stray away from the stage. I am speaking of a service of state; and, upon my word of honour, I can say no more.

tricks . . . but not this one. . . . Come, let us run . . . it is safer. . . .
Hand at the level of your eyes!'

And they fled down the long passage that opened before them.

After a few seconds, that seemed to them like long minutes,
they stopped:

'He doesn't often come this way,' said the Persian. 'This side
has nothing to do with him. This side does not lead to the lake nor
to the house on the lake. . . . But perhaps he knows that we are at
his heels . . . although I promised him to leave him alone and
never to meddle in his affairs again!'

So saying, he turned his head and Raoul also turned his head;
and they again saw the head of fire behind their two heads. It had
followed them. And it must have run also and perhaps faster than
they, for it seemed to be nearer to them.

At the same time, they began to perceive a certain noise of which
they could not guess the nature. They simply noticed that the
sound seemed to move and to approach with the fiery face. It was a
noise as though thousands of nails were being scraped against a
blackboard, the perfectly unendurable noise that is sometimes
made by a little stone inside the chalk grating on the blackboard.

They continued to retreat, but the fiery face came on, came on,
gaining upon them. They could see its features clearly now. The
eyes were round and staring, the nose a little crooked and the
mouth large, with a hanging lower lip, very like the eyes, nose and
lip of the moon, when the moon is quite red, bright red.

How did that red moon manage to glide through the darkness,
at a man's height, with nothing to support it, at least apparently?
And how did it go so fast, so straight before it, with such staring,
staring eyes? And what was that scratching, scraping, grating
sound which it brought with it?

The Persian and Raoul could retreat no farther and flattened
themselves against the wall, not knowing what was going to
happen because of that incomprehensible head of fire and especially now, because of the more intense, swarming, living, 'numer-
ous' sound, for the sound was certainly made up of hundreds of
tiny sounds that moved in the darkness, under the fiery face.

And the fiery face came on . . . with its noise . . . came level with
them! . . .

And the two companions, flat against the wall, felt their hair
stand on end with horror, for they now knew what the thousand
noises meant. They came in a troop, hustled along in the shadow
by innumerable little scurrying waves, swifter than the waves that

rush over the sands at high tide, little night-waves foaming under the moon, under the fiery head that was like a moon. And the little waves passed between their legs, climbed up their legs, irresistibly, and Raoul and the Persian could no longer restrain their cries of horror, dismay and pain. Nor could they continue to hold their hands at the level of their eyes: their hands went down to their legs to push back the waves, which were full of little legs and nails and claws and teeth.

Yes, Raoul and the Persian were ready to faint, like Pampin the fireman. But the head of fire turned round, in answer to their cries, and spoke to them:

'Don't move! Don't move! . . . Whatever you do, don't come after me! . . . I am the rat-catcher! . . . Let me pass, with my rats!.

And the head of fire disappeared, vanished in the darkness, while the passage in front of it lit up, as the result of the change which the rat-catcher had made in his dark lantern. Before, so as not to scare the rats in front of him, he had turned his dark lantern on himself, lighting up his own head; now, to hasten their flight, he lit the dark space in front of him. . . . And he sprang along, dragging with him the waves of scratching rats, all the thousand sounds. . . .

Raoul and the Persian breathed again, though still trembling:

'I ought to have remembered that Erik talked to me about the rat-catcher,' said the Persian. 'But he never told me that the man looked like that . . . and it's funny that I should never have met him before. . . . Of course, Erik never comes to this part!'

'Are we very far from the lake, sir?' asked Raoul. 'When shall we get there? . . . Take me to the lake, oh, take me to the lake! . . . When we are at the lake, we will call out! . . . Christine will hear us! . . . And *he* will hear us too! . . . And, as you know him, we shall talk to him!'

'You baby!' said the Persian. 'We shall never enter the house on the lake by the lake! . . . I myself have never landed on the other bank . . . the bank on which the house stands. . . . You have to cross the lake first . . . and it is well guarded! . . . I fear that more than one of those men – old scene-shifters, old door-shutters – who were never seen again were simply tempted to cross the lake. . . . It is terrible. . . . I myself would have been very nearly killed there . . . if the monster had not recognized me in time! . . . One piece of advice, sir: never go near the lake. . . . And, above all, shut your ears if you hear the voice singing under the water, the siren's voice!'

'But then what are we here for?' asked Raoul, in a transport of fever, impatience and rage. 'If you can do nothing for Christine, at least let me die for her!'

The Persian tried to calm the young man:

'We have only one means of saving Christine Daaé, believe me, which is to enter the house unperceived by the monster.'

'And is there any hope of that, sir?'

'Ah, if I had not that hope, I would not have come to fetch you!'

'And how can one enter the house on the lake without crossing the lake?'

'From the third cellar, from which we were so unluckily driven away. We will go back there now. . . . I will tell you,' said the Persian, with a sudden change in his voice, 'I will tell you the exact place, sir: it is between a set piece and a discarded scene from the *Roi de Lahore*, exactly at the spot where Joseph Buquet died. . . . Come, sir, take courage . . . and follow me! . . . And hold your hand at the level of your eyes! . . . But where are we?'

The Persian lit his lamp again and flung its rays down two enormous corridors that crossed each other at right angles.

'We must be,' he said, 'in the part used more particularly for the water-works. . . . I see no fire coming from the furnaces.'

He went in front of Raoul, seeking his road, stopping abruptly when he was afraid of meeting some waterman. Then they had to protect themselves against the glow of a sort of underground forge which the men were extinguishing and at which Raoul recognized the demons whom Christine had seen on the day of her first captivity.

In this way, they gradually arrived beneath the huge cellars below the stage. They must at this time have been at the very bottom of the 'tub' and at an extremely great depth, when we remember that the earth was dug out at fifty feet below the water that lay under the whole of that part of Paris.[1]

The Persian touched a partition-wall and said:

'If I am not mistaken, this is a wall that might easily belong to the house on the lake.'

He was striking a partition-wall of the 'tub' and perhaps it would be as well for the reader to know how the bottom and the partition-walls of the tub were built. In order to prevent the water

[1] All the water had to be exhausted, in the building of the Opera. To give an idea of the amount of water that was pumped up, I can tell the reader that it represented the area of the courtyard of the Louvre and a height half as deep again as the towers of Notre-Dame. And nevertheless the engineers were obliged to leave a lake.

surrounding the building-operations from remaining in immediate contact with the walls supporting the whole of the theatrical machinery, the architect was obliged to build a double case in every direction. The work of constructing this double case took a whole year. It was the wall of the first inner case that the Persian struck when speaking to Raoul of the house on the lake. To any one understanding the architecture of the edifice, the Persian's action would seem to indicate that Erik's mysterious house was built in the double case formed of a thick wall constructed as an embankment or dam, followed by a brick wall, a tremendous layer of cement and another wall several yards in thickness.

At the Persian's words, Raoul flung himself against the wall and listened eagerly. . . . But he heard nothing . . . nothing except distant steps sounding on the floor of the upper portions of the theatre.

The Persian darkened his lantern again:

'Look out!' he said. 'Keep your hand up! And silence! For we shall try another way of getting in.'

And he led him to the little staircase by which they had ascended lately.

They went up, stopping at each step, peering into the darkness and the silence, till they came to the third cellar. Here the Persian motioned to Raoul to go on his knees; and, in this way, crawling on two knees and one hand – for the other hand was still held in the same position – they reached the end wall.

Against this wall stood a large discarded scene from the *Roi de Lahore*. Close to this scene was a set piece. Between the scene and the set piece there was just room for a body . . . for a body which was found hanging there one day . . . the body of Joseph Buquet.

The Persian, still kneeling, stopped and listened. For a moment he seemed to hesitate and looked at Raoul; then he turned his eyes up, towards the second cellar, which sent down the faint glimmer of a lantern through a cranny between two boards. This glimmer seemed to trouble the Persian.

At last, he tossed his head and made up his mind to act. He slipped between the set piece and the scene from the *Roi de Lahore*, with Raoul close upon his heels. With his free hand, the Persian felt the wall. Raoul saw him bear heavily upon the wall, just as he had pressed against the wall in Christine's dressing-room. Then a stone gave way, leaving a hole in the wall.

This time, the Persian took his pistol from his pocket and made a sign to Raoul to do as he did. He cocked the pistol.

And, resolutely, still on his knees, he wriggled through the hole in the wall. Raoul, who would have liked to pass first, had to be content to follow him.

The hole was very narrow. The Persian stopped almost at once. Raoul heard him feeling the stone around him. Then the Persian took out his dark lantern again, stepped forward, examined something beneath him and immediately extinguished the lantern. Raoul heard him say, in a whisper:

'We shall have to drop a few yards, without making a noise; take off your boots.'

The Persian handed his own shoes to Raoul:

'Put them outside the wall,' he said. 'We shall find them there when we leave.'[1]

He crawled a little further on his knees, then turned right round and, facing Raoul, said:

'I am going to hang by my hands from the edge of the stone and let myself drop *into his house*. You must do exactly the same. Do not be afraid. I will catch you in my arms.'

Raoul soon heard the dull sound of the Persian's fall and then dropped in his turn.

He felt himself clasped in the Persian's arms.

'Hush!' said the Persian.

And they stood motionless, listening. . . .

The darkness was thick around them, the silence heavy and terrible . . .

Then the Persian began to make play with the dark lantern again, turning the rays over their heads, looking for the hole through which they had come and failing to find it:

'Oh!' he said. 'The stone has closed of itself!'

And the light of the lantern swept down the wall and over the floor.

The Persian stooped and picked up something, a sort of cord, which he examined for a second and flung away with horror:

'The Punjab lasso!' he muttered.

'What is it?' asked Raoul.

The Persian shivered:

'It might very well be the rope by which the man was hanged, the rope which they looked for so long! . . .'

[1] These two pairs of boots, which were placed, according to the Persian's papers, just between the set piece and the scene from the *Roi de Lahore*, on the spot where Joseph Buquet was found hanging, were never discovered. They must have been taken by some stage-carpenter or 'door-shutter.'

And, suddenly seized with a fresh anxiety, he moved the little red disc of his lantern over the walls. In this way, he lit up a curious thing: the trunk of a tree, which seemed still quite alive, with its leaves; and the branches of that tree ran right up the walls and disappeared in the ceiling.

Because of the smallness of the luminous disc, it was difficult at first to make out the appearance of things: they saw a corner of a branch . . . and a leaf . . . and another leaf . . . and, next to it nothing at all, nothing but the ray of light that seemed to reflect itself. . . . Raoul passed his hand over that nothing, over that reflection:

'Hullo!' he said. 'The wall is a looking-glass!'

'Yes, a looking-glass!' said the Persian, in a tone of deep feeling And, passing the hand that held the pistol over his moist forehead, he added, 'We have dropped into the torture-chamber!'

What the Persian knew of this torture-chamber and what there befell him and his companion shall be told in his own words, as set down in a manuscript which he left behind him and which I copy as I found it.

CHAPTER XXI

Vicissitudes Of A Persian

The Persian's Narrative

IT WAS THE FIRST TIME that I had entered the house on the lake. I had often begged the 'trap-door lover,' as we used to call Erik in my country, to open its mysterious doors to me. He always refused. I made many attempts, but in vain, to obtain admittance. Watch him as I might, after I first learnt that he had taken up his permanent abode at the Opera, the darkness was always too thick to enable me to see how he worked the door in the wall on the lake. One day, when I thought myself alone, I stepped into the boat and rowed towards that part of the wall through which I had seen Erik disappear. It was then that I came into contact with the siren who guarded the approach and whose charm was very nearly fatal to me.

I had no sooner put off from the bank than the silence amid which I floated on the water was disturbed by a sort of whispered singing that hovered all around me. It was half breath, half music; it rose softly from the waters of the lake; and I was surrounded by it through I knew not what artifice. It followed me, moved with me and was so soft that it did not alarm me. On the contrary, in my longing to approach the source of that sweet and enticing harmony, I leant out of my little boat over the water, for there was no doubt in my mind but that the singing came from the water itself. By this time, I was alone in the boat in the middle of the lake; the voice – for it was now distinctly a voice – was beside me, on the water. I leant over, leant still further. The lake was perfectly calm and a moonbeam that passed through the air-hole on the Rue Scribe showed me absolutely nothing on the surface, which was smooth and black as ink. I shook my head to get rid of a possible humming in the ears; but I soon had to accept the fact that no humming in the ears could equal in harmony the singing whisper that followed and now attracted me.

Had I been inclined to superstition, I should certainly have thought that I had to do with some siren whose business it was to confound the traveller rash enough to venture on the waters of the house on the lake. Fortunately, I come from a country where we are too fond of fantastic things not to know them through and through; and I had no doubt but that I was face to face with some new invention of Erik's. But this invention was so perfect that, as I leant out of the boat, I was impelled less by a desire to discover its trick than to enjoy its charm; and I leant out, leant out . . . until I almost overturned the boat.

Suddenly, two monstrous arms issued from the bosom of the waters and seized me by the neck, dragging me down to the depths with irresistible force. I should certainly have been lost, if I had not had time to give a cry by which Erik knew me. For it was he; and, instead of drowning me, as was certainly his first intention, he swam with me and laid me gently on the bank:

'How imprudent you are!' he said, as he stood before me, dripping with water. 'Why try to enter my house? I did not invite you. I don't want you there, nor anybody! Did you save my life only to make it unbearable to me? However great the service rendered, Erik will perhaps end by forgetting it; and you know that nothing can restrain Erik, not even Erik himself.'

He spoke, but I had now no other wish than to know what I already called the trick of the siren. He satisfied my curiosity, for Erik, who is a real monster – I have seen him at work in Persia, alas! – is also, in certain respects, a regular child, vain and self-conceited and there is nothing he loves so much as, after astonishing people, to prove the really miraculous ingenuity of his mind.

He laughed and showed me a long reed:

'It's the silliest trick you ever saw,' he said, 'but it's very useful for breathing and singing in the water. I learnt it from the Tonkin pirates, who are able to lie hidden for hours at a time in the bed of the rivers.'[1]

I spoke to him severely:

'It's a trick that nearly killed me!' I said. 'And it may have been fatal to others! . . . You know what you promised me, Erik? No more murders!'

'Have I really committed murders?' he asked, putting on his most amiable air.

'Wretched man!' I cried. 'Have you forgotten the rosy hours of Mazenderan?'

'Yes,' he replied, in a sadder tone, 'I prefer to forget them. I used to make the little sultana laugh, though!'

'All that belongs to the past,' I declared; 'but there is the present. . . . And you are responsible to me for the present, because, if I had wished, there would have been none at all for you. . . . Remember that, Erik: I saved your life!'

And I took advantage of the turn in the conversation to speak to him of something that had long been on my mind:

'Erik,' I asked, 'Erik, swear that . . .'

'Swear what?' he retorted. 'You know I never keep my oaths. Oaths are made to catch fools with.'

'Tell me . . . You can tell *me*, at any rate . . .'

'Well? . . .'

'Well, the chandelier . . . the chandelier, Erik? . . .'

'What about the chandelier?'

'You know what I mean.'

'Oh,' he sniggered, 'I don't mind telling you about the chandelier! . . . *It wasn't I!* . . . The chandelier was very old and worn. . . .'

When Erik laughed, he was more terrible than ever. He jumped into the boat, chuckling so horribly that I could not help trembling:

'Very old and worn, my dear daroga![2] Very old and worn, the

---

[1] An official report from Tonkin, received in Paris at the end of July, 1909, relates how the famous pirate chief, the De Tham, was tracked, with his men, by our soldiers; and how all of them succeeded in escaping, thanks to this trick of the reeds.

[2] *Daroga* is Persian for chief of police. Editor's Note.

chandelier! . . . It fell of itself! . . . It came down with a smash! . . . And now, daroga, take my advice and go and dry yourself, or you'll catch a cold in the head! . . . And never get into my boat again. . . . And, whatever you do, don't try to enter my house: I'm not always at home . . . daroga! And I should be sorry to have to dedicate my Requiem Mass to you!'

So saying, swaying to and fro, like a monkey, and still chuckling, he pushed off and soon disappeared in the darkness of the lake.

From that day, I gave up all thought of penetrating into his house by way of the lake. That entrance was obviously too well-guarded, especially since he had learnt that I knew about it. But I felt that there must be another entrance, for I had often seen Erik disappear in the third cellar, while I was watching him, though I could not imagine how.

Ever since I discovered Erik installed in the Opera, I had lived in a perpetual terror of his horrible fancies, not in so far as I was concerned, but I dreaded everything for others.[1] And, whenever some accident, some fatal event happened, I always thought to myself, 'I should not be surprised if that were Erik,' even as others used to say, 'It's the ghost!' How often have I not heard people utter that phrase with a smile! Poor devils! if they had known that the ghost existed in the flesh, I swear they would not have laughed! . . .

Although Erik announced to me very solemnly that he had altered and that he had become the most virtuous of men *since he was loved for himself* – a sentence that, at first, perplexed me most terribly – I could not help shuddering when I thought of the monster His horrible, unparalleled and repulsive ugliness put him without the pale of humanity; and it often seemed to me that, for this reason, he had ceased to believe that he had any duty towards the human race. The way in which he spoke of his love-affairs only increased my alarm, for I foresaw the cause of fresh and more hideous tragedies in this event to which he alluded so boastfully.

On the other hand, I soon discovered the curious moral traffic

[1] The Persian might easily have admitted that Erik's fate also interested himself, for he was well aware that, if the government of Teheran had learnt that Erik was still alive, it would have been all up with the modest pension of the late daroga. It is only fair, however, to add that the Persian had a noble and generous heart; and I do not doubt for a moment that the catastrophes which he feared for others greatly occupied his mind. Besides, his conduct, throughout this business, proves it and is, indeed, above all praise.

established between the monster and Christine Daaé. Hiding in the lumber-room next to the young prima donna's dressing-room, I listened to wonderful musical displays that evidently flung Christine into a marvellous ecstasy; but, all the same, I would never have thought that Erik's voice – which was loud as thunder or soft as angels' voices, at will – could have made her forget his ugliness. I understood all when I learnt that Christine had not yet seen him! I had occasion to go to the dressing-room and, remembering the lessons he had once given me, I had no difficulty in discovering the trick that made the wall with the mirror swing round and I ascertained the means – of hollow bricks and so on – by which he made his voice carry to Christine as though she heard it close beside her. In this way also I discovered the road that led to the well and the dungeon – the Communists' dungeon – and also the trap-door that enabled Erik to go straight to the cellars below the stage.

A few days later, what was not my amazement to learn by my own eyes and ears that Erik and Christine Daaé saw each other and to catch the monster stooping over the little well, in the Communists' road, and sprinkling the forehead of Christine Daaé, who had fainted. A white horse, the horse out of the *Prophète*, which had disappeared from the stables under the Opera, was standing quietly beside them. I showed myself. It was terrible. I saw sparks fly from those yellow eyes and, before I had time to say a word, I received a blow on the head that stunned me.

When I came to myself again, Erik, Christine and the white horse had disappeared. I felt sure that the poor girl was a prisoner in the house on the lake. Without hesitation, I resolved to return to the shore, notwithstanding the certain danger. For twenty-four hours, I lay watching for the monster to appear; for I felt that he must go out, driven by the need of obtaining provisions. And in this connection, I may say that, when he went out in the streets or ventured to show himself in public, he wore a paste-board nose, with a moustache attached to it, instead of his own horrible hole of a nose. This did not quite take away his corpse-like aspect, but it made him almost – I say almost – endurable to look at.

I therefore watched on the bank of the lake and, weary of long waiting, was beginning to think that he had gone through the other door, the door in the third cellar, when I heard a slight splash in the dark, I saw the two yellow eyes shining like candles and soon the boat touched shore. Erik jumped out and walked up to me:

'You've been here for twenty-four hours,' he said, 'and you're annoying me. I tell you, all this will end very badly. And you will have brought it upon yourself; for I have been extraordinarily patient with you. . . . You think you are following me, you silly ass *(sic)*, whereas it's I who am following you; and I know all that you know about me, here. I spared you yesterday, in *my Communists' road*; but I warn you, seriously, don't let me catch you there again! . . . Upon my word, you don't seem able to take a hint!'

He was so furious that I did not think, for the moment, of interrupting him. After puffing and blowing like a walrus, he put his horrible thought into words:

'Yes, you must learn, once and for all – once and for all, I say – to take a hint! I tell you that, with your recklessness – for you have already been twice arrested by the shade in the felt hat, who did not know what you were doing in the cellars and took you to the managers, who looked upon you as an eccentric Persian interested in stage mechanism and life behind the scenes: I know all about it; I was there, in the office: you know I am everywhere – well, I tell you that, with your recklessness, they will begin to wonder you are after here . . . and they will end by knowing that you are after Erik . . . and they will be after Erik themselves . . . and they will discover the house on the lake. . . . If they do, it will be a bad look-out for you, old chap, a bad look-out! . . . I won't answer for anything.'

Again he puffed and blew like a walrus:

'I won't answer for anything! . . . If Erik's secrets cease to be Erik's secrets, *it will be a bad look-out for a large number of the human race!* . . . That's all I had to tell you and, unless you are a sillier ass *(sic)* than I thought, it ought to be enough for you . . . except that you don't know how to take a hint! . . .'

He sat down on the stern of his boat and kicked his heels against the planks, waiting to hear what I had to answer. I simply said:

'It's not Erik that I'm after here!'

'Who then?'

'You know as well as I do: it's Christine Daaé.'

He retorted:

'I have every right to see her in my house. I am loved for my own sake.'

'That's not true,' I said. 'You have carried her off and are keeping her locked up.'

'Listen,' he said. 'Will you promise never to meddle with my affairs, if I prove to you that I am loved for my own sake?'

'Yes, I promise you.' I replied, without hesitation, for I felt convinced that for such a monster the proof was impossible.

'Well, then, it's quite simple . . . . Christine Daaé shall leave this as she pleases and come back again! . . . Yes, come back again, because she wishes . . . come back of herself, because she loves me for myself! . . .'

'Oh, I doubt if she will come back! . . . But it is your duty to let her go.'

My duty, you silly ass (sic)! . . . It is my wish . . . my wish to let her go; and she will come back again . . . for she loves me! . . . All this will end in a marriage . . . a marriage at the Madeleine you silly ass (sic)! Do you believe me, now? When I tell you that my nuptial mass is written . . . wait till you hear the Kyrie.

He beat time with his heels on the planks of the boat and sang:

'Kyrie! . . . Kyrie! . . . Kyrie eleison! . . . Wait till you hear, wait till you hear that mass!'

'Look here,' I said. 'I shall believe you if I see Christine Daaé come out of the house on the lake and go back to it of her own accord.'

'And you won't meddle any more in my affairs?'

'No.'

'Very well, you shall see that to-night. . . . Come to the masked ball. Christine and I will go and have a look round. . . . Then you can hide in the lumber-room and you shall see Christine, who will have gone to her dressing-room, delighted to come back by the Communists' road. . . . And now be off, for I must go and do some shopping! . . .'

To my intense astonishment, things happened as he had said. Christine Daaé left the house on the lake and returned to it several times, without, apparently, being forced to do so. I then tried to cease thinking about this mysterious love-affair, but it was very difficult for me to put Erik out of my mind entirely. However, I resolved to be extremely prudent and did not make the mistake of returning to the shore of the lake or of going by the Communists' road. But the idea of the secret entrance in the third cellar haunted me and I repeatedly went and waited for hours behind a scene from the Roi de Lahore, which had been left there for some reason or other: it was an opera which was not often given. At last, my patience was rewarded. One day, I saw the monster come towards me on his knees. I was certain that he could not see me. He passed between the scene behind which I stood and a set piece, went to the wall and pressed on a spring that moved a stone and afforded him an ingress. He passed through this and the stone closed behind him.

I waited for at least thirty minutes and then pressed the spring in my turn. Everything happened as with Erik. But I was careful not to go through the hole myself, for I knew that Erik was inside. On the other hand, the idea that I might be caught by Erik suddenly made me think of the death of Joseph Buquet. I did not wish to jeopardize the advantages of so great a discovery, which might be useful to many people, to 'a large number of the human race,' in Erik's words; and I left the cellars of the Opera, after carefully replacing the stone.

I continued to be greatly interested in the relations between Erik and Christine Daaé, not from any morbid curiosity, but because of the terrible thought which obsessed my mind that Erik was capable of anything, if he once discovered that he was not loved for his own sake, as he imagined. I continued to wander very cautiously about the Opera and soon learnt the truth about the monster's dreary love-affair. He filled Christine's mind, through the terror with which he inspired her, but the dear child's heart belonged wholly to the Vicomte Raoul de Chagny. While they played about like an innocent engaged couple, keeping to the upper floors of the Opera, to avoid the monster, they little suspected that some one was watching over their safety. I was prepared to go to all lengths: to kill the monster, if necessary, and explain to the police afterwards. But Erik did not show himself; and I felt none the more comfortable for that.

I must state my whole plan. I thought that the monster, being driven from his home by jealousy, would thus enable me to enter it, without danger, through the passage in the third cellar. It was important, for everybody's sake, that I should know exactly what was inside. One day, tired of waiting for an opportunity, I moved the stone and at once heard an astounding music: the monster was working at his *Don Juan Triumphant*, with every door in his house wide open. I knew that this was the work of his life. I was careful not to stir and remained prudently in my dark hole.

He stopped playing, for a moment, and began walking about his place like a madman. And he said aloud, at the top of his voice:

'It must be finished *first*! Quite finished!'

This speech was not calculated to reassure me and, when the music recommenced, I closed the stone very softly.

On the day of the abduction of Christine Daaé, I did not come to the theatre until rather late in the evening, trembling lest I should hear bad news. I had spent a horrible day, for, after reading in a morning paper, the announcement of a forthcoming marriage between Christine and the Vicomte de Chagny, I wondered whether, after all, I should not do better to denounce the monster. But my common sense returned to me and soon showed me that any such action could only precipitate the possible catastrophe.

When my cab put me down before the Opera, I was really almost astonished to see it still standing! But I am something of a fatalist, like all good Orientals, and I entered, ready for anything.

Christine Daaé's abduction in the Prison Act, which naturally surprised everybody, found me prepared. It was quite certain that she had been juggled away by Erik, that prince of conjurors. And I thought positively that this was the end of Christine and perhaps of everybody, so much so that I thought of advising all those people who were staying on at the theatre to make good their escape. I felt, however, that they would be sure to look upon me as mad and I refrained.

On the other hand, I resolved personally to act without further delay. The chances were in my favour that Erik, at that moment, was thinking only of his captive. This was the moment to enter his house through the third cellar; and I resolved to take with me that poor little desperate viscount, who, at the first suggestion, accepted with an amount of confidence in myself that touched me profoundly. I had sent my servant for my pistols. I gave one to the viscount and advised him to hold himself ready to fire, for, after all, Erik might be waiting for us behind the wall. We were to go by the Communists' road and through the trap-door.

Seeing my pistols, the little viscount asked me if we were going to fight a duel. I said:

'Yes. And what a duel!'

But, of course, I had no time to explain things to him. The viscount is a brave little fellow, but he knew hardly anything about his adversary; and that was all the better. My great fear was lest he were already somewhere near us, preparing the Punjab lasso. No one knows better than he how to throw the Punjab lasso, for he is the king of stranglers even as he is the prince of conjurors. When he had finished making the little sultana laugh, at the time of the 'rosy hours of Mazenderan,' she herself used to ask him to amuse her by giving her a thrill. It was then that he introduced the sport of the Punjab lasso. He had lived in India and acquired an incredible skill in the art of strangulation. He would make them lock him into a courtyard to which they brought a warrior – usually, a man condemned to death –

armed with a long pike and a big sword. Erik had only his lasso; and it was always just when the warrior thought that he was going to fell Erik with a tremendous blow that we heard the lasso whizz through the air. With a turn of the wrist, Erik tightened the noose round his adversary's neck and, in this fashion, dragged him before the little sultana and her woman, who sat looking from a window and applauding. The little sultana herself learnt to wield the Punjab lasso and killed several of her women and even of the ladies who came to call. But I prefer to drop this terrible subject of the rosy hours of Mazenderan. I have mentioned it only to explain why, on arriving with the Vicomte de Chagny in the cellars of the Opera, I felt bound to protect my companion against the ever-threatening danger of death by strangling. My pistols could serve no purpose, for Erik was not likely to show himself; but Erik could always strangle us. I had no time to explain all this to the viscount; besides, there was nothing to be gained by complicating the position. I simply told M de Chagny to keep his hand at the level of his eyes, with the arm bent, as though waiting for the command to fire. With his victim in this attitude, it is impossible even to the most expert strangler to throw the lasso with advantage. It catches you not only round the neck, but also round the arm or hand. This enables you easily to unloose the lasso, which then becomes harmless.

After avoiding the commissary of police, a number of door-shutters and the firemen, after meeting the rat-catcher and passing the man in the felt hat unperceived, the viscount and I arrived without obstacle in the third cellar, between the set piece and the scene from the *Roi de Lahore*. I worked the stone and we jumped into the house which Erik had built himself in the double case of the foundation-walls of the Opera. And this was the easiest thing in the world for him to do, because Erik was one of the chief contractors under Philippe Garnier, the architect of the Opera and continued to work, mysteriously, all by himself, when the works were officially suspended, during the war, the siege of Paris and the Commune.

I knew my Erik too well to feel at all comfortable when I jumped into his house. I knew what he had made of a certain palace at Mazenderan. From being the most honest building conceivable, he soon turned it into a house of the very devil, where you could not utter a word but it was overheard or repeated by an echo. With his trap-doors the monster was responsible for endless tragedies of all kinds. His hit upon astonishing inventions. Of these, the most curious, horrible and dangerous was the so-called torture-chamber. Except in special cases, when the little sultana amused herself by inflicting suffering upon some unoffending citizen, no one was let into it but wretches condemned to death. And, even then, when these 'had had enough,' they were always at liberty to put an end to themselves with a Punjab lasso or bowstring, left to their use at the foot of an iron tree.

My alarm, therefore, was great when I saw that the room into which M le Vicomte de Chagny and I had dropped was an exact copy of the torture-chamber of the rosy hours of Mazenderan! At our feet, I found the Punjab lasso which I had been dreading all the evening. I was convinced that this rope had already done duty for Joseph Buquet, who, like myself, must have caught Erik one evening working the stone in the third cellar. He probably tried it in his turn, fell into the torture-chamber and only left it hanged. I could well imagine Erik dragging the body, in order to get rid of it, to the scene from the *Roi de Lahore* and hanging it there as an example, or to increase the superstitious terror that was to help him in guarding the approaches to his lair! Then, upon reflection, Erik went back to fetch the Punjab lasso, which is very curiously made out of catgut and which might have set an examining-magistrate thinking. This explains the disappearance of the rope.

And now I discovered the lasso, at our feet, in the torture chamber! . . . I am no coward, but cold sweat covered my forehead as I moved the little red disc of my lantern over the walls.

M de Chagny noticed it and asked:

'What is the matter, sir?'

I made him a violent sign to be silent.

CHAPTER XXII

In The Torture-Chamber

The Persian's Narrative continued

WE WERE IN THE MIDDLE of a small six-cornered room, the sides of which were covered with mirrors from floor to ceiling. In the corners, we could clearly see the ' joins' in the glasses and the little segments intended to turn on their drums; yes, I recognized them and I recognized the iron tree in the corner, fixed in one of those segments . . . the iron tree, with its iron branch, for the hanged man. . .

I seized my companion's arm: the Vicomte de Chagny was all aquiver, eager to shout to his betrothed that he was bringing her help. I feared that he would not be able to contain himself.

Suddenly, we heard noises on our left. It sounded at first like a door opening and shutting in the next room; and then came a dull moan. I clutched M de Chagny's arm more firmly still; and then we distinctly heard the words;

'You must make your choice! The wedding-mass or the requiem mass!'

I recognized the voice of the monster.

There was another moan, followed by a long silence.

I was persuaded by now that the monster was unaware of our presence in his house, for otherwise he would certainly have managed not to let us hear him. He would only have had to close the little invisible window through which the torture-lovers look down into the torture-chamber. Besides, I was certain that, if he had known of our presence, the tortures would have begun at once.

The important thing was not to let him know; and I dreaded nothing so much as the impulsiveness of the Vicomte de Chagny, who wanted to rush through the walls to Christine Daaé, whose moans, as we thought, we continued to hear at intervals.

'The requiem mass is not at all gay,' Erik's voice resumed, 'whereas the wedding-mass – you can take my word for it – is magnificent! One must take a resolution and know one's mind! I can't go on living like this, like a mole in a burrow! *Don Juan Triumphant is* finished; and now I want to live like everybody else. I want to have a wife like everybody else and to take her out on Sundays. I have invented a mask that makes me look like anybody. People will not even turn round to stare at me. You will be the happiest of women. And we will sing, all by ourselves, till we swoon away with delight. You are crying! You are afraid of me! And yet I am not really wicked. Love me and you shall see! All I wanted was to be loved for myself. If you loved me, I should be as gentle as a lamb; and you could do anything with me that you pleased.'

Soon the moans that accompanied this sort of love's litany increased and increased. I have never heard anything more despairing; and M de Chagny and I recognized that this terrible lamentation came from Erik himself. Christine seemed to stand dumb with horror, without strength to cry out, while the monster was on his knees before her.

Three times over, Erik fiercely bewailed his fate:

'You don't love me! You don't love me! You don't love me!' And then, more gently:

'Why do you cry? You know it gives me pain to see you cry!' A silence.

Each silence gave us fresh hope. We said to ourselves:

'Perhaps he has left Christine, behind the wall.'

And we thought only of the possibility of informing Christine Daaé of our presence, unknown to the monster. We were unable to leave the torture-chamber now, unless Christine opened the door to us; and it was only on this condition that we could hope to help her, for we did not even know where the door might be.

Suddenly the silence in the next room was disturbed by the ringing of an electric bell. There was a sound on the other side of the wall and Erik's voice of thunder:

'Somebody ringing! Come in!'

A sinister chuckle:

'Who has come bothering now? Wait for me here. . . . *I am going to tell the siren to open the door.*'

Steps moved away, a door closed. I had no time to think of the fresh horror that was preparing; I forgot that the monster was only going out, perhaps, to perpetrate a fresh crime; I understand but one thing: Christine was alone behind the wall!

The Vicomte de Chagny was already calling to her:

'Christine! Christine!'

As we could hear what was said in the next room, there was no reason why my companion should not be heard in his turn. Nevertheless, the viscount had to repeat his cry time after time.

At last, a faint voice reached us:

'I am dreaming!' it said.

'Christine, Christine, it is I, Raoul!'

A silence.

'But answer me, Christine! . . . In heaven's name, if you are alone, answer me!'

Then Christine's voice whispered Raoul's name.

'Yes! Yes! It is I! It is not a dream! . . . Christine, trust me! . . . We are here to save you . . . but be prudent! When you hear the monster, warn us!'

Then Christine gave way to fear. She trembled lest Erik should discover where Raoul was hidden, she told us in a few hurried words that Erik had gone quite mad with love and that he had decided *to kill everybody and himself with everybody* if she did not consent to become his wife. He had given her till eleven o'clock the next evening for reflection. It was the last respite. She must then choose, as he said, between the wedding mass and the requiem.

And Erik had then uttered a phrase which Christine did not quite understand:

'Yes or no! If your answer is no, everybody will be dead *and buried!*'

But I understood the sentence perfectly, for it corresponded in a terrible manner with my own dreadful thought.

'Can you tell us where Erik is?' I asked.

She replied that he must have left the house.

'Could you make sure?'

'No. I am fastened. . . I cannot stir a limb.'

When we heard this, M de Chagny and I gave a yell of fury. Our safety, the safety of all the three of us depended on the girl's liberty of movement.

'But where are you?' asked Christine. 'There are only two doors in my room, the Louis-Philippe room of which I told you, Raoul: a door through which Erik comes and goes and another which he has never opened before me and which he has forbidden me ever to go through, because he says it is the most dangerous of the doors, the door of the torture-chamber!'

'Christine, that is where we are!'

'You are in the torture-chamber?'

'Yes, but we cannot see the door.'

'Oh, if I could only drag myself so far! . . . I would knock at the door and that would tell you where it is.'

'Is it a door with a lock to it?' I asked.

'Yes, with a lock.'

'Mademoiselle,' I exclaimed, 'it is absolutely necessary that you should open that door to us!'

'But how?' asked the poor girl, tearfully.

We heard her straining, trying to free herself from the bonds that held her.

'I know where the key is,' she said, in a voice that seemed exhausted by the effort she had made. 'But I am fastened so tight. . . . Oh, the wretch!'

And she gave a sob.

'Where is the key?' I asked, signing to M de Chagny not to speak and to leave the business to me, for we had not a moment to lose.

'In the next room, near the organ, with another little bronze key which he also forbade me to touch. They are both in a little leather bag which he calls the bag of life and death. . . . Raoul! Raoul! Fly! . . . Everything is mysterious and terrible here. . . and Erik will soon have gone quite mad . . . and you are in the torture-chamber! . . . Go back by the way you came! There must be a reason why the room is called by a name like that!'

'Christine,' said the young man, 'we will go from here together or die together!'

'We must keep cool,' I whispered. 'Why has he fastened you, mademoiselle? You can't escape from his house; and he knows it!'

'I tried to commit suicide! The monster went out last night, after carrying me here fainting and half chloroformed. He was going *to his banker*, so he said . . . . When he returned, he found me with my face covered with blood. . . . I had tried to kill myself by striking my forehead against the wall. . . .'

'Christine!' groaned Raoul; and he began to sob.

'Then he bound me. . . . I am not allowed to die until eleven o'clock to-morrow evening! . . .'

'Mademoiselle,' I declared, 'the monster bound you . . . and he shall unbind you. . . . You have only to play the necessary part! . . . Remember that he loves you!'

'Alas!' we heard. 'Am I likely to forget it!'

'Remember it and smile on him . . . entreat him . . . tell him that your bonds hurt you.'

But Christine Daaé said:

'Hush! . . . I hear something in the wall on the lake! . . . It is he! . . . Go away! Go away! Go away! . . .'

'We could not go away, even if we wanted to,' I said, as impressively as I could. 'We cannot leave this! And we are in the torture-chamber!'

'Hush!' whispered Christine again.

Heavy steps dragged slowly behind the wall, stopped and then made the floor creak once more. Next came a tremendous sigh, followed by a cry of horror from Christine, and we heard Erik's voice:

'I beg your pardon for letting you see a face like this! What a state I am in am I not? It's *the other one's* fault! why did he ring? Do I ask people who pass to tell me the time? He will never ask anybody the time again! It is the siren's fault. . . .'

Another sigh, deeper, more tremendous still, came from the abysmal depths of a soul.

'Why did you cry out, Christine?'

'Because I am in pain, Erik.'

'I thought I had frightened you. . . .'

'Erik, unloose my bonds. . . . Am I not your prisoner?'

'You will try to kill yourself again. . . .'

'You have given me till eleven o'clock to-morrow evening Erik, . . .'

The footsteps dragged along the floor once more.

'After all, since we are to die together . . . and since I am just as eager to die as you are . . . yes, I have had enough of this life, you know. . . . Wait, don't move, I will release you. . . . You have only one word to say: *'No!'* And it will at once be finished *with every-body!* . . . You are right, you are right: why wait till eleven o'clock to-morrow evening? True, it would have been grander, finer. . . . But that is childish nonsense. . . . We should only think of our-selves in this life, of our own death . . . the rest doesn't matter. . . . *You're looking at me because I am all wet?* . . . Oh, my dear, it's rain-ing cats and dogs outside! . . . Apart from that, Christine, I believe I am suffering from hallucinations. . . You know, the man who rang at the siren's door just now – I wonder if he's ringing at the bottom of the lake – well, he was rather like . . . There, turn round . . . are you glad? You're free now. . . . Oh, Christine, look at your poor dear wrists: tell me, have I hurt them? . . . That alone deserves death. . . . Talking of death, *I must sing his requiem!*'

Hearing these terrible remarks, I received an awful presenti-ment. . . . I too had once rung at the monster's door . . . and, with-out knowing it, must have set some warning current in motion. . . And I remembered the two arms that had emerged from the inky waters. . . . What poor wretch had strayed to that shore this time! . . . Who was 'the other one,' the one whose requiem we now heard sung? . . .

Erik sang like the god of thunder, sang a *Dies Iras* that enveloped us as in a storm. The elements seemed to rage around us. . . . Suddenly, the organ and the voice ceased so suddenly that M de Chagny and I jumped back, on the other side of the wall, with the shock. And the voice, now changed and transformed, dis-tinctly grated out these metallic syllables:

'*What have you done with my bag?*'

CHAPTER XXIII

The Tortures Begin

The Persian's Narrative continued

THE VOICE REPEATED ANGRILY:

'What have you done with my bag? . . . So it was to take my bag that you asked me to release you!'

We heard hurried steps, Christine running back to the Louis-Philippe room, as though to seek shelter in front of our wall.

'What are you running away for?' asked the furious voice, which had followed her. 'Give me back my bag, will you? Don't you know that it is the bag of life and death?'

'Listen to me, Erik,' sighed the girl. 'As it is settled that we are to live together . . . what difference can it make to you?'

'You know there are only two keys in it,' said the monster. 'What do you want to do?'

'I want to look at this room which I have never seen and which you have always kept hidden from me. . . . It's woman's curiosity!' she said, in a tone which she tried to render playful.

But the trick was too childish for Erik to be taken in by it.

'I don't like curious women,' he retorted, 'and you had better remember the story of Blue-Beard and be careful. . . . Come, give me back my bag! . . . Give me back my bag! . . . Leave the key alone, will you, you inquisitive little thing!'

And he chuckled, while Christine gave a cry of pain. . . . Erik had evidently recovered the bag from her.

At that moment, the viscount could not help uttering an exclamation of impotent rage.

'Hullo, what's that?' said the monster. 'Did you hear, Christine?'

'No, no!' replied the poor girl. 'I heard nothing!'

'I thought I heard a cry.'

'A cry! . . . Are you going mad, Erik? . . . Whom do you expect to give a cry, in this house? . . . I cried out, because you hurt me! . . . I heard nothing.'

'I don't like the way you said that. . . . You're trembling. . . .
You're quite excited. . . . You're lying! . . . There was a cry, there
was a cry! . . . There is some one in the torture-chamber! . . . Ah, I
understand now! . . .'

'There is no one there, Erik! . . .'

'I understand! . . .'

'No one! . . .'

'The man you want to marry, perhaps! . . .'

'I don't want to marry anybody . . . you know I don't.'

Another nasty chuckle:

'Well, it won't take long to find out. . . . Christine, my love, we
need not open the door to see what is happening in the torture-
chamber. . . . Would you like to see? Would you like to see? . . .
Look here! . . . If there is some one, if there is really some one
there, you will see the invisible window light up at the top of the
wall, near the ceiling. . . . We have only to draw back the black
curtain and put out the light here. . . . There, that's it. . . . Let's
put out the light! . . . You're not afraid of the dark, when you're
with your little husband! . . .'

Then we heard Christine's voice of anguish:

'No! . . . I'm frightened! . . . I tell you, I'm afraid of the dark! . . .
I don't care about that room now. . . . You're always frightening
me, like a child, with your torture-chamber! . . . And so I became
inquisitive. . . . But I don't care about it now . . . not a bit . . . not a
bit! . . . .'

And that which I feared above all things began, *automatically*. . . .
We were suddenly flooded with light! . . . Yes, on our side of the
wall, everything seemed aglow. The Vicomte de Chagny was so
much taken by surprise that he staggered where he stood. And the
angry voice roared:

'I told you there was some one! . . . Do you see the window
now? . . . The lighted window, right up there? . . . The man
behind the wall can't see it! . . . But you shall go up the folding
steps: that is what they are there for! . . . You have often asked me
to tell you; and now you know! . . . They are there to give a peep
into the torture-chamber . . . you inquisitive little thing! . . .'

'What do you mean by a torture-chamber? . . . Who is being
tortured? . . . Erik, Erik, say you are only trying to frighten me! . . .
Say it, if you love me, Erik! . . . There are no tortures, are there?'

'Go and look through the little window, dear!'

I do not know if the viscount heard the girl's swooning voice,
for he was too much absorbed by the astounding spectacle that

now appeared before his distracted gaze. As for me, I had seen that sight too often, through the little window, at the time of the rosy hours of Mazenderan; and I cared only for what was being said next door, seeking for a hint how to act, what resolution to take.

'Go and peep through the little window! . . . Tell me what he looks like! . . .'

We heard the steps being dragged against the wall.

'Up with you! . . . No? . . . Then I will go up myself, dear!'

'Oh, very well, I will go up . . . let me go!'

'Oh, my darling, my darling! . . . How sweet of you! . . . How nice of you to save me the exertion, at my age! . . . Tell me what he looks like! . . .'

At that moment, we distinctly heard these words above our heads:

'There is no one there, dear! . . .'

'No one? . . . Are you sure there is no one? . . .'

'Why, of course not . . . no one! . . .'

'Well, that's all right! . . . What's the matter, Christine? You're not going to faint, are you . . . considering there is no one there? . . . Here . . . come down. . . . That's it! . . . Pull yourself together . . . as there is no one there! . . . *But how do you like the landscape?*'

'Oh, very much!'

'There, that's right! . . . You're better now, are you not? . . . That's right, you're much better! . . . No emotions! . . . And what a funny house, isn't it, with landscapes like that inside it?'

'Yes, it's like the Musée Grévin. . . . But, I say, Erik . . . there are no tortures in there! . . . What a fright you gave me! . . .'

'Why . . . considering there is no one there?'

'Did you design that room? . . . It's very handsome, you know! You're a great artist, Erik. . . .'

'Yes, a great artist, in my own line.'

'But tell me, Erik, why did you call that room the torture-chamber?'

'Oh, it's very simple. First of all, what did you see?'

'I saw a forest.'

'And what is in a forest?'

'Trees.'

'And what is in a tree?'

'Birds.'

'Did you see any birds?'

'No, I did not see any birds.'

'Well, what did you see? . . . Think! . . . You saw branches! And

what is in a branch?' asked the terrible voice. *'There's a gibbet!*
That is why I call my forest the torture-chamber! . . . Of course,
it's only a way of talking! . . . It's all a joke, you know! . . . I never
express myself like other people. . . . I never do anything like other
people. . . . But I am getting very tired of it! . . . I 'm sick and tired
of having a forest and a torture-chamber in my house and of living
like a mountebank, in a house with a false bottom! . . . I'm tired of
it! . . . I want a nice, quiet flat, with ordinary doors and windows
and a wife inside it, like anybody else! . . . A wife whom I can love
and take out on Sundays and keep amused on week-days! Oh, you
would have lots of fun with me! I have more than one trick in my
bag, without counting card-tricks. . . . I say, here, shall I show you
a few card-tricks? It will help us pass the time, while waiting for
eleven o'clock to-morrow evening! . . . My dear little Christine! . . .
Are you listening to me? . . . Tell me you love me! . . . No, you
don't love me. . . . but no matter, you will! . . . Once, you could
not look at my mask, because you knew what was behind . . . . And
now you don't mind looking at it and you forget what is behind! . . .
One can get used to everything . . . if one wishes. . . . Plenty of
young people who did not care for each other before marriage
have adored each other since! . . . Oh, I don't know what I am
talking about! . . . But you would have lots of fun with me! . . . For
instance, I am the greatest ventriloquist that ever lived, I am the
finest ventriloquist in the world! . . . You're laughing. . . . Perhaps
you don't believe me? . . . Listen. . . .'

The wretch, who really was the finest ventriloquist in the world,
was only trying to divert the child's attention from the torture-
chamber; but it was a stupid scheme, for Christine thought of
nothing but us! . . . She repeatedly besought him, in the gentlest
tones which she could assume:

'Put out the light in the little window! . . . Erik, do put out the
light in the little window! . . .'

For she saw that this light, which appeared so suddenly and of
which the monster had spoken in so threatening a voice, must
mean something terrible. . . . One thing must have pacified her for
a moment; and that was, seeing the two of us, behind the wall, in
the midst of that dazzling light, alive and well. . . . But she would
certainly have felt much easier if the light had been put out. . . .

Meantime, the other had already begun to play the ventriloquist. He said:

'Here, I raise my mask a little. . . . Oh, only a little! . . . You see
my lips, such lips as I have? They're not moving! . . . My mouth is

closed – such mouth as I have – and yet you hear my voice. . . .
Where will you have it? In your left ear? In your right ear? In the
table? In those little ebony boxes on the mantelpiece. . . . Listen,
dear, it's in the little box on the right of the mantelpiece: what
does it say? *"Shall I turn the scorpion?"* . . . And now, crack! What
does it say in the little box on the left? *"Shall I turn the grasshopper?"* . . . And now, crack! Here it is in the little leather bag. . . .
What does it say? *"I am the little bag of life and death!"* . . . And
now, crack! It is in Carlotta's throat, in Carlotta's golden throat,
in Carlotta's crystal throat, as I live! What does it say? It says, "It's
I, Mr Toad, it's I singing! *I feel without alarm – co-ack! – with its
melody enwind me – co-ack!"* . . . And now, crack! It is on a chair in
the ghost's box and it says, *"Madame Carlotta is singing to-night to
bring the chandelier down!"* . . . And now, crack! Aha! Where is
Erik's voice now? Listen, Christine, darling! Listen! It is behind
the door of the torture-chamber! Listen! It's myself in the torture-
chamber! And what do I say? I say, "Woe to them that have a
nose, a real nose, and come to look round the torture-chamber!
Aha, aha, aha!" '

Oh, the ventriloquist's terrible voice! It was everywhere, everywhere! . . . It passed through the little invisible window, through
the walls . . . it ran around us, between us. . . . Erik was there,
speaking to us! . . . We made a movement as though to fling ourselves upon him. . . . But, already, swifter, more fleeting than the
voice of the echo, Erik's voice had leapt back behind the wall! . . .

Soon, we were able to hear nothing more at all, for this is what
happened:

'Erik! Erik!' said Christine's voice. 'You tire me with your voice.
. . . Don't go on, Erik! . . . Isn't it very hot here?'

'Oh yes,' replied Erik's voice, 'the heat is unendurable!'

'But what does this mean? . . . The wall is quite hot! . . . The
wall is burning! . . .'

'I'll tell you, Christine, dear: it is because of the forest next
door.'

'Well, what has that to do with it? . . . The forest? . . .'

'Why, didn't you see that it was an African forest?'

And the monster laughed so loudly and hideously that we could
no longer distinguish Christine's beseeching cries! . . . The
Vicomte de Chagny shouted and banged against the walls like a
madman. . . . I could not restrain him. . . . But we heard nothing
except the monster's laughter . . . and the monster himself can
have heard nothing else . . . . And then there was the sound of a

body falling on the floor and being dragged along . . . and a door slammed . . . and then nothing, nothing more around us save the scorching silence of the tropics . . . in the heart of an equatorial forest! . . .

CHAPTER XXIV

'Barrels! Barrels!'

The Persian's Narrative continued

I HAVE SAID that the room in which M le Vicomte de Chagny and I were imprisoned was a regular hexagon, lined throughout with mirrors. Plenty of these rooms have been seen since, mainly at exhibitions: they are called 'palaces of illusion,' or some such name. But the invention belongs entirely to Erik, who built the first room of this kind under my eyes, at the time of the rosy hours of Mazenderan. A decorative object, such as a column, for instance, was placed in one of the corners and immediately produced a hall of a thousand columns; for, thanks to the mirrors, the real room was multiplied by six hexagonal rooms, each of which, in its turn, was multiplied indefinitely. But the little sultana soon tired of this childish illusion, whereupon Erik altered his invention into a 'torture-chamber.' For the architectural motive placed in one corner, he substituted an iron tree. This tree, with its painted leaves, was absolutely true to life and was made of iron so as to resist all the attacks of the 'patient' imprisoned in the torture-chamber. We shall see how the scene thus obtained was twice altered into two successive other scenes, produced instantaneously by means of the automatic rotation of the drums or rollers in the corners. These were divided into three sections fitting into the angles of the mirrors and each supporting a decorative scheme that came into sight as the roller revolved upon its axis.

The walls of this strange room gave the patient nothing to lay hold of, because, apart from the solid decorative object, they were simply furnished with mirrors, thick enough to withstand any onslaught of the victim, who was flung into the chamber empty-handed and barefoot.

There was no furniture. The ceiling was capable of being lit up. An ingenious system of electric heating, which has since been imitated, allowed the temperature of the walls and room to be increased at will. . . .

I am reciting all these details of a perfectly straightforward invention, giving, with the aid of a few painted branches, the supernatural illusion of an equatorial forest blazing under the tropical sun, so that no one may doubt the present balance of my brain or feel entitled to say that I am mad or lying or that I take him for a fool.[1]

I now return to the facts where I left them. When the ceiling lit up and the forest became visible around us, the viscount's stupefaction was immense. That impenetrable forest, with its innumerable trunks and branches, threw him into a terrible state of consternation. He passed his hands over his forehead, as though to drive away a dream; his eyes blinked; and, for a moment, he forgot to listen.

I have already said that the sight of the forest did not surprise me at all; and therefore I listened for both of us to what was happening next door. Lastly, my attention was especially attracted, not so much to the scene, as to the mirrors that produced it. These mirrors were broken in parts. Yes, they were marked and scratched; they had been 'starred,' in spite of their solidity; and this proved to me that the torture-chamber in which we now were *had already served a purpose.*

Yes, some wretch, whose feet were not bare like those of the victims of the rosy hours of Mazenderan, had certainly fallen into this 'mortal illusion' and, mad with rage, had kicked against those mirrors which, nevertheless, continued to reflect his agony. And the branch of the tree on which he had put an end to his own sufferings was arranged in such a way that, before dying, he had seen, for his last consolation, a thousand men writhing in his company.

Yes, Joseph Buquet had been through all this! . . . Were we to die as he had done? I did not think so, for I knew that we had a few hours before us and that I could employ them to better purpose than Joseph Buquet was able to do. After all, I was thoroughly acquainted with most of Erik's 'tricks;' and now or never was the time to turn my knowledge to account.

[1] It is only natural that, at the time when the Persian was writing, he should take so many precautions against any spirit of incredulity on the part of those who were likely to read his narrative. Nowadays, when we have all seen this sort of room, his precautions would be superfluous.

To begin with, I abandoned any idea of returning to the passage which had brought us to that accursed chamber. I did not trouble about the possibility of working the inside stone that closed the passage; and this for the simple reason that to do so was out of the question. We had dropped from too great a height into the torture-chamber; there was no furniture to help us reach the passage; not even the branch of the iron tree, not even each other's shoulders were of any avail.

There was only one possible outlet, that opening into the Louis-Philippe room in which Erik and Christine Daaé were. But, though this outlet looked like just an ordinary door on their side, it was absolutely invisible to us. We must therefore try to open it without even knowing where it was.

When I was quite sure that there was no hope for us from Christine Daaé's side, when I had heard the monster dragging the poor girl from the Louis-Philippe room *lest she should interfere with our tortures,* I resolved to set to work without delay.

But I had first to calm M de Chagny, who was already walking about like a madman, uttering incoherent cries. The snatches of conversation which he had caught between Christine and the monster had contributed not a little to drive him beside himself: add to that the shock of the magic forest and the scorching heat which was beginning to make the perspiration stream down his temples and you will have no difficulty in understanding his state of mind. He shouted Christine's name, brandished his pistol, knocked his forehead against the glass in his endeavours to rush down the glades of the illusive forest. In short, the torture was beginning to work its spell upon a brain unprepared for it.

I did my best to induce the poor viscount to listen to reason. I made him touch the mirrors and the iron tree and the branches and explained to him, by optical laws, all the luminous imagery by which we were surrounded and of which we need not allow ourselves to be the victims, like ordinary, ignorant people.

'We are in a room, a little room; that is what you must keep saying to yourself . . . . And we shall leave the room as soon as we have found the door. . . .'

And I promised him that, if he let me act, without disturbing me by shouting and walking up and down, I would discover the trick of the door in less than an hour's time.

Then he lay flat on the floor, as one does in a wood, and declared that he would wait until I found the door of the forest, as there was nothing better to do! And he added that, from where he was, 'the view was splendid!' The torture was working, in spite of all that I had said.

Myself, forgetting the forest, I tackled a glass panel and began to finger it in every direction, hunting for the spot which I must press in order to turn the door in accordance with Erik's system of pivots. This spot might be a mere speck on the glass, a speck no larger than a pea, under which the spring lay hidden. I hunted and hunted. I felt as high as my hands could reach. Erik was about the same height as myself and I considered that he would not have placed the spring higher than suited his stature.

While groping over the successive panels with the greatest care, I endeavoured not to lose a minute, for I was feeling more and more overcome with the heat and we were literally roasting in that blazing forest.

I had been working like this for half an hour and had finished three panels, when, as ill-luck would have it, I turned round on hearing a muttered exclamation from the viscount:

'I am stifling,' he said. 'All these mirrors are sending out an infernal heat! . . . Do you think you will find that spring soon? . . . If you are much longer about it, we shall be roasted alive!'

I was not sorry to hear him talk like this. He had not said a word of the forest and I hoped that my companion's reason would hold out for some time longer against the torture. But he added:

'What consoles me is that the monster has given Christine until eleven to-morrow evening. If we can't get out of here and go to her assistance, at least we shall be dead before her! Then Erik's mass can serve for all of us!'

And he gulped down a breath of hot air that nearly made him faint.

As I had not the same desperate reasons as M le Vicomte de Chagny for accepting death, I returned to my panel, after giving him a word of encouragement; but I had made the mistake of taking a few steps while speaking and in the tangle of the illusive forest, I was no longer able to make sure of the panel! I had to begin all over again, at random, feeling, fumbling, groping.

Now the fever laid hold of me in my turn . . . for I found nothing, absolutely nothing. . . . In the next room, all was silence. We were utterly lost in the forest, without an outlet, a compass, a guide or anything. Oh, I knew what awaited us if nobody came to our aid . . . or if I did not find the spring! . . . But, look as I might, I found nothing but branches . . . beautiful branches that stood straight up before me or spread gracefully over my head . . . . But they gave no shade. And this was natural enough, as we were in an equatorial forest, with the sun right above our heads, an African forest. . . .

M de Chagny and I had repeatedly taken off our coats and put them on again, finding at one time that they made us still hotter and at another that they protected us against the heat. I continued to offer a moral resistance, but M de Chagny seemed to me quite 'gone.' He pretended that he had been walking in that forest for three days and nights, without stopping, looking for Christine Daaé! From time to time, he thought he saw her behind the trunk of a tree, or gliding between the branches; and he called to her with words of supplication that brought the tears to my eyes. And then, at last:

'Oh, how thirsty I am!' he cried, in delirious accents. I too was thirsty . . . my throat was on fire. . . . And, yet, squatting on the floor, I went on hunting, hunting, hunting for the spring of the invisible door . . . especially as it was dangerous to remain in the forest as evening drew nigh. . . . Already the shades of night were beginning to surround us. . . . It had happened very quickly – night falls quickly in tropical countries – suddenly, with hardly any twilight. . . .

Now night, in the forest of the equator, is always dangerous, particularly when, like ourselves, one has not the materials for a fire to keep off the beasts of prey. I did indeed try for a moment to break off the branches, which I would have lit with my dark lantern, but I knocked against the mirrors also and remembered, in time, that we had only images of branches to do with. . . .

The heat did not disappear with the daylight; on the contrary, it was now still hotter under the blue rays of the moon. I urged the viscount to hold our weapons ready to fire and not to stray from camp, while I went on looking for my spring.

Suddenly, we heard a lion roar a few yards away.

'Oh,' whispered the viscount, 'he is quite close! . . . Don't you see him? . . . There . . . through the trees . . . in that thicket! . . . If he roars again, I will fire! . . .'

And the roars were repeated, louder than before. And the viscount fired, but I do not think that he hit the lion; only, he smashed a mirror, as I perceived the next morning, at daybreak. We must have covered a good distance during the night, for we suddenly found ourselves on the edge of the desert, an immense desert of sand, stones and rocks. It was really not worth while leaving the forest to come upon the desert. Tired out, I flung myself down beside the viscount, for I had had enough of looking for springs which I could not find.

I was quite surprised – and I said so to the viscount – that we had encountered no other dangerous animals during the night. Usually, after the lion came the leopard and sometimes the buzz of the tsetse fly. These effects were easily obtained; and I explained to M de Chagny how Erik imitated the roar of a lion on a long tabour or timbrel, with an ass's skin at one end. Over this skin he tied a string of catgut, which was fastened at the middle to another similar string passing through the whole length of the tabour. Erik had only to rub this string with a glove smeared with resin and, according to the manner in which he rubbed it, he imitated to perfection the voice of the lion or the leopard, or even the buzzing of the tsetse fly.

The idea that Erik was probably in the room beside us, working his trick, made me suddenly resolve to enter into a parley with him, for we must obviously give up all thought of taking him by surprise. And, by this time, he must be quite aware who were the occupants of his torture chamber. I called him:

'Erik! Erik!'

I shouted as loud as I could across the desert, but there was no answer to my voice. . . . All around us lay the silence and the bare immensity of that stony desert. . . . What was to become of us in the midst of that awful solitude?

We were beginning literally to die of heat, hunger and thirst . . . of thirst especially. . . . At last, I saw M de Chagny raise himself on his elbow and point to a spot on the horizon. . . . He had discovered an oasis! . . .

Yes, far in the distance was an oasis . . . an oasis with limpid water, which reflected the iron tree! . . . Tush, it was the scene of the mirage. . . . I recognized it at once . . . the worst of all the three scenes! . . . No one had been able to fight against it . . . no one. . . . I did my utmost to keep my head *and not hope for water*, because I knew that, if a man hoped for water, the water that reflected the iron tree, and if, after hoping for water, he struck against the mirror, then there was but one thing for him to do: to hang himself on the iron tree! . . .

So I cried to M de Chagny:

'It's the mirage! . . . It's the mirage! . . . Don't believe in the water! . . . It's another trick of the mirrors! . . .'

Then he flatly told me to shut up, with my tricks of the mirrors, my springs, my revolving doors and my palaces of illusion! He angrily declared that I must be either blind or mad to imagine that all that water flowing over there, among those countless, splendid trees, was not real water! . . . And the desert was real! . . . And so was the forest! . . . And it was no use trying to take him in: he was an old, experienced traveller; he had been all over the place! . . .

And he dragged himself along, saying:

'Water! Water! . . .'

And his mouth was open, as though he were drinking. . . .

And my mouth was open too, as though I were drinking. . . .

For we not only saw the water, but *we heard it*! . . . We heard it flow, we heard it ripple! . . . Do you understand that word 'ripple'? . . . *It is a sound which you hear with your tongue!* . . . You put your tongue out of your mouth to listen to it better! . . .

Lastly – and this was the most pitiless torture of all – we heard the rain; and it was not raining! This was an infernal device. . . . Oh, I knew well enough how Erik obtained it! He filled with little stones a very long and narrow box, broken up inside with wooden and metal projections. The stones, in falling, struck against these projections and rebounded from one to the other; and the result was a series of pattering sounds exactly like a rainstorm.

Ah, you should have seen us putting out our tongues and dragging ourselves towards the rippling river-bank! Our eyes and ears were full of water, but our tongues were hard and dry as horn! . . .

When we reached the mirror, M de Chagny licked it . . . and I also licked the glass. . . .

It was burning hot! . . .

Then we rolled on the floor with a hoarse cry of despair. M de Chagny put the one pistol that was still loaded to his temple; and I stared at the Punjab lasso at the foot of the iron tree. I knew why the iron tree had returned, in this third change of scene! . . . The iron tree was waiting for me! . . .

But, as I stared at the Punjab lasso, I saw a thing that made me start so violently that M de Chagny delayed his attempt at suicide. I seized him by the arm. And then I caught the pistol from him . . . and then I dragged myself on my knees towards what I had seen.

I had discovered, near the Punjab lasso, in a groove in the floor, a black-headed nail whose use I knew. At last I had found the spring!

I felt the nail. . . . I lifted a radiant face to M de Chagny. . . . The black-headed nail yielded to my pressure. . . .

And then . . .

And then we saw, not a door opening in the wall, but a cellar-flap released in the floor. Cool air came up to us from the black hole below. We stooped over that square of darkness as though over a limpid well. With our chins in the cool shade, we drank it in.

And we bent lower and lower over the trap-door. What could there be in that cellar which opened before us? Water? Water to drink? . . .

I thrust my arm into the darkness and came upon a stone and another stone . . . a staircase . . . a dark staircase leading into the cellar. The viscount wanted to fling himself down the hole; but I, fearing a new trick of the monster's, stopped him, turned on my dark lantern and went down first.

The staircase was a winding one and led down into pitchy darkness. But oh, how deliciously cool were the darkness and the stairs! The lake could not be far away. . . .

We soon reached the bottom. . . . Our eyes were beginning to accustom themselves to the dark, to distinguish shapes around us . . . circular shapes . . . on which I turned the light of my lantern. . . .

Barrels!

We were in Erik's cellar: it was here that he must keep his wine and perhaps his drinking-water . . . . I knew that Erik was a great lover of good wine. . . . Ah, there was plenty to drink here! . . .

M de Chagny patted the round shapes and kept on saying:

'Barrels! Barrels! . . . What a lot of barrels! . . .'

Indeed, there was quite a number of them, symmetrically arranged in two rows, one on either side of us. They were small barrels and I thought that Erik must have selected them of that size to facilitate their carriage to the house on the lake. . . .

We examined them successively, to see if one of them had not a funnel, showing that it had been tapped at some time or another. But all the barrels were hermetically closed.

Then, after half lifting one to make sure that it was full, we went on our knees and, with the blade of a small knife which I carried, I prepared to stave in the bung-hole.

At that moment, I seemed to hear, coming from very far, a sort of monotonous chant which I knew well, for I had very often heard it in the streets of Paris:

'Barrels! . . . Barrels! . . . Any barrels to sell? . . .'

My hand desisted from its work. M de Chagny had also heard. He said:

'That's funny! . . . It sounds as if the barrel was singing! . . .'

The song was repeated, farther away:

'Barrels! . . . Barrels! . . . Any barrels to sell? . . .'

'Oh,' said the viscount, 'I swear the tune is dying away *inside* the barrel! . . .'

We stood up and went to look behind the barrel.

'It's *inside,*' said M de Chagny, 'it's *inside!*'

But we heard no more and were driven to accuse the disturbed condition of our senses. And we returned to the bunghole. M de Chagny put his two hands together underneath it and, with a last effort, I burst the bung.

'What's this?' cried the viscount. 'This isn't water!'

The viscount put his two full hands close to my lantern. . . . I stopped to look . . . and, at the same moment, flung away my lantern with such violence that it broke and went out, leaving us in utter darkness. . . .

What I had seen in M de Chagny's hands . . . was gunpowder!

CHAPTER XXV

Which Shall She Turn?

The Persian's Narrative concluded

THE DISCOVERY FLUNG US into a state of alarm that made us forget all our past and present sufferings. We now knew what the monster meant to convey when he said to Christine Daaé:

'Yes or no! If your answer is no, everybody will be dead *and buried!*'

Yes, buried under the ruins of the Paris Opera-house!

The monster had given her until eleven o'clock in the evening. He had chosen his time well. There would be many people up there, many 'of the human race' in the brilliant theatre. What finer attendance could he expect at his funeral? He would go down to the tomb escorted by the whitest shoulders in the world, decked with the richest jewels. . . .

Eleven o'clock to-morrow evening! . . .

We were all to be blown up in the middle of the performance . . . if Christine Daaé said no!

Eleven o'clock to-morrow evening! . . .

And what else could Christine say but no? Would she not prefer to espouse death itself rather than that living corpse? She did not know that on her acceptance or refusal depended the awful fate of many members of the human race! . . .

Eleven o'clock to-morrow evening! . . .

And we dragged ourselves through the darkness, feeling our way to the stone steps, for the light in the trap-door overhead that led to the room of mirrors was now extinguished; and we repeated to ourselves:

'Eleven o'clock to-morrow evening! . . .'

At last, I found the staircase . . . but, suddenly, I drew myself up on the first step, for a terrible thought had come to my mind:

'What is the time?'

Yes, what was the time? . . . For, after all, eleven o'clock to-morrow evening might be now, might be this very moment! . . . Who could tell us the time? We seemed to have been imprisoned in that hell for days and days . . . for years . . . since the beginning of the world. . . . Perhaps we should be blown up then and there! . . . Ah, a sound! . . . A crack!

'Did you hear that? . . . There, in the corner . . . good heavens! . . . Like a sound of machinery! . . . Again! . . . Oh, for a light! . . . Perhaps it's the machinery that is to blow everything up! . . . I tell you, a cracking sound: are you deaf?'

M de Chagny and I began to yell like madmen. . . . Fear spurred us on. . . We rushed up the treads of the staircase, stumbling as we went . . . anything to escape the dark, to return to the mortal light of the room of mirrors! . . .

We found the trap-door still open, but it was now as dark in the room of mirrors as in the cellar which we had left. . . . We dragged ourselves along the floor of the torture-chamber, the floor between us and the powder-magazine. . . . What was the time? . . . We shouted, we called out: M de Chagny to Christine, I to Erik. I reminded him that I had saved his life. . . . But no answer, save the echoing cry of our despair, our madness: what was the time? We argued, we tried to calculate the time which we had spent there . . . but we were incapable of reasoning. . . . If only we could see the face of a watch! . . . Mine had stopped, but M de Chagny's was still going. . . . He told me that he had wound it up before dressing for the Opera. . . . We had not a match upon us. . . . And yet we must know. . . . M de Chagny broke the glass of his watch and felt the two hands. . . . He questioned the hands of the watch with his finger-tips, going by the position of the ring of the watch. . . . Judging by the space between the hands, he thought it might be just eleven o'clock! . . .

But perhaps it was not the eleven o'clock of which we stood in dread. . . . Perhaps we had still twelve hours before us! . . .

Suddenly, I exclaimed:

'Hush!'

I thought I heard footsteps in the next room. Some one tapped against the wall. Christine Daaé's voice said:

'Raoul! Raoul!'

We now all began to talk at once, on either side of the wall. Christine sobbed: she had not felt sure that she would find M de Chagny alive. . . . The monster had been terrible, it seemed, had done nothing but rave, waiting for her to give him the 'yes' which she refused. And yet she had promised him that 'yes,' if he would take her to the torture-chamber. But he had obstinately declined and had uttered hideous threats against all the members of the human race! . . . At last, after hours and hours of that hell, he had this moment gone out . . . leaving her alone to reflect for the last time. . . .

'Hours and hours? What is the time now? What is the time, Christine?'

'It is eleven o'clock! . . . Eleven o'clock, all but five minutes!'

'But which eleven o'clock?'

'The eleven o'clock that is to decide life or death! . . . He told me so before he went. . . . He is terrible. . . . He is quite mad: he tore off his mask and his yellow eyes shot flames! . . . He did nothing but laugh! . . . He said, "Five minutes! I leave you alone, to spare your blushes! Here," he said, taking a key from the little bag of life and death, "here is the little bronze key that opens the two ebony caskets on the mantelpiece in the Louis-Philippe room. . . . In one of the caskets, you will find a scorpion, in the other, a grasshopper, both very cleverly done in Japanese bronze: they will say yes or no for you. If you turn the scorpion I shall understand, when I come back, that you have said yes. The grasshopper will mean no." And he laughed like a drunken demon. I did nothing but beg and entreat him to give me the key of the torture-chamber, promising to be his wife if he granted me this request. . . . But he told me that there was no further need for that key and that he was going to throw it into the lake! . . . And he again laughed like a drunken demon and left me. . . . Oh, his last words were, "The grasshopper! . . . Mind the grasshopper! . . . A grasshopper not only turns: it hops! . . . It hops! . . . And it hops jolly high!"'

The five minutes had nearly elapsed and the scorpion and the

grasshopper were scratching at my brain. Nevertheless, I had suf-
ficient lucidity left to understand that, if the grasshopper were
turned, it would hop . . . and with it many members of the race!
There was no doubt that the grasshopper controlled an electric
current intended to blow up the powder magazine! . . .

M de Chagny, who seemed to have recovered all his strength of
mind at hearing Christine's voice, explained to her, in a few hurried words, the situation in which we and all the Opera were. . . .
He told her to turn the scorpion at once. . . .

There was a pause.

'Christine,' I cried, 'where are you?'

'By the scorpion.'

'Don't touch it!'

The idea had come to me – for I knew my Erik – that the monster had perhaps deceived the girl once more. Perhaps it was the
scorpion that would blow everything up. After all, why wasn't he
there? The five minutes were long past . . . and he was not back. . . .
Perhaps he had taken shelter and was waiting for the explosion! . . .
Why had he not returned? . . . He could not really expect Christine ever to consent to become his voluntary prey! . . . Why had he
not returned?

'Don't touch the scorpion!' I said.

'Here he comes!' cried Christine. 'I hear him! Here he is! . . .'

We heard his steps approaching the Louis-Philippe room. He
came up to Christine, but did not speak. Then I raised my voice:

'Erik! It is I! Do you know me?'

With extraordinary calmness, he at once replied:

'*So you are not dead in there?* . . . Well, then, keep quiet!'

I tried to speak, but he said, coldly:

'Not a word, daroga, or I shall blow everything up.' And he
added, 'The honour rests with mademoiselle. . . . Mademoiselle
has not touched the scorpion' – how deliberately he spoke! –
'mademoiselle has not touched the grasshopper' – with what com-
posure! – 'but it is not too late to do the right thing. There, I open
the caskets without a key, for I am a trap-door lover and I open
and shut what I please and as I please . . . . I open the little ebony
caskets; mademoiselle, look at the little dears inside. Aren't they
pretty? . . . If you turn the grasshopper, mademoiselle, we shall all
be blown up. . . . There is enough gunpowder under our feet to
blow up a whole section of Paris. . . . If you turn the scorpion,
mademoiselle, all that powder will be soaked and drowned. . . .
Mademoiselle, to celebrate our wedding, you shall make a very

handsome present to a few hundred Parisians who are at this moment applauding a poor masterpiece of Meyerbeer's: you shall make them a present of their lives. . . . For, with your own fair hands, you shall turn the scorpion. . . . And merrily, merrily, we will be married!'

A pause; and then:

'If, in two minutes, mademoiselle, you have not turned the scorpion, I shall turn the grasshopper . . . and the grasshopper, I tell you, *hops jolly high!* . . .'

The terrible silence began anew. The Vicomte de Chagny, realizing that there was nothing left to do but pray, went down on his knees and prayed. As for me, my blood beat so fiercely that I had to take my heart in both my hands, lest it should burst. . . .

At last, we heard Erik's voice:

'The two minutes are past. . . . Good-bye, mademoiselle! . . . Hop, grasshopper! . . .'

'Erik,' cried Christine, 'do you swear to me, monster, do you swear to me that the scorpion is the one to turn? . . .'

'Yes, to hop at our wedding. . . .'

'Ah, you see! You said, to hop!'

'At our wedding, ingenuous child! . . . The scorpion opens the ball . . . . But that will do! . . . You won't have the scorpion? Then I turn the grasshopper!'

'Erik!'

'Enough!'

I was crying out in concert with Christine. M de Chagny was still on his knees, praying.

'Erik! I have turned the scorpion!'

Oh, the second through which we passed!

Waiting!

Waiting to find ourselves in fragments, amid the roar and the ruins! . . .

Feeling something crack beneath our feet, hearing an appalling hiss through the open trap door, a hiss like the first sound of a rocket!

It came softly, at first, then louder, then very loud. . . .

But it was not the hiss of fire.

It was more like the hiss of water.

And now it became a gurgling sound:

'Guggle! Guggle!'

We rushed to the trap-door. All our thirst, which had vanished when the terror came, now returned with the lapping of the water.

The water rose in the cellar, above the barrels, the powder barrels – 'Barrels! . . . Barrels! . . . Any barrels to sell?' – and we went down to it with parched throats. It rose to our chins, to our mouths. And we drank. We stood on the floor of the cellar and we drank. And we went up the stairs again in the dark, step by step, went up with the water. . . .

The water came out of the cellar with us and spread over the floor of the room. . . . If this went on, the whole house on the lake would be swamped. The floor of the torture-chamber had itself become a regular little lake, in which our feet splashed. Surely there was water enough now! Erik must turn off the tap!

'Erik! Erik! That is water enough for the gun-powder! Turn off the tap! Turn off the scorpion!'

But Erik did not reply. . . . We heard nothing but the water rising: it was half-way up to our waists!

'Christine!' cried M de Chagny. 'Christine! The water is up to our knees!'

But Christine did not reply. . . . We heard nothing but the water rising.

No one, no one in the next room, no one to turn the tap, no one to turn the scorpion!

We were all alone, in the dark, with the dark water that seized us and clasped us and froze us!

'Erik! Erik!'

'Christine! Christine!'

By this time, we had lost our foothold and were spinning round in the water, carried away by an irresistible whirl, for the water turned with us and dashed us against the dark mirrors, which thrust us back again; and our throats, raised above the whirlpool, roared aloud. . . .

Were we to die here, drowned in the torture-chamber? . . . I had never seen that. Erik, at the time of the rosy hours of Mazenderan, had never shown me that, through the little invisible window.

'Erik! Erik!' I cried. 'I saved your life! Remember! . . . You were sentenced to death! . . . But for me, you would be dead now! . . . Erik!'

We whirled round in the water like so much wreckage. But, suddenly, my straying hands seized the trunk of the iron tree! I called M de Chagny and we both clung to the branch of the iron tree.

And the water rose still higher.

'Oh! Oh! Can you remember? How much space is there between the branch of the tree and the dome-shaped ceiling? Do try to remember! . . . After all, the water may stop, it must find its level! . . . There, I think it is stopping! . . . No, no, oh, horrible! . . . Swim! Swim for your life!'

Our arms became entangled in the effort of swimming; we choked; we struggled in the dark water; already we could hardly breathe the dark air above the dark water, the air which escaped, which we could hear escaping through some vent-hole or other. . . .

'Oh, let us turn and turn until we find the air-hole and then glue our mouths to it!'

But I lost my strength, I tried to lay hold of the walls! Oh, how those glass walls slipped from under my groping fingers! . . . We whirled round again! . . . We began to sink! . . . One last effort! . . . A last cry:

'Erik! . . . Christine! . . .'

'Guggle, guggle, guggle!' in our ears. 'Guggle! Guggle!' At the bottom of the dark water, our ears went, 'Guggle! Guggle!'

And, before losing consciousness entirely, I seemed to hear, between two gurgles:

'Barrels! . . . Barrels! . . . Any barrels to sell? . . .'

CHAPTER XXVI

The End Of The Ghost

THE PREVIOUS CHAPTER marks the conclusion of the written narrative which the Persian left behind.

Notwithstanding the horrors of a situation which seemed definitely to abandon them to their deaths, M de Chagny and his companion were saved by the sublime devotion of Christine Daaé. I had the rest of the story from the lips of the daroga himself.

When I went to see him, he was still living in his little flat in the Rue de Rivoli, opposite the Tuileries. He was very ill and it took all my ardour as an historian pledged to tell the truth to persuade him to live the incredible tragedy over again for my benefit. His faithful old servant Darius showed me in. The daroga received me at a window overlooking the garden of the Tuileries. He still had his magnificent eyes, but his poor face looked very worn. He had shaved the whole of his head, which was usually covered with an astrakhan cap; he was dressed in a long, very plain coat and amused himself by unconsciously twisting his thumbs inside the sleeves; but his mind was quite clear and he told me his story with perfect lucidity, as follows.

It seems that, when he opened his eyes, the daroga found himself lying on a bed. M de Chagny was asleep on a sofa, beside the wardrobe. An angel and a devil were watching over them. . . .

After the deceptions and illusions of the torture-chamber, the precision of the middle-class details in that quiet little room seemed invented for the express purpose of once more puzzling the mind of the mortal rash enough to stray into that abode of living nightmare. The wooden bedstead, the beeswaxed mahogany chairs, the chest of drawers, the brasses, the little square anti-macassars carefully placed on the backs of the chairs, the clock on the mantelpiece and the harmless-looking ebony caskets at either end . . . lastly, the what-not filled with shells, with red pin-cushions, with mother-of-pearl boats and an enormous ostrich-egg . . . the whole discreetly lighted by a shaded lamp standing on a small round table: this collection of ugly, peaceable, reasonable furniture, *at the bottom of the Opera cellars*, bewildered the imagination more than all the late fantastic happenings.

And the figure of the masked man seemed all the more formidable in this old-fashioned, neat and trim little frame. It bent down over the Persian and said in his ear:

'Are you better, daroga? . . . You are looking at my furniture? . . . It is all I have left of my poor unhappy mother. . . .'

Christine Daaé did not say a word: she moved about noiselessly, like a sister of charity who had taken a vow of silence. She brought a cup of cordial, or of hot tea, he did not remember which. The man in the mask took it from her hands and gave it to the Persian. M de Chagny was still sleeping.

Erik poured a drop of rum into the daroga's cup and, pointing to the viscount, said:

'He came to himself long before we knew if you were still alive, daroga. He is quite well. He is asleep. We must not wake him. . . .

Erik left the room for a moment and the Persian raised himself on his elbow, looked around him and saw Christine Daaé sitting by the fireside. He spoke to her, called her . . . but he was still very weak and fell back on his pillow. Christine came to him, laid her hand on his forehead and went away again. And the Persian remembered that, as she went, she did not so much as glance at M de Chagny, who, it is true, was sleeping peacefully; and she sat down again in her chair by the chimney-corner, silent as a sister of charity who had taken a vow of silence. . . .

Erik returned with some little bottles which he placed on the mantelpiece. And, again in a whisper, so as not to wake M de Chagny, he said to the Persian, after sitting down and feeling his pulse:

'You are now saved, both of you. And soon I shall take you up to the surface of the earth, *to please my wife.*'

Thereupon he rose, without further explanation, and disappeared once more.

The Persian now looked at Christine's quiet profile under the lamp. She was reading a tiny book, with gilt edges, like a religious book. There are editions of the *Imitation* that look like that. The Persian still had in his ears the natural tone in which the other had said, 'to please my wife.' Very gently, he called her again; but Christine was rapt in her book and did not hear him. . . .

Erik returned, mixed the daroga a draught and advised him not to speak to 'his wife' again nor to any one, *because it might be very dangerous to everybody's health.*

Eventually, the Persian fell asleep, like M de Chagny, and did not wake until he was in his own room, nursed by his faithful Darius, who told him that, on the night before, he was found propped against the door of his flat, where he had been brought by a stranger who rang the bell before going away.

As soon as the daroga recovered his strength and his wits, he sent to Count Philippe's house to enquire after the viscount's health. The answer was that the young man had not been seen and that Count Philippe was dead. His body was found on the bank of the Opera lake, on the Rue-Scribe side. The Persian remembered the requiem mass which he had heard from behind the wall of the torture-chamber and had no doubt regarding the crime and the criminal. Knowing Erik as he did, he easily reconstructed the tragedy. Thinking that his brother had run away with Christine Daaé, Philippe must have dashed in pursuit of him along the Brussels road, where he knew that everything was prepared for the elopement. Failing to find the pair, he hurried back to the Opera, remembered Raoul's strange confidence about his fantastic rival and learnt that the viscount had made every effort to enter the cellars of the theatre and that he had disappeared, leaving his hat in the prima donna's dressing-room beside an empty pistol-case. And the count, who no longer entertained any doubt of his brother's madness, in his turn darted into that infernal underground maze. This was enough, in the Persian's eyes, to explain the discovery of the Comte de Chagny's corpse on the shore of the lake, where the siren, Erik's siren, kept watch.

The Persian did not hesitate. He determined to inform the police. Now the case was in the hands of an examining magistrate called Faure, an incredulous, commonplace, superficial sort of person (I write as I think), with a mind utterly unprepared to receive a confidence of this kind. M Faure took down the daroga's depositions and proceeded to treat him as a madman.

Despairing of ever obtaining a hearing, the Persian sat down to write. As the police did not want his evidence, perhaps the press would be glad of it; and he had just written the last line of the narrative which I have quoted in the preceding chapters, when Darius announced the visit of a stranger who refused his name, who would not show his face and who declared simply that he did not intend to leave the place until he had spoken to the daroga. The Persian at once felt who his singular visitor was and ordered him to be shown in. The daroga was right. It was the ghost, it was Erik.

He looked extremely weak and leant against the wall, as though afraid of falling. Taking off his hat, he revealed a forehead white as wax. The rest of the face was hidden by the mask.

The Persian rose to his feet as Erik entered:

'Murderer of Count Philippe, what have you done with his brother and Christine Daaé?'

Erik staggered under the direct attack, kept silent for a moment, dragged himself to a chair and heaved a deep sigh. Then, speaking in short phrases and gasping for breath between the words:

'Daroga, don't talk to me . . . about Count Philippe. . . . He was dead . . . by the time . . . I left my house . . . he was dead . . . when . . . the siren sang. . . . It was an . . . accident . . . a sad . . . a very sad . . . accident. . . . He fell very awkwardly . . . but simply and naturally . . . into the lake! . . .'

'You lie!' shouted the Persian.

Erik bowed his head and said:

'I have not come here . . . to talk about Count Philippe . . . but to tell you that . . . I am going . . . to die. . . .'

'Where are Raoul de Chagny and Christine Daaé? . . .'

'I am going to die. . . .'

'Raoul de Chagny and Christine Daaé?' . . .

'Of love . . . daroga. . . . I am dying . . . of love. . . . That is how it is. . . . I loved her so! . . . And I love her still . . . daroga . . . and I am dying of love for her, I . . . tell you! . . . If you knew how beautiful she was . . . when she let me kiss her . . . alive. . . . It was the first . . . time, daroga, the first . . . time I ever kissed a woman. . . . Yes, alive . . . I kissed her alive . . . and she looked as beautiful as if she had been dead! . . .'

The Persian shook Erik by the arm:

'Will you tell me if she is alive or dead?'

'Why do you shake me like that?' asked Erik, making an effort to speak more connectedly. 'I tell you I am going to die . . . . Yes, I kissed her alive. . . .'

'And now she is dead?'

'I tell you I kissed her just like that, on her forehead . . . and she did not draw back her forehead from my lips! . . . Oh, she is a good girl! . . . As to her being dead, I don't think so; but it has nothing to do with me. . . . No, no, she is not dead! And no one shall touch a hair of her head! She is a good, honest girl and she saved your life, daroga, at a moment when I would not have given twopence for your Persian skin. After all, who cared about you? What were you there for, with that little chap? You would have died as well as he! . . . My word, how she entreated me on behalf of her little chap! But I told her that, as she had turned the scorpion, she had, through that very fact and of her own free will, become engaged to me and that she did not want two men engaged to her, which was true enough. . . . As for you, you did not exist, you had ceased to exist, I tell you, and you were going to die with the other! . . . Only, mark me, daroga, when you were yelling like the devil, because of the water, Christine came to me, with her beautiful blue eyes wide open, and swore to me, as she hoped to be saved, that she would be *my living wife*! . . . Until then, in the depths of her eyes, daroga, I had always seen my dead wife; it was the first time I saw *my living wife* there. She was sincere, as she hoped to be saved. She would not kill herself. It was a bargain. . . . Half a minute later, all the water was back in the lake; and I had a hard job with you, daroga, for, upon my honour, I thought you were done for! . . . However! . . . There you were! . . . It was understood that I was to take you both up to the surface of the earth. When at last, I cleared the Louis-Philippe room of you, I came back alone. . . .'

'What have you done with the Vicomte de Chagny?' asked the Persian, interrupting him.

'Ah, you see, daroga, I couldn't carry him up like that at once. . . . He was a hostage. . . . But I could not keep him in the house on the lake either, because of Christine; so I locked him up comfortably, I chained him up nicely – a whiff of the Mazenderan perfume had left him as limp as a rag – in the Communists' dungeon, which is in the most remote and deserted part of the Opera, below the fifth cellar, where no one ever comes and no one ever hears you. Then I went back to Christine. She was waiting for me. . . .

Erik here rose solemnly. Then he continued, but, as he spoke, he was overcome by all his former emotion and began to tremble all over like a leaf:

'Yes, she was waiting for me . . . waiting for me erect and alive, a real, living bride . . . as she hoped to be saved. . . . And, when I . . . came forward, more timid than . . . a little child, she did not run away . . . no, no . . . she stayed . . . she waited for me. . . . I even believe . . . daroga . . . that she put out her forehead . . . a little . . . oh, not much . . . just a little . . . like a living bride. . . . And . . . and . . . I . . . kissed her! . . . I! . . . I! . . . I! . . . And, she did not die! . . . Oh, how good it is, daroga, to kiss a person! . . . You can't tell, you can't! . . . But I! I! . . . My mother, daroga, my poor, unhappy mother would never . . . let me kiss her. . . . She used to run away . . . and throw me my mask! . . . Nor any other woman . . . ever, ever! . . . Ah, you can understand, my happiness was so great, I cried. . . . And I fell at her feet, crying . . . and I kissed her feet . . . her little feet . . . crying. . . . You're crying too, daroga . . . and she also cried . . . the angel cried! . . .'

Erik sobbed aloud and the Persian himself could not restrain his tears in the presence of that masked man, who, with his shoulders shaking and his hands clutching at his chest, was moaning with pain and love by turns:

'Yes, daroga . . . I felt her tears flow on my forehead . . . on my forehead, my forehead, mine! . . . They were hot . . . they were sweet! . . . They trickled under my mask . . . they mingled with the tears in my eyes . . . they flowed between my lips. . . . Listen, daroga, listen to what I did. . . . I tore off my mask so as not to lose one of her tears . . . and she did not run away! . . . And she did not die! . . . She remained alive . . . weeping . . . over me . . . with me. . . . We cried together! I have tasted all the happiness the world can offer! . . .'

And Erik fell into a chair, choking for breath:

'Ah, I am not going to die yet . . . presently I shall . . . but let me cry! . . . Listen, daroga . . . listen to this . . . . While I was at her feet . . . I heard her say . . . "Poor, unhappy Erik!" . . . *And she took my hand!* . . . I had become no more, you know, than a poor dog ready to die for her. . . . I mean it, daroga! . . . I held in my hand a ring, a plain gold ring which I had given her . . . which she had lost . . . and which I had found again . . . a wedding-ring, you know. . . . I slipped it into her little hand and said, "There! . . . Take it! . . . Take it for you . . . and him! . . . It shall be my wedding-present . . . a present from your poor, unhappy Erik. . . . I know you love the boy . . . don't cry any more!" . . . She asked me, in a very soft voice, what I meant. . . . Then I made her understand that, where she was concerned, I was only a poor dog, ready to die for her . . . and that she should marry the young man when she pleased, because she had cried with me and mingled her tears with mine! . . .'

Erik's emotion was so great that he had to tell the Persian not to look at him, for he was choking and must take off his mask. The daroga went to the window and opened it. His heart was full of pity, but he took care to keep his eyes fixed on the trees in the Tuileries gardens, lest he should see the monster's face.

'I went and released the young man,' Erik continued, 'and told him to come with me to Christine. . . . They kissed before me in the Louis-Philippe room. . . . Christine had my ring. . . . I made Christine swear to come back, one night when I was dead, crossing the lake from the Rue-Scribe side, and bury me in the greatest secrecy with the gold ring, which she was to wear until that moment. . . . I told her where she would find my body and what to do with it. . . . Then Christine kissed me, for the first time, herself, here, on the forehead – don't look, daroga! – here, on the forehead . . . on my forehead, my forehead, mine – don't look, daroga! – and they went off together. . . . Christine had stopped crying. . . . I alone cried. . . . Daroga, daroga, if Christine keeps her promise, she will come back soon! . . .'

Erik ceased speaking. The Persian asked him no questions. He was quite reassured as to the fate of Raoul de Chagny and Christine Daaé: no one could have doubted the word of the weeping Erik that night.

The monster resumed his mask and collected his strength to leave the daroga. He told him that, when he felt his end to be close at hand, he would send him, in gratitude for the kindness which the Persian had once shown him, the things which he held dearest in the world: all Christine Daaé's papers, letters which she had written to Raoul, at the time of that adventure, and left with Erik, together with a few objects belonging to her, such as a pair of gloves, a shoe-buckle and two pocket-handkerchiefs. In reply to the Persian's question, Erik told him that the young people, as soon as they found themselves free, had resolved to go and look for a priest in some lonely spot where they could hide their happiness and that, with this object in view, they had started from 'the northern railway-station of the world.' Lastly, Erik relied on the Persian, as soon as he received the promised relics and papers, to inform the young couple of his death and to advertise it in the *Epoque*.

That was all. The Persian saw Erik to the door of his flat and Darius helped him down to the street. A cab was waiting for him. Erik stepped in; and the Persian, who had gone back to the window, heard him say to the driver:

'Go to the Opera.'

And the cab drove off into the night.

The Persian had seen the poor, unhappy Erik for the last time. Three weeks later, the *Epoque* published this advertisement:

'ERIK IS DEAD.'

EPILOGUE

I HAVE NOW TOLD the singular, but veracious story of the Opera ghost. As I declared on the first page of this work, it is no longer possible to deny that Erik really lived. There are now so many proofs of his existence, within the reach of all, that we can trace Erik's actions logically throughout the tragedy of the Chagnys.

There is no need here to repeat how greatly the case excited the capital. The kidnapping of the singer, the death of the Comte de Chagny under such exceptional conditions, the disappearance of his brother, the drugging of the gas-man at the Opera and of his two assistants: what tragedies, what passions, what crimes had surrounded the idyll of Raoul and his sweet and charming Christine! . . . What had become of that wonderful, mysterious artist of whom the world was never, never to hear again? . . . She was represented as the victim of a rivalry between the two brothers; and nobody suspected what had really happened, nobody realized that, as Raoul and Christine had both disappeared, they had both retired far from the world to enjoy a happiness which they would not have cared to make public after Count Philippe's unaccountable death. . . . They took the train one day from 'the northern railway-station of the world.' . . . Possibly, I too shall take the train at that station, one day, and go and seek around thy lakes, O Norway, O silent Scandinavia, for the perhaps still living traces of Raoul and Christine and also of Mamma Valerius, who disappeared at the same time! . . . Possibly, some day, I shall hear the lonely mountains of the north echo the singing of her who knew the Angel of Music! . . .

Long after the case was pigeon-holed by that most unintelligent magistrate, M Faure, the newspapers made desultory efforts to fathom the mystery. One evening-paper alone – a paper which made a feature of theatrical gossip – said:

'We recognize the touch of the Opera ghost.'

And even that was written ironically!

The Persian alone knew the whole truth and held the main evidence, which came to him with the pious relics promised by the ghost. It fell to my lot to complete that evidence with the aid of the daroga himself. Day by day, I kept him informed of the progress of my enquiries, which he himself directed. He had not been to the Opera for years and years, but he had preserved the most accurate recollection of the building and there was no better guide than he to help me discover its most secret recesses. He also told me where to gather further information, whom to ask; and he sent me to call on M Poligny, at a moment when the poor man was almost on the point of drawing his last breath. I had no idea that he was so very ill and I shall never forget the effect which my questions about the ghost produced upon him. He looked at me as if I were the devil and answered only in a few incoherent sentences, which showed, however – and that was the main thing – the extent of the perturbation which 'O.G.,' in his time, had wrought in that already very restless life (for M Poligny was what people call a man of pleasure).

When I came and told the Persian of the poor results of my visit to M Poligny, the daroga gave a faint smile and said:

'Poligny never knew the full extent to which that extraordinary scoundrel of an Erik humbugged him.' – The Persian, by the way, spoke of Erik sometimes as a demi-god and sometimes as the lowest of the low – 'Poligny was superstitious and Erik knew it.

Erik knew most things about the public and private affairs of the Opera. When M Poligny heard a mysterious voice tell him, in Box 5, of the manner in which he used to spend his time and abuse his partner's confidence, he did not wait to hear more. Thinking at first that it was a voice from heaven, he believed himself damned; and then, when the voice began to ask for money, he saw that he was being victimized by a shrewd blackmailer to whom Debienne himself had fallen a prey. Both of them, already tired of management for various reasons, resigned without trying to pry further into the personality of that curious O. G., who had added such a singular set of clauses to their lease. They bequeathed the whole mystery to their successors and heaved a sigh of relief when they were rid of a business that had bothered them, without providing them with the least amusement

I then spoke of their two successors and expressed my surprise that, in his *Memoirs of a Manager*, M Moncharmin should describe the Opera ghost's behaviour at such length in the first part of the book and hardly mention it in the second. In reply to this, the Persian, who knew the Memoirs as thoroughly as if he had written them himself, observed that I should find the explanation of the whole matter if I would just recollect the few lines which Moncharmin devotes to the ghost in the second part aforesaid. I quote these lines, which are particularly interesting because they describe the very simple manner in which the famous incident of the twenty-thousand francs was closed:

'As for O.G., some of whose curious tricks I have related in the first part of my Memoirs, I will only say that he atoned by one spontaneous fine action for all the worry which he had caused my dear friend and partner and, I am bound to say, myself. He felt, no doubt, that there are limits to a jest, especially when it is so expensive and when the commissary of police has been informed, for, a few days after the disappearance of Christine Daaé, when we had made an appointment in our office with M Mifroid to tell him the whole story, we found, on Richard's table, a large envelope, inscribed, in red ink, *"With O. G.'s compliments."* It contained the large sum of money which he had playfully succeeded in extracting, for the time being, from the treasury. Richard at once declared that we must be content with that and drop the subject. I agreed with Richard. All's well that ends well. What say you, O. G.?'

Of course, Moncharmin continued to believe, especially after the money had been restored, that he had been, for a little while, the butt of Firmin Richard's sense of humour, whereas Richard, on his side, was convinced that Moncharmin had amused himself by inventing the whole affair of the Opera ghost, in order to revenge himself for a few jokes.

I asked the Persian to tell me by what trick the ghost had taken twenty-thousand francs from Richard's pocket in spite of the safety-pin. He replied that he had not gone into this little detail, but that, if I myself cared to make an investigation on the spot, I should certainly find the solution to the riddle in the managers' office by remembering that Erik had not been nicknamed the trap-door lover for nothing. I promised the Persian to do so as soon as I had time; and I can tell the reader at once that the results of my investigation were perfectly satisfactory. In fact, I hardly thought that I should ever discover so many undeniable proofs of the authenticity of the feats ascribed to the ghost.

The Persian's manuscript; Christine Daaé's papers; the statements made to me by the people who used to work under MM Richard and Moncharmin, by little Meg herself (the worthy Mme Giry, I am sorry to say, is no more) and by Sorelli, who is now living in retirement at Louveciennes: all these documents relating to the existence of the ghost, which I propose to deposit in the archives of the Opera, have been checked and confirmed by a number of important discoveries of which I am justly proud.

I have not been able to find the house on the lake, Erik having definitely blocked up all the secret entrances.[1] On the other hand, I have discovered the secret passage of the Communists, the planking of which is falling to pieces in parts, and also the trap-door through which Raoul and the Persian penetrated into the cellars of the Opera-house. In the Communists' dungeon, I noticed numbers of initials traced on the walls by the poor wretches confined in it; and among these were an 'R' and a 'C' – R. C.: Raoul de Chagny! The letters are there to this day.

If the reader will visit the Opera one morning and ask leave to

[1] Even so, I am convinced that it would be easy to reach it by draining the lake, as I have repeatedly requested the Ministry of Fine-Arts to do. I was speaking about it to M Dujardin-Beaumetz, the under-secretary for fine-arts, only forty-eight hours before the first serial publication of this book. He was interested and gave me some hope. There is no doubt that Erik was an incomparable artist. Who knows but that the score of *Don Juan Triumphant* might yet be discovered in the house on the lake?

stroll about where he pleases, without being accompanied by a stupid guide, let him go to Box 5 and knock with his stick or knuckles on the enormous column that separates this from the stagebox. He will find that the column sounds hollow. After that do not be astonished by the suggestion that it was occupied by the voice of the ghost: there is room inside the column for two men. If you are surprised that, when the various incidents occurred, no one turned round to look at the column, you must remember that it presented the appearance of solid marble and that the voice contained in it seemed rather to come from the opposite side, for, as we have seen, the ghost was an expert ventriloquist. The column is elaborately carved and decorated with the artist's chisel; and I do not despair of one day discovering that the piece of sculpture could be raised or lowered at will, so as to give passage to the ghost's mysterious correspondence with Mame Giry and to his generous tips.

However, all these discoveries are nothing, to my mind, compared with that which I was able to make, in the presence of the acting-manager, in the managers' office, within a couple of inches from the desk-chair. It consisted of a trap-door, the width of a board in the flooring and the length of a man's forearm and no longer; a trap-door that falls back like the lid of a box: a trap-door through which I can see a hand come and dexterously fumble at the pocket of a swallow-tail coat. . . .

That is the way the forty-thousand francs went! . . . And that also is the way by which, through some trick or other, they were returned. . . .

Speaking about this to the Persian, I said:

'So we may take it, since the forty-thousand francs was returned, that Erik was simply amusing himself with that amended lease of his?'

'Don't you believe it!' he replied. 'Erik wanted money. Thinking himself without the pale of humanity, he was restrained by no scruples and he employed the extraordinary gifts of dexterity and imagination which he had received by way of compensation for his extraordinary ugliness to prey upon his fellow-men. His reason for restoring the forty-thousand francs of his own accord was that he no longer needed it. He had relinquished his marriage with Christine Daaé. He had relinquished everything above the surface of the earth.'

According to the Persian's account, Erik was born in a small town not far from Rouen. He was the son of a master-mason. He ran away at an early age from his father's house, where his ugliness was a subject of horror and terror to his parents. For a time, he frequented the fairs, where a showman exhibited him as the 'living corpse.' He seems to have crossed the whole of Europe, from fair to fair, and to have completed his strange education as an artist and magician at the very fountain-head of art and magic, among the gipsies. A period of Erik's life remained quite obscure. He was seen at the fair of Nijni-Novgorod, where he displayed himself in all his hideous glory. He already sang as nobody on this earth had ever sung before; he practised ventriloquism and gave displays of legerdemain so extraordinary that the caravans returning to Asia talked about it during the whole length of their journey. In this way, his reputation penetrated the walls of the palace at Mazenderan, where the little sultana, the favourite of the Shah-in-Shah, was boring herself to death. A fur-trader, returning to Samarkand from Nijni-Novgorod, told of the marvels which he had seen performed in Erik's tent. The trader was summoned to the palace and the Daroga of Mazenderan was told to question him. Next, the daroga was instructed to go and find Erik. He brought him to Persia, where, for some months, Erik's will was law. He was guilty of not a few horrors, for he seemed not to know the difference between good and evil. He took part calmly in a number of political assassinations; and he turned his diabolical inventive powers against the Emir of Afghanistan, who was at war with the Persian Empire. The Shah took a liking to him.

This was the time of the rosy hours of Mazenderan, of which the daroga's narrative has given us a glimpse. Erik had very original ideas on the subject of architecture and thought out a palace much as a conjuror contrives a trick-casket. The Shah ordered him to construct an edifice of this kind. Erik did so; and the building appears to have been so ingenious that His Majesty was able to move about in it unseen and to disappear without a possibility of the trick's being discovered. When the Shah-in-Shah found himself the possessor of this gem, he ordered Erik's yellow eyes to be put out. But he reflected that, even though blind, Erik would still be able to build another, equally remarkable house for another sovereign; and also that, as long as Erik was alive, there would be some one who knew the secret of the wonderful palace. Erik's death was therefore decided upon, together with that of all the labourers who had worked under his orders. The execution of this abominable decree devolved upon the Daroga of Mazenderan. Erik had shown him some slight services and procured him many a hearty laugh. He saved Erik by providing him with the means of escape, but nearly paid with his head for his generous weakness.

Fortunately for the daroga, a corpse, half-devoured by the birds of prey, was found on the shore of the Caspian Sea and was taken for Erik's body, because the daroga's friends had dressed the remains in clothing that belonged to Erik. The daroga was let off with the loss of the imperial favour, the confiscation of his property and an order of perpetual banishment. As a distant connection of the Shah's family, however, he continued to receive a small allowance of a few hundred francs a month, from the Persian Treasury; and on this he came to live in Paris.

As for Erik, he went to Asia Minor and thence to Constantinople, where he entered the Sultan's employment. In explanation of the services which he was able to render a monarch haunted by perpetual terrors, I need only say that it was Erik who constructed all the famous trap-doors and secret chambers and mysterious strong-boxes which were found at Yildiz-Kiosk after the last Turkish revolution. He also invented those automata, dressed like the Sultan and resembling the Sultan in all respects,[1] which made people believe that the Commander of the Faithful was awake at one place when, in reality, he was asleep elsewhere.

Of course, he had to leave the Sultan's service for the same reasons that made him fly from Persia: he knew too much. Then, tired of his adventurous, formidable and monstrous life, he longed to be some one 'like everybody else.' And he became a contractor like any ordinary contractor, building ordinary houses with ordinary bricks. He tendered for part of the foundations in the Opera. His estimate was accepted. When he found himself in the cellars of the enormous playhouse, his artistic, fantastic, wizard nature resumed the upper hand. Besides, was he not as ugly as ever? He dreamt of creating for his own use a dwelling unknown to the rest of the earth, where he could hide from men's eyes for all time.

The reader knows and guesses the rest. It is all in keeping with the incredible and yet veracious story. Poor, unhappy Erik! Shall we pity him? Shall we curse him? He asked only to be 'some one, ' like everybody else. But he was too ugly! And he had to hide his genius *or use it to play tricks with*, when, with an ordinary face, he would have been one of the most distinguished of mankind! He had a heart that could have held the empire of the world; and in

[1] See the interview of the special correspondent of the *Matin* with Mohammed-Ali Bey, on the day after the entry of the Salonika troops into Constantinople.

the end he had to content himself with a cellar. Surely we may pity the Opera ghost!

I have prayed over his mortal remains, that God might show him mercy notwithstanding his crimes. Yes, I am certain, quite certain that I prayed beside his body, the other day, when they took it from the spot where they were burying the phonographic records. It was Erik's skeleton. I did not recognize it by the ugliness of the head, for all men are ugly when they have been dead as long as that, but by the plain gold ring which he wore and which Christine Daaé must have slipped on his finger, when she came to bury him in accordance with her promise.

The skeleton was lying near the little well, in the place where the Angel of Music first held Christine Daaé fainting in his trembling arms, on the night when he carried her down to the cellars of the Opera-house.

And, now, what do they mean to do with that skeleton? Surely they will not bury it in the common grave! . . . I say that the skeleton of the Opera ghost is no ordinary skeleton and that its proper place is in the archives of the National Academy of Music.

WORDSWORTH CLASSICS

General Editors: Marcus Clapham & Clive Reynard

DISTRIBUTION

**AUSTRALIA
& PAPUA NEW GUINEA
Peribo Pty Ltd**
58 Beaumont Road, Mount Kuring-Gai
NSW 2080, Australia
Tel: (02) 457 0011 Fax: (02) 457 0022

**CYPRUS
Huckleberry Trading**
3 Othos Avvey, Tala Paphos
Tel: 06 653585

**CZECH REPUBLIC
Bohemian Ventures spol s r o**
Delnicka 13, 170 00 Prague 7
Tel: 02 877837 Fax: 02 801498

**FRANCE
Copernicus Diffusion**
23 Rue Saint Dominique, Paris 75007
Tel: 1 44 11 33 20 Fax: 1 44 11 33 21

**GERMANY
GLBmbH (Bargain, Promotional
& Remainder Shops)**
Schönhauser Strasse 25
D-50968 Köln
Tel: 0221 34 20 92 Fax: 0221 38 40 40

**Tradis Verlag und Vertrieb GmbH
(Bookshops)**
Postfach 90 03 69
D-51113 Köln
Tel: 022 03 31059
Fax: 022 03 3 93 40

**GREAT BRITAIN & IRELAND
Wordsworth Editions Ltd**
Cumberland House, Crib Street
Ware, Hertfordshire SG12 9ET

**INDIA
OM Book Service**
1690 First Floor
Nai Sarak, Delhi – 110006
Tel: 3279823-3265303 Fax: 3278091

**ISRAEL
Timmy Marketing Limited**
Israel Ben Zeev 12
Ramont Gimmel, Jerusalem
Tel: 02-865266 Fax: 02-880035

**ITALY
Magis Books SRL**
Via Raffaello 31/C
Zona Ind Mancasale
42100 Reggio Emilia
Tel: 1522 920999 Fax: 0522 920666

**NEW ZEALAND & FIJI
Allphy Book Distributors Ltd**
4-6 Charles Street, Eden Terrace
Auckland,
Tel: (09) 3773096 Fax: (09) 3022770

**NORTH AMERICA
Universal Sales & Marketing**
230 Fifth Avenue, Suite 1212
New York, NY 10001, USA
Tel: 212 481 3500 Fax: 212 481 3534

**PHILIPPINES
I J Sagun Enterprises**
P O Box 4322 CPO Manila
2 Topaz Road, Greenheights Village
Taytay, Rizal
Tel: 631 80 61 TO 66

**PORTUGAL
International Publishing Services Ltd**
Rua da Cruz da Carreira, 4B,
1100 Lisbon
Tel: 01 570051 Fax: 01 3522066

**SOUTHERN, CENTRAL
& EAST AFRICA
P.M.C.International Importers &
Exporters CC**
Unit 6, Ben-Sarah Place, 52-56 Columbine
Place, Glen Anil, Kwa-Zulu Natal 4051
  P.O.Box 201520
  Durban North, Kwa-Zulu Natal 4016
  Tel: (031) 844441 Fax: (031) 844466

**SCOTLAND
Lomond Books**
36 West Shore Road, Granton
Edinburgh EH5 1QD

**SINGAPORE,
MALASIA & BRUNEI
Paul & Elizabeth Book Services Pte Ltd**
163 Tanglin Road No 03-15/16
Tanglin Mall, Singapore 1024
Tel: (65) 735 7308 Fax: (65) 735 9747

**SLOVAK REPUBLIC
Slovak Ventures spol s r o**
Stefanikova 128, 94901 Nitra
Tel/Fax: 087 25105

**SPAIN
Ribera Libros, S.L.**
Poligono Martiartu, Calle 1 - no 6
48480 Arrigorriaga, Vizcaya
Tel: 34 4 6713607 (Almacen)
     34 4 4418787 (Libreria)
Fax: 34 4 6713608 (Almacen)
     34 4 4418029 (Libreria)